UNEXPECTED DEVELOPMENTS

UNEXPECTED DEVELOPMENTS

R.B. Dominic

A Joan Kahn BOOK

ST. MARTIN'S PRESS
NEW YORK

Copy editor Mildred Maynard

Library of Congress Cataloging in Publication Data

Dominic, R. B.
    Unexpected developments.

    "A Joan Kahn book."
    I. Title.
PS3562.A755U5   1984   813'.54   83-21111
ISBN 0-312-83278-8

First Edition

10 9 8 7 6 5 4 3 2 1

Unexpected Developments

1

The steps of the House of Representatives are among the most photographed backdrops in Washington. But congressmen are rarely sighted there. Except when the cameras belong to a TV network, most legislative work is still conducted indoors. Tourists usually have to train their Kodaks on marble, granite and other tourists.

One fine afternoon in early April proved to be an exception. Traffic up and down included high-school classes from seventeen states, a visiting Japanese trade delegation, many energetic young staffers and two real live congressmen.

Furthermore, the Honorable Benton Safford (D., Ohio) and the Honorable Anthony Martinelli (D., R.I.) were, in fact, talking about affairs of state.

"What burns me is that Providence voted big for him last November," said Tony Martinelli.

"Newburg did, too," Safford replied.

"So why are they yelling at us?"

Martinelli's question was rhetorical. Now that the new President's belt-tightening programs had been unveiled, the American electorate was doing what it always did—complaining.

"Well, I'm not just sitting still and taking it," Martinelli continued. "I'm sending out a form letter. 'Dear Constituent—you want to kick somebody, go find a Republican. Sincerely yours . . .'"

"I could never get away with it," said Ben regretfully.

There were more Republicans in southern Ohio than in Provi-

1

dence and plenty of them crossed party lines to help Congressman Safford back to Washington every other year.

"Anyway," he said, "you can't blame it all on the Republicans, Tony. It's really a conservative coalition."

Fairness had not gotten Martinelli where he was. "The Republicans nominated this weirdo and elected him. He's their baby," he said, conveniently forgetting a recent Democratic performance along these lines.

Ben was not going to argue. The last election had been an unqualified disaster from his—and Tony's—point of view. With the White House and the Senate in ultraconservative hands, the House of Representatives was beginning to resemble Valley Forge.

"Well, I'd better get back to the front line," he said as they proceeded indoors.

With the Speaker conducting delaying action, the battles in the House were being fought in committee, not on the floor. There had been virtually no roll calls all session. But this did not materially lighten the workload. Ben, and every other member of Congress, had been hearing from home.

"Yeah, and you've got farmers, too," said Tony, referring to the administration's plan to dismantle the Soil Conservation Service. "Thank God I don't. All I've got are the school-lunch people. And Social Security. And, don't let me forget, they want to close the veterans' hospital. See you around, Ben."

On this note, he peeled off to his own quarters, jaunty as ever. Despite the dapper silk tailoring, Martinelli was fighting as hard as any soldier.

Ben's uniform was less elegant, and rumpled at that. Jauntiness was not his style, but he was ready to go into the trenches for the farmers of Newburg County. Before he could do so, however, other Newburg interests claimed his attention.

"Oh, Mr. Safford," said one of his secretaries, halting him as he entered his suite. "Mrs. Lundgren—"

The administrative aide who guided Ben through the darker thickets of the budget looked up from the computer. "CBO is right on the button, and OMB is smoking something funny. Say, did Janet get hold of you?"

Just then Madge Anderson materialized. "There you are," she said.

"Don't tell me, let me guess," said Ben. "Janet called."

The secretary and the administrative assistant went back to their appointed rounds and left him in Madge's competent hands. She was already dialing.

"You don't happen to know what it's about, do you?" he asked.

"I think Mrs. Lundgren wants to tell you herself," said Madge. Then, to the phone: "Mrs. Lundgren, please. . . . What? . . . Well, she gave me this number. . . . Would you look around and see if you can find her?" Cupping the receiver, she told Ben, "They're getting her."

"Fine," he said, without paying attention. When Janet and Madge got going, he usually found it wiser to wait and see.

Madge Anderson had started out as Ben's personal secretary. But as his seniority, committee assignments and staff grew, she had become something closer to his deputy. It was Madge who ran the Washington office, Madge who kept tabs on the bright young people who worked there, Madge who organized his schedule. Madge was ornamental, industrious and loyal to Ben's best interests. She frequently knew what they were before he did.

Janet always knew. She was his older sister and, with her husband, Fred, his major weapon in Newburg. At election time, second-generation Lundgrens came home to beat the bushes for every possible vote.

Without Mrs. Lundgren and Miss Anderson, a confirmed bachelor like Ben could have been at a serious disadvantage, politically speaking. He knew this very well. But, as he had once told his brother-in-law, he sometimes got the feeling that he wasn't measuring up to their high standards.

"Here he is, Mrs. Lundgren," said Madge.

Rousing himself, Ben took the phone. "Hi, Janet," he said.

3

Then, possibly because he had been thinking of farmers, he said, "How's the weather?"

"Just look out the window," she said.

"I don't want to jump to conclusions," he said, "but that sounds as if you're in Washington."

"I am."

It was not unknown for Janet to visit the capital, but Ben could not recall her doing it unannounced.

"Spur of the moment?" he suggested, testing the waters.

"You could say that," she replied carefully. "I did try to get you last night."

Last night, Ben told her, had been the National Association of Buying Agents.

Janet was not interested. "Ben, you've got to come over right away."

"Fine," he replied. "Where are you?"

"The Pentagon," she jolted him by replying. "What room is this? . . . Three . . . three . . . oh— Here, this young man can give you directions."

A resonant baritone came on the line. "Congressman Safford? If you'll just come to the East Entrance . . ."

While instructions rolled on, Madge got on the extension.

"Do you want me to repeat that?" the baritone asked.

"No," said Madge. "We've got it."

"Well then, here's Mrs. Lundgren."

"Janet," said Ben firmly, "just what are you doing at the Pentagon?"

As was to be expected, her firmness was more than a match for his.

"I'll tell you when you get here," she replied. "But, Ben, hurry. It's terribly important."

"I'm on my way."

Before the connection was broken, he heard her comment to a third party. "There, what did I tell you, Peg? Ben is coming right over."

"Madge," he said, rising. "I don't like the sound of this one bit."

Thoughtfully, Madge nibbled a pencil. "All Mrs. Lundgren said to me was that she didn't want to say anything over the phone."

Ben liked that even less.

Room 3306-78-B in the Pentagon proved to be an outpost of the United States Air Force. It was a large waiting room, furnished with a desk, file cabinets and a line of benches along the wall. Presiding over it was a crisp young woman in corporal's uniform.

Entering, Ben saw his sister waiting expectantly. Janet had the knack of never looking out of place, and it had not deserted her in the Pentagon. Her clothes were well chosen, her eyes attested to humor and character and, all in all, the Air Force would have been lucky to have her.

Her companion must have been about Janet's age, but there the similarity ended. She was as unmatronly as possible, with modish ash-blonde hair, an elegant figure and long, silken legs. Her olive-green dress was as simple and understated as Janet's, but even Ben could see that the overall effect was different.

"Ben," said Janet, jumping to her feet. "This is Mrs. Conroy. Peg, you said you hadn't met my brother Ben, didn't you?"

Despite her sleek Georgetown look, Peg Conroy's voice, like her smile, was pure Newburg. "How do you do, Mr. Congressman," she greeted him pleasantly. But obviously something was worrying her.

"Peg's a clothes buyer at Berman's," Janet explained. "When I went shopping yesterday, I happened to run into her."

Ben nodded encouragingly although they were not making much progress. Berman's was Newburg's Home-Owned Department Store, and Ben had known the Bermans, father and son, all his life. This still did not explain the Pentagon.

"So I told Janet all about Neil," Peg said quickly, "and she said that maybe you could help us." She paused, then added breathlessly, "You don't know what I'm talking about, do you. Neil is my son."

The young corporal was studiously ignoring them, but Janet lowered her voice anyway. "Neil's a captain in the Air Force, Ben."

Since this was not the time or the place for delicacy, Ben was deliberately blunt: "What's the trouble?"

Helpless for an instant, Mrs. Conroy lost her self-possession. Janet picked up the narrative in resolutely matter-of-fact tones. "Peg just heard from Neil yesterday," she reported. "They're holding some sort of board of inquiry in there"—she waved at the door behind the clerk—"and they're handing down a decision right now."

Before Ben could get any details, the door Janet had indicated suddenly opened, and a wave of uniforms surged out. Air Force brass of all ranks filed from the inner room in total silence. Not a word was said as sergeants, captains, majors and generals marched into the corridor. Only one officer stopped at the desk.

Then, while Ben was still mesmerized by this unexpected parade, a final uniformed figure appeared in the doorway.

Peg Conroy was the first to notice him. "Neil!"

The young officer slowly focused on her. "Mom?" he said incredulously. "My God, what are you doing here?"

Almost too quickly, she said, "Never mind that. What happened in there, Neil?"

Conroy moved forward, either to join his mother or to put distance between himself and the desk. He towered over her, a tall fair young man who just missed being handsome. At the moment, his blue eyes were deeply shadowed and there was a bitter twist to his lips. Drawing a deep breath, he said, "The crash was caused by pilot error."

Wordlessly, Peg Conroy reached out a hand toward him. As she did, the officer at the desk turned.

"Captain Conroy, don't forget you're still in the Air Force."

"No, General Farrington," said Conroy, while his mother's hand slowly fell to her side.

The general flicked a cold suspicious glance in Safford's direction, then briskly followed his fellow officers out of the waiting room.

His departure left an aching silence. Ben, irritated by the show of force, was happy to break it. "Captain Conroy, I'm Congressman Safford," he announced, noticing the girl at the desk raise her head slightly.

"How do you do, sir," Conroy replied automatically.

With a fair assumption of normalcy, Peg said, "Neil, Congressman Safford says that maybe he can help you."

Ben would have shuddered at the implications of this if he had not been concentrating on Conroy. An impenetrable mask had settled over the captain's face.

"There's no need for a congressman," he said expressionlessly. "This is Air Force business."

"But, Neil—"

It did not require a nudge from Janet to show Ben his next step. "Yes, we all heard that it's Air Force business, but it won't do any harm to go someplace and talk, will it?"

Before Conroy could turn him down flat, Janet went into action.

"Peg and I missed lunch," she said promptly. She then improved on perfection and slipped her arm through Conroy's so that, short of an undignified tussle, he was obliged to escort her out of room 3306-78-B.

The restaurant they stumbled into was appropriate. The food was appalling, the air was stale and the walls were mud brown. Ben remained in the dark in more ways than one. What little information he obtained came from the women, with Neil occasionally forced into a few grudging monosyllables.

Peg made a point of emphasizing her son's career. After Newburg High School, he had been a star at the Air Force Academy and a success in the service, with assignments all over the world on some of the most sophisticated equipment the Air Force had.

"But in spite of all this moving around, you're still one of my constituents?" Ben asked.

"I vote in Newburg."

It sounded more like a threat than an answer.

Janet, openly bidding for her brother's sympathy, made sure he knew Peg's story as well. Left a widow with a young baby, Mrs. Conroy had become head buyer at Berman's. When she was encouraged to talk about herself, she emerged as an energetic, resilient woman who was amused by the world of fashion that was her bread and butter.

"Oh, there are people in Newburg who can afford Paris originals," she said in reply to a question. "But they want the fun of going to Paris to buy them. I stick with the New York shows."

But background could do only so much. Ben squared his shoulders and tackled his subject. "Captain Conroy, I don't know anything about this board of inquiry. It will save time if you tell me."

After carefully considering the proposal, Conroy provided an answer of sorts. "Last February, I was piloting a VX-92 and we crashed."

"This year?" said Ben, feeling the first flicker. Neil nodded.

Justice delayed may be justice denied, but try telling that to the powers that be. The military are as bad as anyone else. Moving from an accident in February to a verdict in April was, Ben would have said, impossible.

"Action with the speed of sound," he remarked. Undue haste always rings a warning bell. "Tell me the specifics."

"We plowed into a schoolyard in Utah. Three kids were hit. Billy, my co-pilot was killed. I walked away with a couple of broken ribs."

The stark presentation was clearly intended as discouragement. Ben knew when to sidestep. "Usually accidents like that get a lot of coverage."

Janet seconded him. "I went to the library last night. It was the same day as that assassination attempt on the Queen of England."

"That explains it," said Ben. No one could ever forget those headlines. Like all politicians, he knew how thoroughly big stories can blanket everything else.

As these thoughts flashed through his mind, Peg Conroy spoke up. "But how could they say it was your fault, Neil? You weren't even flying the plane. It was your co-pilot."

Ignoring his mother, Conroy stiffened and addressed Ben.

8

"The responsibility for the flight is the pilot's," he said, speaking by rote. "Any negligence is his fault. It's that simple."

"Simple!" Peg Conroy gasped, choking over her coffee. "That isn't what you've been saying for the past two months."

"I misunderstood the situation," her son said.

"If it was that simple, how could you?" demanded Peg, putting the very question that had occurred to Ben. "You weren't even worried about this board. When they moved it up, you said you were glad. You'd gotten all your technical material together and you wanted to get it over with."

Like most young men, Neil Conroy sounded more childish when he was talking to his mother than at any other time. "Anybody would want to get it over with," he said sulkily.

"It never crossed your mind that you'd be blamed," she charged, perilously close to explosion. "And you expected the board to go on for days, if not weeks. Don't bother to deny it."

"Mom, for God's sake will you—" he began in a furious undertone.

But now she was not speaking to him. Swinging to Ben, Peg let the words pour out in a cataract. "When Neil called me yesterday, he sounded punch-drunk. They hadn't let him introduce his evidence, they hadn't called some of his witnesses and they were going to report their decision today. He couldn't believe it."

"Is this true?" Ben demanded.

Conroy was once again in full control of himself. "It is true that I didn't get a chance to say as much as I expected, sir. The members of the board were satisfied they had sufficient evidence to make their finding. They were all experienced officers, and they knew what they were doing."

Ben wanted it signed, sealed and delivered. "And are you satisfied with the verdict?"

Neil Conroy could not have been more emphatic if he had been standing in front of a firing squad.

"Yes, sir, I am."

2

After lunch, Ben took Janet back to his office, picking up company en route. Congressman Eugene Valingham Oakes (R., S.Dak.) and Congresswoman Elsie Hollenbach (R., Calif.) were old and valued colleagues. They had already been briefed on the reason for Janet's latest visit.

"I just wish you'd been along with us, Val," said Janet.

Congressman Oakes did not pretend to misunderstand her. "It's true that when it comes to the ladies, I have a lighter hand than Ben," he murmured complacently.

"And all this couldn't have happened at a worst time for Peg," Janet added. "She was planning to get married again in a few weeks."

Val shook his massive head in sympathy but Ben, tired of sisterly pressure, was impatient. "I don't see what that has to do with anything. Look, I like Peg Conroy, and I hope she'll be very happy, but—"

"Well, you don't think she'll go off and marry Earl Mohr while Neil's career is going up in smoke, do you?"

Wisely, Ben ignored her question. "The trouble is that Neil's mixed up in something too complicated for mother love."

"And Captain Conroy is a problem himself, too," Val pointed out. "Didn't you say he was satisfied with the verdict? If he thinks justice has been done, it's hard to see what Ben can do—no matter what a white-haired mother back home may hope."

Ben grinned. "Peg's not the white-haired type."

"The principle is the same."

"Anyway," said Ben, "you've put your finger on what's really bothering me, Val. This about-face by Conroy. For months he hasn't exhibited the slightest concern about this hearing and, after all, he knows what happened in Utah. Then, within twenty-four hours, he turns himself into a robot, playing the same record over and over again—the pilot is always responsible, the service knows what it's doing, will civilians please stand aside. It's fishy as hell."

Janet applauded this conclusion. "They've brainwashed Neil. I was afraid they'd brainwash you, too."

"Come on, Janet, you know better than that. No general tells me to keep my hands off because it's Air Force business."

"Worthy of Elsie," said Val with deliberate provocation.

Congresswoman Hollenbach, far-famed as the scourge of the Department of Defense, immediately lived up to her reputation. Inclining her gray head regally, she said, "There are elements in this situation of legitimate concern to you, Ben. The speed and secrecy with which the board was convened, the haste to conclude the inquiry without hearing all the evidence and, finally, the open attempt to coerce a young officer into silence. You would be amply justified in demanding an explanation."

Ben hesitated. Too often Elsie's lofty formulations were mere camouflage for her natural inclinations. Needling the military was not one of his hobbies.

"There!" said Janet triumphantly. "How can you say no after that?"

"Because it may be too complicated for me, as well as Peg Conroy. I don't know anything about pilot error or jet aircraft, let alone some supersonic miracle plane like the VX-92. I won't get to first base if the Air Force wants to brush me off."

Mrs. Hollenbach smiled grimly. "There will be no question of brushing you off, Ben. Not while you're a member of the committee."

"My God, of course!"

For Janet's sake, Val spelled out the obvious. "We're all on the Uniform Weaponry Committee. The Air Force can't afford to offend Congressman Safford these days, not if they give a damn about their appropriations."

In other words, Congress was finally getting down to the task of establishing a system of uniform weapons with NATO. The funding for many missiles was at stake.

"And I'm holding another ace," Ben recalled. "A couple of weeks ago, Preston Goodrich was appointed Undersecretary of Defense."

Janet gave a cry of pleasure. "Pres Goodrich? From back home? Why, then you won't have any trouble at all."

This was too unrealistic for Val Oakes. "If there's one thing that can strain the sacred ties of friendship, Janet, it's politics."

The sacred ties were at least partly operational the next day. Instead of enthroning himself behind a massive desk, Preston Goodrich was waiting for Ben in the doorway.

"Ben, good to see you," he said, shaking hands enthusiastically.

A tall, thin man with slicked-back hair and owlish glasses, he looked like the ideal team player. But as Ben knew, Goodrich's conservative appearance was misleading. He had a Yugoslavian wife, played the bagpipes and liked to backpack in remote wilderness areas.

People who should know said that Preston Goodrich was also a sharp, hard-nosed businessman. Ben both liked and respected him.

After the usual inquiries about wife, children and housing, Ben asked: "You've been here long enough to know. How are you liking Washington, Pres?"

"Well, it's not what I'm used to," said Goodrich frankly. "It's a new set of working conditions for me."

Since Goodrich was serving a Republican President, Ben decided it would be tactless to press the point.

"Tell me what I can do for you," said Goodrich. "Unless this is just a courtesy call—which I doubt."

"Far from it," said Ben, and proceeded to outline the Conroy situation as he knew it.

As he spoke, he got a vivid impression that Preston Goodrich promptly confirmed. "That's Captain Neil Conroy, right? Let's get the record. . . ."

He pressed buttons and, within minutes, files of material had been delivered to the undersecretarial desk.

"It sounds like a real shame," said Goodrich, riffling rapidly through a thick, bound volume of typescript. "Conroy had an outstanding service record until the VX-92 crash."

"To tell you the truth, I'm taking that on faith," Safford said. "I just met Conroy, and I don't really know a lot about him. But, Preston, what's got me worried is the board of inquiry. It seems to me it was pushed through very fast. Then, too, there's this strange lack of publicity—"

Without consulting any documents, Goodrich interrupted. "That was the weekend somebody shot at the Queen, remember?"

"You really are up to date on things that happened a long time before you took office, Pres," Ben said quietly.

Instead of answering directly, Goodrich made an offer. "Do you want to look at the record yourself? The vote was three to two."

Ben had been responsible for too many transcripts himself to put much faith in them. "No, thanks, Pres. What I really would like to do is to talk to the members of the board—including the two who didn't go along."

Goodrich had not been expecting this. But after a brief internal debate, he made a decision: "I don't see why that couldn't be arranged. It's probably a good idea, too. After you've talked to the board, you'll have a pretty good picture of why they voted the way they did."

"Well, if it can be worked out, I'd appreciate it," said Ben, knowing something more was coming.

"But before we go any further," said Goodrich, doodling as he spoke, "there's one thing I will tell you. The word did go out to expedite the Conroy hearing."

Even from old friends, Ben mistrusted concessions.

"Care to tell me why?"

Goodrich smiled at him, without a lot of humor. "I guess I'm going to have to. It's because the situation in the Middle East is so damn tricky—and getting trickier by the minute. Keeping as quiet as possible about Ibn Billeni—frankly, Ben, that was a high-level policy decision. The very highest level, if you want to know."

Startled, Ben said, "You've lost me. Who's Ibn Billeni?"

Goodrich looked at him quizzically. "I see what you mean about not knowing Conroy very well. Ibn Billeni was the co-pilot. He was sent over here from Saudi Arabia for training on advanced planes like the VX-92."

"I heard something about a co-pilot," said Ben, thinking back. "Conroy called him Billy."

Goodrich nodded. "As you know, the Saudis are important— and sensitive. We had the State Department breathing down our neck, telling us how bad this would look on television. So . . ."

"So the word went out," Ben finished for him.

"That's right," said Preston Goodrich.

There was a full stop, as deliberate as a musical interval. Then, resuming as if there had been no mention of anything out of the way, Goodrich said, "What I'll try to do is set up appointments for you next week with every member of Conroy's board. That should convince you that he didn't get a raw deal even though there were some special conditions."

"Fine," said Ben.

"And Ben," said Goodrich, sounding embarrassed. "Maybe you can do us a favor, too. If Conroy is making waves about Ibn Billeni—"

"It isn't Conroy, Pres," said Ben. "It's me. And don't worry, once I'm sure Neil Conroy got a fair hearing—I'll forget all about Saudi Arabians."

"Fair enough," said Undersecretary Goodrich.

3

These days, Brigadier General Reynold Farrington was more used to giving orders than taking them.

"What do you mean, be prepared to review the Conroy hearing with some congressman? Who says so?"

"The Undersecretary," his aide replied. "He said every member of the board, without fail."

Farrington gave a short bark of derisive laughter. "I wish they'd make up their minds. First they get together with the State Department and decide to keep the whole thing under wraps. Now they're pretending to open up. I suppose they want us to bury Safford with technical detail."

"I expect so, sir. Are there any instructions about the appointments?"

"There certainly are!" Farrington snapped. "Give him the majority view first. Start with me, then Colonel Yates and Captain Perini. With any luck, we'll wear him out before he ever gets to Severance and Kruger."

Reynold Farrington sounded like a man dealing with a routine problem before returning to his real work. Nevertheless, after the aide left his office, he remained motionless, staring into space.

Lieutenant Colonel Lawrence Yates reacted less professionally.

"Hey! It's Friday afternoon," he protested.

"Don't worry, Larry," Farrington's aide soothed him. "We're not doing anything until next week. I've put the general down for

Monday, you for Tuesday afternoon and Julian Perini on Wednesday. How does that sound?"

"Okay with me," Yates drawled into the phone.

Strangers were often surprised by Lawrence Yates' rank. A lanky frame, a full head of hair and a Texas smile camouflaged his forty years. But he had been flying for twenty of those years, he held an advanced engineering degree and he understood General Farrington's tactics at once.

"But I'll bet it doesn't work," he remarked. "Sooner or later, Safford will get to the ones who held out for Conroy."

"A technical avalanche is what the general is counting on," said the aide. "But anyway, your weekend is safe."

Yates chuckled. "Thank God for that. I've got better things to do than going over that pile of transcripts again."

"I'll bet you have."

Colonel Yates' post-divorce life-style was becoming an Air Force legend.

General Farrington's aide was not the only one who got busy on the phone. Some of the calls had gone as far as California.

At Dorland Aircraft, the president's office was vast and lavish, but it was still too small for the two men in it. Walter Wellenmeister, at sixty, was stepping down as president of Dorland to serve as Ambassador to France. George Kidder, at fifty, was stepping up to take Wellenmeister's place. The transfer of power was not going smoothly. Fixed smiles could not conceal simmering hostility.

"You couldn't be taking over at a better time, George—a great new fighter system being tested by the Air Force, and the Paris Air Show in a couple of weeks as the perfect showcase." Wellenmeister sighed theatrically. "I only wish it had been such smooth sailing when I walked into this office."

He looked around the room with a proprietary air undiminished by the cardboard box at his feet. The last hour had been spent packing the trophies and mementos of his long career.

"As far as the Paris Air Show is concerned," said Kidder, "Dorland's major effort will be selling Sky Freighter."

George Kidder, tall, smooth and urbane, was the one who

16

should have become a diplomat. Wellenmeister was a rotund little man with bristling eyebrows and a scrappy style. What's more, Kidder had just neatly landed some telling blows. The VX-92 was Wellenmeister's baby, developed while Kidder, a long way from headquarters, was overseeing the birth of Dorland's new transport, Sky Freighter.

And he had also underlined the distance soon to yawn between Dorland and its ex-president.

Reddening with anger, Wellenmeister fell back on the brisk authoritative style he used so often with subordinates. "Use your head, George! You can't have a precision flying demonstration with cargo planes. And that's what people remember."

But Kidder was no longer a subordinate. "They remember crashes, too. Which reminds me, Walter, some congressman is asking questions about the VX-92 that smashed up last February. Maybe you haven't heard?"

"I've heard," Wellenmeister grunted. "Don't forget, I have a lot of friends in Washington right now."

Some quirk of personality made him revel in his recent prominence as crony and benefactor of the new President of the United States. His pride in going to Paris was almost childlike. But as Kidder knew to his cost, however foolish Walter might sometimes look, he was far from being a fool.

"Let's hope you don't need those friends too soon," Kidder said amiably.

Wellenmeister's small eyes were suddenly gunslinger cold. "Don't lose any sleep over it, George. I'm not going to."

But George Kidder had stopped believing what Wellenmeister said a long time ago.

Ben Safford was only too happy to speed his sister and Peg Conroy on their way back to Ohio with promises of early reports.

"Is Neil going back with you?" he asked.

"Not for a couple of days," Peg said. "Then he'll be sitting at home waiting for the decision on disciplinary action. And I mean sitting."

Janet translated. "Peg doesn't want him lying down and taking it. She wants him fighting."

"Cheer up," Ben urged. "Maybe he'll start after I've talked to the members of his board. Anyway, I'll take another crack at him then."

"Good luck to you," said Neil's devoted mother. "I've talked to him until I'm blue in the face, and I could have saved myself the trouble."

Inspired by the desire to give her something concrete, Ben went further than he intended. "One thing I can tell you. I've already started getting hints about national security."

"National security!" Janet sniffed. "That's what people start yelling whenever there's dirty work."

If Janet wanted to see dirty work, Ben reflected later, she should have stayed another half hour. Madge Anderson had just announced an unprecedented visit.

"Congressman Atamian would like a few minutes, if you can spare the time," she said, rolling her eyes.

Ben stared at her, bemused. Congressman Michael Atamian (D., Calif.), during his five terms in Congress, had sponsored no legislation, skipped most committee work and missed too many roll calls. All his efforts were devoted to taking care of the interests of Dorland Aircraft.

"Send him in," said Ben genially. "I should have remembered who makes the VX-92."

Atamian, compact, sleek and dark-browed, entered Ben's office without his usual strut.

"I suppose you want to talk about Dorland, Mike," Ben said by way of greeting.

Far from taking offense, Atamian was grateful for the lead. "That's right," he said, reaching into his pocket for a cigar. After fussing with his lighter, he added, "Dorland's headquartered in my district."

Ben had to hand it to Atamian. A skin that thick must be a real asset in his particular line of work.

18

"Yes, I'd heard," he said. "Have they been on your tail about the Conroy board of inquiry?"

Lost in reverie, Atamian contemplated his smoke. "I keep in touch," he said ambiguously. "That's why I wanted to have this little talk with you. I don't know how up you are on Dorland. I can tell you confidentially that the Air Force is real enthusiastic about the VX-92—and so are the Europeans. Now's no time to rock the boat, Ben. All you'll do is make a lot of enemies."

"Is that a warning?" Ben asked mildly. "Or a threat?"

Atamian did not like this. "Who's talking about threats? All I'm telling you is that Dorland has a lot of clout."

"It has more clout in California than it does in Newburg," Ben replied.

"Dorland's got plenty of clout in Washington, don't forget," said Atamian. "Anyway, tell me what you've got to gain by hassling them."

"I'm not going after Dorland," said Ben, losing patience. "I'm making sure that my constituent's rights were respected."

Atamian was too tenacious to give up. "Why should the Air Force give Conroy a raw deal? Hell, it was an open-and-shut case."

"Then there's nothing for Dorland to worry about, is there?" said Ben.

Atamian's dark eyes narrowed, but his smile did not falter. "They're not worrying, Ben. It's just that they don't want a lot of grief right now."

"Thanks for telling me," said Ben.

As fate would have it, Elsie Hollenbach was entering just as Mike Atamian exited.

"Afternoon, Elsie," Atamian said with breezy familiarity.

Mrs. Hollenbach's reply was as stony as a vote of censure.

"Ben," she said. "I'd like you to look at these deficiency appropriations before you take off for the weekend."

The implication was that he intended to play truant and Ben knew why. Atamian might be gone, but the memory lingered on.

"I'll look it over tonight, Elsie," he said. "Tell me, how do you feel about Dorland? Atamian was pleading their cause."

She was a study in conflicting emotions. "Dorland is important to the economy of the whole state," she said. "All of us in the California delegation are concerned for their well-being. At least fifty thousand jobs are at stake. However, I need scarcely tell you, Atamian is the only one who regards himself as a lobbyist for Dorland."

"I don't think Mike was talking about jobs."

"Then what was he talking about?" she pressed.

"The Conroy board of inquiry, I think," said Ben. "I'm beginning to wonder what I've stirred up. First I get a lot of heavy pointers about Saudi Arabia. Then Atamian sails in here with hints about Dorland wanting to avoid bad publicity. God knows I'm not suspicious by nature, but it does make you think."

Mrs. Hollenbach preferred to stick with facts. "Did Preston Goodrich cooperate?"

"To the hilt," said Ben. "I'm having interviews with every member of the Conroy board—"

Just then the phone rang.

"Congressman Safford?" The voice was young and apologetic. "Yes?"

"This is Captain Julian Perini speaking. Someone made an appointment for me to talk to you about the Conroy board of inquiry next Wednesday."

"That's right," said Ben, with a glance toward Elsie, who was unabashedly eavesdropping.

Perini grew more apologetic. "I'm afraid that won't be possible."

"Do you want to explain that, Captain?" said Ben sternly. "Undersecretary Goodrich told me that every member of the board would be available."

"I guess they didn't know that I'm flying out to the Coast tonight for a two-week course."

"A two-week delay is out of the question," said Ben promptly.

Elsie was more practical. "Tell him," she whispered, "that you will take this up with his superiors."

But strong-arm tactics were not necessary.

"There is a way we could get together," said Perini hesitantly. "Not that I want to inconvenience you."

With Mrs. Hollenbach breathing dedication to duty, what did inconvenience matter? "Go on," said Ben.

"I'm at Quantico right now, and I'll be stopping at my place in Fairfax on my way to the airport. If you could meet me there in an hour . . ." Perini did not sound happy. "Of course, I realize it's a long way for you to come, especially at five o'clock on Friday."

This was an odd request from a junior officer, and Ben was tempted to refuse. In fact, he could not help wondering if he was expected to refuse.

If so, somebody was in for a big surprise.

"Give me your address," he said crisply, reaching for a pencil. "I'll start right away."

In spite of the usual difficulties with suburban geography, Ben arrived in record time. As he paid off the cabby, he observed that Captain Perini was at least setting the stage. In the driveway, a car was parked with its hatchback raised. On the ground, ready for stowage, stood two suitcases.

Ben marched up the walk to the front entrance and applied his finger to the push-button. When the musical notes failed to produce any result, Ben was not surprised. The same chimes back home in Ohio had never been audible in the kitchen. He headed for the back door and was almost there when he heard a persistent whining.

"Hello there! What's your problem?" said Ben with his hand on the knob.

The whimpers were emanating from a dejected beagle lying on the other side of the screen door. For one brief moment, the situation seemed commonplace. There was a pile of luggage by a car, and there was a pet bewailing its significance. Suddenly, as Ben opened the door, the beagle streaked forward. Ben instinctively grabbed him, and the far corner of the room came into view.

A man was sprawled face down on a desk, half his head blown away.

As Ben froze, transfixed by shock, a final ghastly dimension was added to the scene. The beagle flung back his head and gave vent to a full-throated howl of desolation.

21

4

Never in his life had Ben wanted to leave a house more. Nonetheless, five minutes later he was huddled in a kitchen chair waiting for the police. He had not backed out onto the street, yelling as he went; he had not even gone next door to use the phone. He had resisted every instinct because of one small detail. In the larger horror, Ben barely registered the pistol clutched in a dangling hand or the Air Force jacked draped over the chair. But alarm bells had sounded loud and clear at the sight of hundred-dollar bills spilling from a large manila envelope.

After that, Ben had not dared leave the scene. He had stumbled blindly into the kitchen, called out several times, then located the wall telephone. Now he was clasping the beagle on his lap, more to dispel his own sense of isolation than to comfort the shivering animal.

In Washington, D.C., there are over five hundred legislators and, like everybody else, they park in tow-away zones, they get mugged, they are picked up in vice raids. Unlike everybody else, they react to these events entirely in terms of probable publicity. Even with blood pouring from his wounds, your average senator is worrying about how he will look next November.

The suburban police have not had as much experience with this phenomenon as their metropolitan colleagues.

"You want what?" the detective, Sergeant Dunnet, asked blankly.

"I want to be searched," Ben repeated. "There's a lot of money

22

by that body, and I don't want anyone saying some of it left with me."

Even before ABSCAM, most congressmen disliked being found with stacks of unmarked bills.

"All right, all right," growled the sergeant. "We'll search you before you go. Right now we've got other things to do."

They were standing in the doorway of the family room, waiting for the doctor to finish his examination. Ben, who had been averting his eyes, gave a sigh of relief when the medics wheeled their burden to the ambulance.

The doctor snapped his case shut and prepared to depart.

"You'll get the report tomorrow but don't expect any surprises," he said on his way out. "It looks pretty straightforward."

"Yes," Dunnet agreed, strolling forward and gesturing Ben to follow. "The poor guy gave himself a couple of belts to get up his nerve, took a last look at his girl's picture and put the gun to his head."

For the first time, Ben inspected the desk calmly. On one side an empty glass, with a fly droning around its rim, stood next to a half-empty bottle of bourbon. On the other side, there was a large photograph of a pretty young woman smiling radiantly. It was inscribed: *With all my love, Nancy.*

"Of course, none of that explains why he did it," the sergeant continued.

"There's no point looking at me," Ben said grumpily. "I've told you that I never heard the name of Julian Perini before today. And I still don't know if that was him with his brains spattered all over the desk."

Dunnet was unruffled. "The stuff in his wallet says it was Perini. All right, so you didn't know him. But you had business with him, and it was important enough to trek out here to his house."

With as little emphasis as possible, Ben explained the conflict in Perini's schedule. "So you see, I didn't come rushing out here because of some emergency. I just wanted to catch him before he left town."

Unfortunately, Sergeant Dunnet had a gift for separating the wheat from the chaff. After several moments' concentration, he reached the conclusion Ben had arrived at in the kitchen.

"It doesn't make much sense that way, does it?" he remarked. "You're asking me to believe that he comes back here from Quantico expecting to meet with you, packs his things for his trip, carries the stuff out to the car, then decides to shoot himself."

"We don't know what else may have come up," Ben offered weakly.

Dunnet ignored him. "It's more reasonable to say he was here all the time. He was planning to skip town. He gets himself a ticket, collects his gear and then, at the last possible minute, gives you a ring to say there's no way he can get into Washington. But you throw a monkey wrench into the works by deciding to come here. Hell, he never expected that. Now there's only one way left. So he gets some Dutch courage, then blows his brains out. What do you think of that reading?"

Ben did not like it at all. He did not care for the role of nemesis, hounding young officers to their deaths.

"A lot of things could have happened in that hour that we don't know about."

"Sure. But let's stick with the probabilities. What kind of axe were you going to drop on the guy?"

"Look, Sergeant, I really am more ignorant than you're ready to believe. I don't know why Perini shot himself. But I can tell you this much. You'd be better off putting these questions to the Air Force. If there is a mess—and I don't say there is—it's the Air Force's mess. Let them straighten it out."

Ben was doing his best to honor his obligations. Preston Goodrich had cooperated with him, and he was trying to reciprocate. On the other hand, he had no intention of being front man for a tangle that could be far more complex than he—or Goodrich, for that matter—ever anticipated.

"If I were you, I'd start with the Undersecretary's office," he went on. "They're the ones who suggested I see Perini."

"I'll get right on to them," Dunnet promised. "Thanks for the starting point."

His tone suggested that the matter was closed and he was moving on.

"You see, the problem is that there's no note. Nobody wants to make the family feel worse than they're going to, nobody wants to drag things out," he said conversationally. "Still, before Headquarters closes the file, they're going to want a reason for all this."

But Ben was quite as adept as the sergeant at reading between the lines, and he could see where they were heading.

"I suppose so," he stalled.

"Of course, that money lying there almost looks as if it's supposed to be a substitute for a note, as if it's supposed to explain everything."

"In Washington, that amount of money in cash usually means there's been some hanky-panky," Ben agreed.

General observations were not what Dunnet was after.

"Other places besides Washington," he grunted. "It didn't do the poor guy much good, did it? He didn't spend it on wine, women and song. Maybe he was so ashamed he couldn't bring himself to use it. But then you'd be surprised how few people commit suicide because of simple remorse. More often, they're about to be caught. This money here could just be a final installment."

He paused to look at Safford with open speculation. "You did say you had a whole list of people you were going to see, Congressman? Does that mean we can expect bodies cropping up all over the place?"

"I doubt it." Grudgingly, Ben expanded. "I'm questioning the members of an Air Force board of inquiry. There might be one rotten apple, but that would be it."

Dunnet nodded to himself, either because he had succeeded in breaking through Safford's reserve or because he had confirmed a suspicion.

"What was it? Quartermaster Corps kickbacks? PX thefts?" he suggested alertly.

Ben, treading his cautious line of noninvolvement, was not volunteering information, but neither was he encouraging mistakes.

"Pilot error," he said baldly.

Dunnet was taken aback. "Pilot error?" he echoed. "Since when is that into dirty money?"

"There's no point asking me. I haven't seen a single member of that board yet, and I certainly didn't expect things to start off with a suicide. I doubt if the Air Force did, either."

"Great!" Dunnet brooded for a moment before shooting out a sudden question. "You know anything about flying planes?"

"Not a damned thing."

"Neither do I. Well, that settles it. The Air Force is going to have to come in whether they like it or not. Why the hell did Perini have to snuff himself out here? If he'd done it on an Air Force base, it would be theirs all the way."

The policeman's attitude toward the dead man, Safford noticed, had hardened considerably. With PX shortages, Julian Perini would have been another poor slob looking for easy money. Now, however, with service scandal and specialized detail looming, he was a serious nuisance to the Fairfax Police Department.

"This is still just guessing," Ben said halfheartedly. "It may be very simple. Perini's girl friend could have given him the gate, and he took it too hard."

"Ha!" Dunnet bleated. "And the money spilling all over the place is a coincidence, I suppose? Don't you believe it!"

Ben shrugged. "I don't, but it's the best I can do. And now, if you're done with me, I have to go. But I still want to be searched."

"Sure thing. But congressmen aren't the only ones people are suspicious of when it comes to loose cash. You'd better stay and witness our count."

Dunnet called over two of his men, emptied the envelope completely and began the tally. With the efficiency of long experience, he was soon finished.

"Fifteen thousand even," he announced, poising a pen over his report. "Right?"

His two men nodded.

26

"Congressman Safford!" he snapped. "Is that right by you?"

"Yes, it's fifteen thousand," Ben said absently, his attention elsewhere.

When he had first seen the money on the desk, the manila envelope had appeared blank. Now, lying where Dunnet had tossed it aside, it was closer to Ben, and he realized that his first impression had been wrong. The envelope bore no address, but there was a small letterhead in the upper corner. The typeface was so ornate it almost defeated his efforts to read it upside down.

As he signed the report, Ben was barely able to stifle the question drumming through his mind.

Why had Julian Perini received fifteen thousand dollars from the Saudi Arabian Embassy?

5

Unlike some metropolitan newspapers, the Washington dailies can spare only a limited amount of space for local items. Economic troubles, turmoil in Central America, the nuclear arms race—these swallow the lion's share. To fill the few remaining columns, the city editor has more than enough crime and mayhem. The death of an unknown Air Force office by his own hand did not justify any journalistic manpower. Sergeant Dunnet was careful not to transform drabness into drama, so the story was buried in the back pages of the weekend editions. There was no reference to unmarked bills, Saudi envelopes, recent boards of inquiry, or to Congressman Benton Safford.

The paper was delivered in Chevy Chase at seven-thirty. Congressman Michael Atamian did not get around to it until ten. In tribute to one of Washington's perfect spring days, he and Mrs. Atamian were breakfasting on the patio. Since Atamian relished gracious living, there was no hurried gulping of coffee and orange juice. Saturday morning began with a substantial serving of bacon and eggs. Only then was the *Post* unfurled. Somewhere between the boysenberry jam and the tupelo honey, Atamian's eye fell on the Perini item. One look, and he rose so abruptly that he startled his wife.

"I thought you weren't playing golf until noon, Mike," she observed.

"That's right, but I've got a few calls to make first," he announced importantly.

He should have known better than to waste the effort. The

woman sharing his coffeepot was not the wife who had put him through law school, raised his children and shared his first campaign. Helen had been traded in for a newer model. The current Mrs. Atamian was twenty years younger than her predecessor, varnished from head to toe and, at the moment, deep in a list of decorating schemes for the California spread she had coaxed Atamian into buying.

"Have a good time, sweetie," she said, barely noticing that he had already disappeared inside.

Walter Wellenmeister had not come to Washington to read the papers. He made this clear when Atamian, after fruitless calls to the West Coast, finally tracked him to a Connecticut Avenue hotel.

"I glanced at the front page, but I didn't read the *Post* from cover to cover," said Wellenmeister, breathing impatience over the phone. "I'm only in town for two days, and I've been running, I can tell you. I've been taking George Kidder around—the Senate, DOD, the works. Then, last night, there was a private party in Georgetown. What is it you want, Mike? I'm due over at the State Department in ten minutes."

Atamian could not afford to take offense. Almost all the good things in his life were paid for by Dorland, including the new house in California and, for that matter, the second Mrs. Atamian. So, gritting his teeth, he said, "That suicide in Virginia last night—he was a captain on the Conroy board of inquiry."

"Why did he kill himself?"

"I don't know," said Atamian, rattled. "The *Post* didn't say."

After a long silence, Wellenmeister said, "Then you'd better find out."

"That's just what I'm going to start doing," said Atamian. "But I thought—"

Unceremoniously, Wellenmeister cut him off. "In any event, I don't see how this has anything to do with us. Do you?"

"No, but—"

"I didn't think so. Look, Mike, I've got to go, but there is one thing you should bear in mind. Conditions aren't what they were.

You're not working with me anymore. I'm going to be in Paris. From now on, you'll be reporting to George Kidder."

Kidder was still an unknown quantity to Atamian. Since caution always pays, he said, "Do you think I should tell him·about this Perini suicide?"

For a man in a tearing hurry, Wellenmeister spoke very slowly. "If I were you, Mike, I'd think twice about that."

Unlike Mike Atamian, Undersecretary Goodrich spent his Saturday mornings in the office. So when the Air Provost Marshal reported the suicide, Goodrich requested, and got, the salient facts in writing.

Only then did he let himself think about the implications of Julian Perini's suicide—and the Saudi Arabian bribe. He thought also about a significant footnote inserted by the Air Provost Marshal: the body had been discovered by Congressman Benton Safford.

Twice, Goodrich made to reach for the phone and twice let his hand drop in midair. Finally, reflecting that Ben Safford knew as much as he did, if not more, he made up his mind.

"Ben, let's get together and talk," he was saying not much later. "I'll come by and pick you up. We can go out to the house."

So Saturday afternoon found Ben Safford in Chevy Chase. Although he did not know it, he was a scant three blocks from Congressman Mike Atamian's residence. This patio, however, was not a riot of expensive garden furnishings. It was occupied by an easel, many dirty rags, a cardboard box with three puppies, and Zinka Goodrich. She was a large untidy woman who cooked, painted, and raised children and cocker spaniels with exuberant gusto. She greeted Ben with a bear hug, then returned to her art.

Goodrich led Ben into a small book-lined room. "Zinka calls this my study," he said, straight-faced. "Just move that pile of laundry and sit down, Ben."

How this man became a Republican, Ben would never understand.

"Now what do we do?" said Goodrich.

The Undersecretary was getting down to brass tacks with a

speed that Ben appreciated. Rehashing Julian Perini's suicide, with all the gory details, was the last thing he wanted to do.

Ben responded in kind. "It seems to me that the Air Force is going to have to make it up to Neil Conroy. Unless your people have a different reason for Perini's taking a Saudi bribe?"

But the Air Provost Marshal had been definite. Investigation was still continuing, but the early returns painted Julian Perini as an exemplary officer. His only contact with Saudi interests had been the Conroy hearing. Barring unexpected developments, it seemed to be a straight-line progression: the Saudis had paid Perini to vote against Neil Conroy, saddling him with the guilt for the VX-92 crash and protecting their own national. When Congressman Safford appeared with questions, Perini had been afraid to face him.

"This Ibn Billeni," Ben said, reverting to a nagging detail. "Was he a prince or something?"

"Not that I know of," Goodrich replied. "Why?"

Ben shrugged. The inescapable fact of the bribe was what counted, not the motives. For all he knew, it had something to do with Saudi Arabian codes of honor.

"When you say make it up to Conroy, what do you have in mind, Ben?" asked Goodrich, returning to the main theme.

Before Ben could formulate an answer, Zinka appeared in the doorway. "Preston," she said with rich irony. "They want you again. Very important! Very, very important."

"I thought it would take them a little more time to get their act together," said Goodrich almost to himself as he obeyed the summons.

In his absence, Zinka entertained Ben with an irreverent description of life in Washington. "They do not like women," she informed him.

"Oh, I don't know about that."

"No, only the Secretary's wife. Me, I am an undersecretary's wife. This is nothing. Then, the telephone. It is always immediate, top priority. Never does anybody say hello, goodbye . . . Preston, you are back," she said as her husband returned. "Why do you look that way? Have they fired you, so we are going back to Cleveland? I tell you, it would make me happy."

Still talking, she left.

Goodrich did look bewildered. "It was about Neil Conroy. Ben, there's been a top-level policy decision. They want to offer him a total exoneration. He's to be reinstated without prejudice."

When there was no response, he continued challengingly, "Of course, that's what you want, isn't it?"

Despite Peg Conroy, Neil, and his own sister, Janet, Ben did not bother to field that one. "I expected them to reopen the case, but exonerating him? Right off the bat?"

Goodrich did not pretend to misunderstand. "It's consistent, at least. From the start, the emphasis has been on minimizing all publicity."

"We're bending over backward to keep from offending the Saudis, aren't we?" said Ben. "I suppose the official line is that they don't know a thing about Julian Perini, or Neil Conroy."

"Thank God that's up to the State Department. The Air Force has plenty of problems of its own."

"I'm beginning to see what you mean," said Ben Safford.

General Khalid, head of the purchasing mission at the Embassy of Saudi Arabia, did not rely on the State Department or anybody else to safeguard his interests. By Sunday, he was taking precautions of his own.

"You say this envelope was lying on the desk beside the body?" he demanded.

His informant nodded mutely.

"And the money was actually inside the envelope?" he persisted.

"Yes, General."

Khalid was a favorite among Washington hostesses, partly because of his distinguished, hawklike appearance, partly because of his cosmopolitan air but mostly because of his suave and courtly manner. To a woman, they would have been shocked by the explosion of wrath he now let loose. At its conclusion, the informant was grateful to scuttle away with nothing worse than a curt dismissal. Even the general's assistant, hardened by experience, entered on cat feet.

"The file you requested," he said softly, depositing it on the desk.

"Wait!"

Barely breathing, the assistant waited as Khalid rapidly scanned the thin sheaf of papers. Neither man was conscious of the bizarre appearance they presented in combination. Khalid, who was due at a formal dinner within the hour, wore full-dress uniform. His assistant, unceremoniously yanked from the squash court, was still wearing a sweatband and shorts.

"Just as I thought," Khalid said at last, slamming the folder shut. "There is absolutely nothing here."

"No, but after all Ibn Billeni was a man of no importance."

Khalid smiled grimly. "Not while he was alive. It may be a different story now."

With the immediate crisis over, the assistant ventured a suggestion. "It's a shame the money was actually inside the envelope. That makes things more difficult. But surely we can still come up with some explanation."

"I am not sure that would be wise." Khalid plucked his lower lip thoughtfully. "Explanations, justifications—they would all mean renewed inquiry. We do better to live with the admitted facts, however distasteful, than to court headlines."

Ruefully, the assistant recalled the possibility of headlines. "Certainly not now."

"Exactly. I am about to start negotiating with Dorland for the Sky Freighter. It is imperative that we be on good terms." Khalid shoved aside the file and prepared to rise. "And who knows? We may be on better terms than I expected."

6

On Monday morning, Ben's colleagues listened raptly to an account of his weekend's adventures. True to their calling, they began by congratulating him on his avoidance of publicity.

"A lot of things are crawling under that rock you turned over," Tony Martinelli said sagely. "You don't want the people in your district connecting you."

By then Ben was determined to have something to show for his unpleasant experience. "I only wish I could get hold of Neil Conroy to wrap this up. He hasn't been available in Washington or Newburg, and I'd like to deliver the good news."

"It's the only way you'll get any credit," Val Oakes reasoned.

"Getting credit isn't bothering me," Ben said slowly. "The thing is, everybody in the administration is worrying about the big problem. They don't care about a lowly captain, and they could withdraw their offer any minute they want."

In any negotiation, it always makes sense to grab an attractive deal before it evaporates.

"I'll go along with that," said Tony. "The way they've tried to keep things under cover and this last-minute switch on Conroy— it's enough to make you smell a rat."

Mrs. Hollenbach, who could have given lessons in strategy to the Red Army, said thoughtfully, "You still have those appointments at the Pentagon, Ben?"

"Well, I assume that's all washed out now . . ." Ben began, before he realized what she was suggesting.

For a moment, the steely glint in Mrs. Hollenbach's eye was reflected in his own appreciative smile.

"That's not a bad idea, Elsie," he murmured. "Not bad at all."

Ben's arrival at the Pentagon caused instant consternation.

"I'm sorry, Congressman. The general isn't back from the weekend yet."

"My appointment with him was at ten o'clock," Ben pointed out.

The good aide shoulders blame whenever possible. "I should have checked with your office. I assumed that you wouldn't still want to talk to the board, under the circumstances."

How many people were making that assumption? Briskly, Ben said, "No, I'm going ahead as planned. Since I'm here, let's avoid wasting the trip. What about Captain Severance and Major Kruger? I know they were last on the list, but I could knock them off right now."

Farrington's aide made one final attempt. "Maybe you'd like to talk about it with the general first. He'll be back—"

"No," said Ben. "You see, I've already talked to the Undersecretary."

The aide had no alternative.

After two hours, Ben had no progress to show for these forceful tactics.

Major Carl Kruger was laboriously explaining his vote to exonerate Neil Conroy.

"As far as I was concerned, we didn't have enough evidence for a decision of any kind. That VX-92 could have gone down because of pilot error or a gummed-up guidance system. Or it could have been unavoidable—that happens."

"But didn't you get any pointers?" Ben asked

Kruger was gruff. "That's what I'm telling you, Mr. Congressman. There wasn't a hell of a lot of testimony of any kind. Of course, with an Arab on board, I knew there'd be pressure to speed things up. But from where I sit, they overdid."

Trying a new tack, Ben pressed on. "Tell me, why didn't Conroy blame the accident on the co-pilot?"

Kruger let him in on an Air Force fact of life. "Dumping on a dead crew member doesn't sit so good. What Conroy should have done was get the facts on record and let them speak for themselves."

"Then why didn't he?"

"He tried, and in case anyone's forgotten, I'm one of the ones who backed him." Kruger's satisfaction lasted only briefly. "And now it turns out that Perini was on the take—which makes monkeys out of all of us."

Grievance makes everybody talk, and Ben capitalized on this. "That's another thing I don't understand, Major. Perini was a junior officer on the board. Why bribe him? His opinion couldn't carry a lot of weight with senior officers like you—or General Farrington."

Kruger shook his head. "That's not the way it works. Look, the Air Force really sweats to get impartial boards. All the prospective names go into the computer to make sure they aren't old buddies. But when the case is technical, you go for skills because they're in short supply. Perini was a fighter pilot qualified on the Dorland VX-92. That's why Farrington would listen to him. Rank doesn't make all that much difference."

"What about you?" Ben asked bluntly. "Did Perini try to change your mind?"

"He never said a word to me," said Major Kruger. "I just wish he had. And if I were Neil Conroy—"

"Was that because you were as qualified as he was?" Ben put in hastily, trying to cut off an outburst.

Kruger shook his head. "No, I wasn't up there with Perini. It's been four or five years since I was in fighters. Given the state of the art these days, I'm a generation or two behind."

"What about the rest of the board?"

Kruger reflected. "Well, Perini and Yates and Severance were all fighter pilots. Farrington's flying days are long past. Now he's an administrator thinking about his retirement. You can't fault the makeup of Conroy's board."

"The problem wasn't the makeup, it was Julian Perini," said Ben incautiously.

He set Major Kruger off again. The tirade lasted until Lieutenant Colonel Lawrence Yates arrived, levered Kruger up and out, then turned to Safford. "I'm sorry about the snafu over appointments, Mr. Congressman. They told me as soon as I got back from Hilton Head. Look, if you'd be willing to talk over lunch, General Farrington should get in by two."

Lunch was not in the cafeteria but in a special Pentagon dining room. After refusing wine, oysters and pâté, Ben protested, "Colonel Yates, I'll settle for a beer and a corned beef sandwich. I appreciate lunch, but I don't have to be stuffed with food before I listen to your version of the Conroy case."

Yates blinked. "Conroy?"

"That's what we're here to talk about."

"Yes, I know, but—" Abruptly, Yates abandoned this thought. Then, with a grin, he said, "Farrington's office did say you're on the Uniform Weaponry Committee."

Ben realized that brandishing his committee assignment had given the Pentagon the wrong idea.

"I am, but right now I'm operating as Neil Conroy's congressman," he said loud and clear.

Yates unbent noticeably. "Conroy got a raw deal, and Julian Perini turned out to be an SOB. That's all there is to say."

"Not quite," said Ben. "Colonel Yates, why did you hold Conroy responsible, not the co-pilot?"

Yates was not another Major Kruger. Raising an ironic eyebrow, he drawled, "Well, it wasn't because the Saudis paid me off, Mr. Congressman."

"I didn't think it was, Colonel," said Ben.

With that out of his system, Yates was ready to cooperate.

"Mr. Safford, Conroy's co-pilot was a trainee, but he was already a professional. That made it a judgment call." He frowned in the effort to communicate. "Ideally, the trainee corrects his own mistakes. If he's not fast enough, the pilot jumps in. The question of how long the pilot waits is the kicker. I'm conservative about it. I

37

thought Conroy waited too long, then didn't want to admit it. It wasn't the kind of thing he'd like in his record."

Something in Yates' tone alerted Ben. "And now?"

Yates laughed shortly. "Put it this way. I've got a lot more sympathy for him today than I did a week ago. From here on, anybody looking at my sheet is going to notice that I was part of the Conroy board—the one that was crooked."

If this was a bid for sympathy, Ben was having none of it. "You mean Conroy wasn't Perini's only victim?" he said.

"Not by a long shot," said Yates. But he was not self-pitying. "I suppose I should have expected it. Board duty is nobody's favorite assignment, and this one has been a can of worms all the way. First of all, civilians got killed. That makes the service very, very edgy. Then, there's a Saudi in the plane. So the State Department gets into the act. Now it turns out that the Saudis were spreading cash around—"

"And Perini took a bribe to shove the blame on Conroy," said Ben, ruthlessly going from the general to the particular. "Did he shove hard?"

"He pushed all right," said Yates, "But I put it down to his being a captain."

Ben looked inquiring.

"They're all the same," Yates explained so tolerantly that he looked every year of his age. "As long as they're at the Academy, or just out, they're still practicing. When they make captain, they really are pretty expert at something. Suddenly, they're sure as hell of themselves. At least that's what I thought then. Perini's suicide puts a different complexion on the whole damned thing."

To break the somber silence, Ben agreed with him. "It's going to make a difference all the way around—starting with Neil Conroy."

Yates cocked his head thoughtfully, then said, "I wouldn't be too sure of that, Mr. Safford. Even if the Air Force calls a new board, the findings could be the same."

Ben saw nothing useful to be gained by arguing the point. "You're entitled to your opinion, Colonel Yates, but I don't think the Air Force is planning to reconvene any boards. I've heard it suggested that they give Conroy a clean bill of health and forget the whole thing as soon as possible."

Colonel Yates did not reject the notion out of hand.

"You mean, throwing out the rule book?" he mused. "It could be. The people upstairs wanted this VX-92 crash kept real quiet, and I guess they still do." Glancing at his watch, he straightened. "If there's anything else I can do for you, let me know. But by now, the general's got to be back."

"And he doesn't like to be kept waiting?" Ben suggested.

Rising, Yates grinned. "That's one of the reasons we all buck so hard to end up as generals."

General Farrington's apology for the misunderstanding was perfunctory. "Didn't expect you to show up," he said briefly, proceeding straight to business. "You're still digging into the Conroy board. I suppose you've decided we did a sloppy job."

"I haven't decided anything," Ben replied mildly. "I'm just trying to get a feel for what happened."

"What happened," said Farrington evenly, "is that I was ordered to expedite the hearing. There's nothing sinister about that. I'll bet there have been times on the Hill when one of your committees has been told to push right along."

When Ben remained silent, Farrington expanded: "And that doesn't mean the outcome has been prejudged. It means that you plow ahead, cutting out the frills. I certainly had no reason to expect an Air Force officer to be taking bribes from a foreign power."

"No," said Ben. "I can see that."

Farrington was not getting the response he wanted. "God knows I'm ashamed of Perini. Everybody in the Air Force is. But let me tell you, Congressman Safford, that's still no reason for Neil Conroy to act like a goddamned fool!"

Up to this point, Ben had had no difficulty following Farrington. But he had lost him on the turn. "A fool?" he said.

Farrington modulated into persuasiveness. "He's a fine young officer, and I hate to see him throw his career away. He's getting a second chance, and if you have his best interests at heart, you'll advise him not to boot it."

"I'm not sure I understand what you're getting at, General," said Ben.

"Well, you know the Air Force is offering Conroy a full and unqualified clearance, don't you?"

Ben nodded

"Well, Conroy took his sweet time about answering," Farrington said irritably. "But just before you came in, the Undersecretary's office called. Conroy's refusing to go along. He insists on a second full-scale board of inquiry."

Unguardedly, Ben voiced his first thought. "I wonder what he's up to."

"God knows! But it's the worst thing he could do," Farrington said, "Believe me, Congressman Safford, you'll be doing that boy a favor—a big favor—if you talk him out of it."

"I'll *talk* to him," said Congressman Safford, "but that's as much as I can promise, General, until I find out exactly why Conroy is digging his heels in."

An involuntary grunt from Farrington told Ben he had somehow scored a point. It would have been helpful if he knew what it was.

7

Ben Safford's original intention had been to spend the following weekend brushing up on the supplementary budget. Nevertheless, the next Friday night saw him in Newburg, Ohio.

"I decided at the last minute to have it out with Neil Conroy. All week long, Pres Goodrich has been after me, and that means the White House is leaning on him. The least I can do is find out what Conroy's got up his sleeve."

Ben was in the entrance hall at 8 Plainfield Road, the big old house that had been his father's. It belonged to Janet and Fred now, with the ell serving as Ben's bachelor quarters.

"You should have called from the airport," said his brother-in-law, watching the taxi speed off. "We didn't know what time you were getting in, otherwise I could have picked you up. How much are they charging for the trip these days?"

"Eleven-sixty," said Ben, depositing a battered two-suiter.

"Highway robbery," said Fred Lundgren. The objection sprang from principle, not pocketbook. Lundgren's Ford Agency serviced Newburg, Curryville and a large part of southern Ohio. Business was bad these days, but Fred still did not have to worry about taxi fares. "It wouldn't have taken me ten minutes—"

"Ben, there you are!" Drawn by their voices, Janet emerged from the kitchen, wiping her hands on an apron. "We held dinner, then we decided you might be coming in early tomorrow."

"Tomorrow morning I'm grilling Neil Conroy," he said, after returning her greeting. "Besides, they fed me on the plane."

"Well, come in and have some coffee and cake."

As he munched, Ben learned without surprise that Janet had seized the opportunity to pack his weekend schedule.

So, shortly after eight o'clock the following morning, Fred dropped him off outside the Federal Building. Early as this was, it was not too early for Nick Minakis, who ran Ben's Newburg office. Fresh from the University of Ohio, Nick was a budding political hotshot. He was also a numbers man.

". . . ten requests for information from the Library of Congress. Then we've got two illegal-alien cases pending. I've set up appointments with Immigration. And, Ben, the mail on the new Social Security bill is running two-to-one against."

Roughly speaking, every United States congressman represents half a million citizens. So Minakis, and the rest of the new breed, were right. Numbers, tables and graphs were the only way to keep tabs.

". . . get Weizman and Wylie to poll the first week in September," said Minakis, getting to the most important numbers of all. "That gives us plenty of time before the election."

Nodding, Ben said, "I'll do my best to generate some good publicity."

Nick suspected a joke, but let it pass. "That reminds me. Here are some computer printouts we ought to go over."

Before Nick could bury him, Ben was reprieved.

"Good morning," said Neil Conroy, sticking his head around the door.

"Come on in," said Ben heartily. "Nick, I'll get cracking on all this stuff as soon as I can. Sit down, Captain Conroy."

Sighing eloquently, Nick departed.

"Every day is election day if you've got the right kind of staff," Ben observed when the door closed.

Conroy forced a polite smile but did not relax.

Ben studied him. Blue jeans, a sweat shirt and sneakers took the place of the knife-edged uniform but, oddly, this did not make Conroy look younger. Instead, it placed him in the ranks of Newburg's solid workingmen, currently filling the streets outside. Taking in the strong jawline and the solid, competent hands, Ben deliberately moved to a less formal approach.

"I appreciate your coming in, Neil. I bet you know what I want to talk about."

With a ghost of a smile, Conroy said, "I can guess."

"Your mother doesn't understand why you're refusing official exoneration either?" Ben suggested.

"No," said Conroy, withdrawing into himself. "She doesn't."

Ben was not very imaginative, but he suddenly felt sorry for Conroy. Family pressure can be the worst of all.

"Look," he said decisively, "let me say my piece. Then, if you're willing, we can talk. If not, I'll leave you alone. Okay?"

Conroy hesitated. Then, warily, he said, "Okay."

"I know you're not Peg Conroy's little boy Neil. You've managed your own affairs for a long time, and pretty well. You don't need me or anyone else barging in between you and the Air Force. It's your career and your future."

He paused while Neil Conroy sat tight.

"But this whole situation is turning out to be a lot more complicated than you or anyone else realized. My God, Neil, look at Perini. When he committed suicide, he proved that Saudi Arabia and dirty money were part of the picture. You didn't know that—and neither did the Air Force."

"So?" Conroy asked unencouragingly.

"So you were in the dark at your hearing," Ben fired back. "I'm suggesting you could be in the dark now."

Whether or not he was getting through, he could not tell. Doggedly he went on: "Now look, the Saudis are bad enough. But I've got to warn you, there's a political smell coming my way. Maybe it's just because of the Saudis, the way the administration is claiming. But, Neil, it could be something else. Believe me, with politics you never can tell. If you've got some idea it's just you and the Air Force cleaning up the record, I'd advise you to forget it."

He gave these words time to sink in, then added: "That's why I wish you'd tell me why you're refusing their deal. You see, if you went along—well, you might be helping the Air Force as well as yourself."

Nobody had ever called Ben a silver-tongued orator, and he was conscious of his limitations. But he had struck a chord.

"Like hell!" said Conroy explosively. "Holding out is the only way I *can* help the Air Force."

Ben was glad to hear Conroy talking, even if he was saying the wrong thing.

"Neil, be reasonable. What can a second board acccomplish? Your co-pilot and Perini are both dead. Whatever they did is over and done with."

There was a long silence. Then Conroy came to a decision. Speaking deliberately, he said: "Billy didn't do anything. It was the plane. That's what they're trying to keep me from saying."

Ben was out of his depth. "The plane?" he repeated. "You mean it wasn't working right? It hadn't been properly serviced, or something like that?"

Conroy looked him straight in the eye. "No," he said levelly. "I mean the whole design of the VX-92 is flawed."

Ben Safford might not know about supersonic aircraft but he recognized a bombshell when it hit him. Any possibility of a design flaw in the VX-92 could escalate them into another arena entirely. They were no longer talking about the plight of a single constituent. They could be talking about a national issue.

He looked across the desk. Did Conroy realize the forces he might be taking on—Congressman Michael Atamian for one, Dorland Aircraft and, when you stopped to think about it, the whole damned administration?

Stalling for time, Ben asked, "Neil, did you report this to the Air Force?"

"What do you think all my technical evidence was about? I never dreamed they wouldn't let me introduce it. Next time, things will be a lot different."

It was one version of what had happened. There were, as Ben reminded himself, others. But there was no use raising the specter of Julian Perini and Saudi envelopes again, at least not directly.

"You keep thinking the Air Force will play it by the book," he said. "What if they're not calling the shots on this one?"

"The Air Force has to give me another board."

They had reached an impasse, and Ben did his best to break it.

"Neil, I don't know whether you're right or wrong about the VX-92. Don't bother to explain, I wouldn't follow you anyway. But one thing I want to tell you as seriously as I can. This is too important for too many people. They're not going to let you slip this into the record. Not without one hell of a fight."

"Who cares about the record?" Conroy said contemptuously. "Tell them I'm going to ground every VX-92 in the Air Force."

"Oh, my God!" said Congressman Safford.

Ten minutes later, after Conroy had left without yielding an inch, Ben was still gripped by foreboding. Thanks to Janet, however, he did not have unlimited time at his disposal. He gave Nick Minakis another hour on the backlog, then set forth across Courthouse Square. Just outside the Federal Building, he encountered an old acquaintance.

"Well, Ben," said Mayor William Wilhelm, falling into step beside him.

"Morning, Will," Ben replied in the same measured cadence. He and the mayor went back a long, long way.

"In town for the VFW banquet tonight?"

"No," said Ben. Then he corrected himself. "At least, not that I know of."

Mayor Wilhelm was distracted by a passing matron, to whom he doffed his hat. He was one of the vanishing breed of politicians who know how to wield a Panama.

"Mrs. Carens," he confided after the lady passed. "Ten kids. You don't see that much anymore in Newburg. Why, I remember . . ."

Tales of old Newburg, which were Wilhelm's stock in trade, occupied them as they waited for the light to change.

". . . sixteen living sons," said Wilhelm nostalgically. "Of course, that was with four wives, two of them sisters. Before your time, Ben. They lived out by the old mill."

Suddenly, the squeal of brakes and an outburst of honking tore him and Ben away from the good old days. A panel truck had cut across traffic to double-park near the two men. The drivers who were not honking were shouting.

In the midst of the din, a patrolman emerged.

"That's more like it," said Mayor Wilhelm.

Traffic Officer Mellow was pulling out the inevitable pad when the passenger door flung open, nearly knocking the mayor off his feet.

"Ben!" said Peg Conroy. Even in slacks and sandals, she looked more fashionable than every other woman in sight. "Neil's coming downtown to talk to you."

"I just left him, Peg," said Ben. "Oh, excuse me, do you know the mayor?"

"We're old friends," she replied with a grin.

According to Val Oakes, you were supposed to treat good women like courtesans and rambling roses like angels. Wilhelm, who had perfect pitch for these nuances, beamed at Peg and said roguishly, "Peg is one of my best girl friends. I just wish we had a few more like her."

In other words, as Ben learned, Mrs. Conroy was a charter member of the Mayor's Committee to Make Newburg the Petunia City.

Downtown was not what it had been. Main Street showed signs of wear and tear. The mayor was forever seeking federal funds, wooing investors and cooking up schemes like the petunias. The theory was that all householders and businesses would plant petunias around trees, install window boxes and transform Newburg into a bower.

"I see," said Ben, keeping to himself reservations about petunias as agents of urban revitalization.

Meanwhile, Earl Mohr had lumbered around the truck and come to rest beside the others.

"First ticket I've had in three years," he observed ruefully.

"Oh, Earl, I'm sorry," said Mrs. Conroy. "But when I caught sight of Ben, I didn't stop to think. I shouldn't have yelled."

46

A shrug of massive shoulders was Mohr's only response.

"You know the mayor, Earl, but have you met Congressman Safford?"

"Nope," said Mohr, proffering a hand that was huge, work-scarred and gentle.

"I told you how Ben is helping Neil," Peg said.

Mohr nodded, but it was Wilhelm who said, "Real glad to hear that, Ben. Neil is a fine young man, and we're mighty proud of him in Newburg."

He continued in this vein for several moments. Ben, listening gravely, glanced at Mohr and was surprised to catch unmistakable glee in those round blue eyes.

"Well, I'd best be getting along," Wilhelm concluded, doffing his hat and resuming his promenade.

Ben decided Janet's schedule could wait. "What about a cup of coffee at Kolmar's?" he suggested.

"I'd better drive," said Mohr, although Kolmar's was just a block away. "Otherwise Teddy Mellow could give me another ticket."

Kolmar's had been a Newburg institution for generations. The food was home cooked, the drinks were reasonable and most of the waitresses were grandmothers. More important, it was a place where you could talk. The booths were as secure as confessionals.

"About Neil," said Ben, plunging in as soon as they were settled. "Has he told you what he told me about the plane?"

"Yes," Peg said soberly. "Ben, what do you think?"

"To tell you the truth, I don't know what to think," he replied. "But I've got a nasty feeling that Neil is sticking his neck way, way out."

"Me, too," she said unhappily. Then, trying to see the bright side, she said, "Neil says that once the Air Force gives him this second hearing, everything will be cleared up."

She needed reassurance, but Ben did not feel he could give it. "He's an optimist, Peg."

"That's what I'm afraid of," she said, biting her lip.

"If there is anything seriously wrong with the VX-92," said

Ben, half convincing himself, "we've got a Grade A mess on our hands. There are millions of dollars and some pretty big names riding on that plane. Neil—and any board he has—would be so much small-fry, just like the original Watergate burglars."

This pessimism silenced both of them until Mohr, looking from Peg to Ben, said, "Neil isn't dumb."

"I wasn't saying—"

"Earl means," Peg Conroy interrupted, "that Neil is smart enough to know that too."

"That's what I mean," Mohr agreed. Having attracted their attention, he was compelled to go on. "And Neil knows a lot about the Air Force. More than anybody here. He saw the pressure go on once."

"He saw it and hates to admit it," said Ben.

"That's Neil all over," Peg exclaimed.

Mohr waited to see if they had anything more substantial to say, then proceeded: "So he's got to be thinking that maybe it could happen again."

"Yes, but—"

"That makes sense—"

Defeating each other by speaking simultaneously, Peg and Ben provided a space for the slow-talking Mohr. "I got thinking," he ruminated aloud. "I've know Neil for a long time."

With an impulsive gesture, Peg put a hand over his. He covered it with his other hand and placidly continued. "He's a good kid, but he knows his own mind, Peg. You've got to admit that. So, if I'm figuring him right, he's got some sort of backup plan."

"Do you think so?" she asked anxiously.

"Yes," said Earl Mohr.

Ben could believe almost anything of Neil Conroy. "What could it be?"

"Search me," said Mohr. Before a sense of letdown could spread, he went on: "That's why I'm not coming over to dinner tonight, Peg."

She blinked at this abrupt conversational swerve. Ben was totally lost.

"Instead, I'm going to take Neil out to Russell's for a steak and a couple of beers," Mohr continued stolidly. "Just him and me."

"Well, for his sake, I hope you have better luck than I did," Ben observed.

"I think I will," said Mohr, without boasting. "You see, I'm not a congressman."

Ben was not offended, but Mohr, belatedly realizing he might be, offered an apology of sorts.

"One of the things that has to be getting to Neil is all the big shots tanking over him. You don't have to be a captain in the Air Force to have that burn you up."

It was a more profound remark than Ben Safford realized at the time.

8

Congressman Michael Atamian was spending that particular weekend in his hometown, too. He did not waste time on the West Coast equivalent of Mayor Wilhelm but reported directly to Dorland Aircraft. Atamian liked to tell himself, and anybody who would listen, that he was simply extending a courtesy to an important constituent.

From the moment he left his Mercedes, it was a hard posture to maintain. In Washington, Atamian worked out of Capitol Hill, while Dorland occupied a modest lobbying office. But in California, Dorland flaunted the lavish headquarters of a worldwide empire, with the big corner suite housing an emperor.

To make things more uncomfortable for Mike Atamian, he was introducing himself to a new man in the role.

"I've got a tight schedule today," George Kidder said as the door closed behind his secretary. "I can't give you more than a few minutes, Congressman."

"I don't want to keep you," said Atamian, sounding apologetic despite himself. "But I thought you should know the latest on the Conroy case."

"Conroy?" Kidder repeated.

"The pilot in that VX-92 crash in Utah," said Atamian.

Kidder, his eyebrows drawn into a level bar, simply waited.

"It turns out that the Saudis were scared because one of their men was actually flying," said Atamian, rushing his words. "They paid off a member of the board of inquiry. Now, if all this comes out in the open, it could be a real tricky situation—"

"Not for us," said Kidder coolly. "I understand the State De-

50

partment is taking care of the Saudi end. It's their problem, Atamian, not Dorland's."

Atamian scowled. "Well, there's one more thing," he said antagonistically. "From what I hear, the pilot is digging his heels in. He wants a full-scale second hearing."

Not a flicker of expression showed on Kidder's face. "That's a matter for the Air Force to decide."

Atamian was still in the dark about how much George Kidder knew. Choosing his words, he said, "Dorland was lucky on publicity once. That kind of luck can run out."

Kidder responded by looking pointedly at his watch.

Flushing, Atamian got to his feet. "I won't take any more time, at least not now. We'll be seeing each other tonight, and maybe we'll get a chance to talk some more."

For a moment, the new president of Dorland was at a loss. Then, without enthusiasm, he said, "Oh, you're on our guest list, are you?"

Atamian was fuming as he rode the elevator down to the lobby. But self-respect was one of the few luxuries he could not afford. He would have to play it any way Kidder wanted. Dorland was too profitable to lose because of crossed signals.

George Kidder was thinking, too. Did Dorland's man in Congress have to be such a cheap little hustler? Or was he simply another one of Walter Wellenmeister's mistakes?

For the time being, Congressman Atamian was too insignificant to be worth George Kidder's attention.

The same could not be said of his next visitor.

"I'm glad to see you again, General Khalid," Kidder said, ushering the Saudi Arabian into his office.

Since Khalid was shopping for an entire fleet of cargo planes, George Kidder meant every word. Within half an hour, he was selling hard.

". . . enormous capacity coupled to economy of operation. Sky Freighter will let you leapfrog the railroad and truck systems and introduce a really cost-effective distribution network."

"That," Khalid agreed, "is certainly what we have in mind."

"That's why we put so much effort into the engineering of these planes," said Kidder. "We can give you top performance, together with routine maintenance that doesn't make heavy demands on your technical people."

Khalid had heard a lot of sales pitches. The world's richest oil reserves had guaranteed that.

"But, Mr. Kidder, routine maintenance does not present the problem. That can be scheduled for the home base. It is the unexpected repairs that create—"

"We've thought of that, too," said Kidder quickly.

During the next hour, he convinced General Khalid that there was very little that Dorland had not thought of. Then Khalid's negotiating instinct told him that the time had come to introduce uncertainty.

"Mr. Kidder, you have given me much to think about. I would like to study your proposals for a day or two, before we meet again. But I must tell you how impressed I am by the care and attention Dorland has devoted to this project. It is all the more remarkable when one considers that the chief claim on your resources must be your line of fighter aircraft."

"Thank you, General," said Kidder, stiffening. "I assure you we are putting our best efforts into Sky Freighter."

Khalid was not going to let him escape from the VX-92 so easily.

"That unfortunate crash," he murmured. "No doubt, plane manufacturers must be prepared for such incidents. Nevertheless, it must be a matter of deep concern."

"We don't like accidents, but it's a fact we have to live with," said Kidder forthrightly. "The auto industry probably feels the same way."

"No doubt," said Khalid gently. "They are not, however, in the unenviable position of supplying one customer, and one customer with investigative procedures of its own."

Kidder did some rapid thinking. For some reason, Khalid wanted to talk about the Conroy case, without giving it a name.

Was he testing the waters about bribes? Cautiously, he said, "Dorland has always been willing to accept the findings of the Air Force."

Khalid's eyelids flickered appreciatively. "I agree that is the most prudent attitude for all parties," he said with approval. "These things take their course and are forgotten."

"That's the way it usually works," said Kidder, closing the subject. "About our proposals—I can meet you anytime you want. But while you're out here, I hope you'll be able to drop in on our little celebration this evening. All our top management people will be there."

"I look forward to the occasion," said General Khalid.

The little celebration was Dorland's obligatory farewell party for Walter Wellenmeister. It was like all such rituals, with one difference. How many presidents leave the company to become Ambassador to France?

"Boy, Walter's going to be a new experience for the French, isn't he?" said the treasurer of Dorland, passing George Kidder with a conspiratorial grin.

"That's one way to put it," said Kidder reflectively.

For twenty hard-hitting years, Wellenmeister had ruled Dorland with a rod of iron. Staff jokes about him, inspired by nervousness, dislike or fear, had never been very funny. Nobody had ever found Wellenmeister ridiculous. Now almost everybody did.

A shrill outburst of feminine laughter from the far corner pinpointed one reason for the Wellenmeister descent into comedy. From the moment that the President of the United States had announced the appointment, Mrs. Walter Wellenmeister had sprung into prominence.

"Will you look at Deedee! That getup might do for Buckingham Palace. But the Sandy Pines Country Club?"

The swirling throng had deposited Mrs. George Kidder at her husband's side.

"Never mind Deedee," he said single-mindedly. "General Khalid's the one to keep an eye on tonight."

Joan Kidder was the perfect corporation wife. George had made it abundantly clear that selling Sky Freighter to Saudi Arabia was absolutely necessary.

"Don't worry," she said calmly. "I got him together with John Tubby and his top engineer."

"Good," said Kidder.

"And now that your mind's at rest, do look at Deedee," she urged.

With Khalid taken care of, he was willing to obey. A sudden break in the crowd let him take in Deedee's full magnificence.

"I haven't seen so many feathers since the early Marlene Dietrich," he observed judiciously. "She looks ready to molt."

Joan was about to top this when the arrival of Walter Wellenmeister forced her to assume a welcoming smile instead.

"There you are, George!" Tonight, Wellenmeister was putting on a show. "Tell me, how does Dorland look from the top?"

Both Kidders knew every detail of Wellenmeister's losing fight to handpick his successor. So Joan decoyed them with a long, ruthless burble about the Paris Embassy.

". . . and George will get a chance to see it when he goes over to Paris for the Air Show," she prattled. "Oh, how I wish I was as lucky."

"Deedee's got big plans," Wellenmeister replied with immense satisfaction. "Let me tell you, she's really looking forward to the challenge. But Deedee's not forgetting her old friends, Joanie. She asked me to tell you especially that if there are any little hints she can give you about being the president's wife, all you have to do is ask."

He beamed at her benevolently.

Mrs. Kidder, who would sooner have consulted the inmates of the local reformatory, beamed right back. It was wonderful of Deedee to think of others when she had so much on her hands.

"It's just like her, isn't it, George? And I'm going to take her up on it right away. Just as soon as I introduce General Khalid to some people."

With a last flutter, she was gone.

Wellenmeister stayed. "Khalid?" he said sharply. "How's the Sky Freighter push going, George?"

"Fine," said Kidder repressively.

Wellenmeister looked around, lowered his voice and said, "I don't have to tell you that the competition's ready to play hardball."

"We can handle it."

"Just don't take anything for granted," Wellenmeister said, with a grunt.

Under the new Ambassador, Kidder recognized the old Walter, bigger than life.

But now that he was at the top at Dorland, Kidder no longer had to exercise the iron self-discipline that had got him there.

"By the way, Walter, an old friend of yours dropped by to see me today."

"Who was that?" Wellenmeister asked suspiciously.

"Congressman Atamian," said Kidder with unconcealed distaste.

Wellenmeister, who had been moving through the crowd of well-wishers with majestic geniality, stopped short.

"George, Atamian isn't an old friend of mine," he said emphatically. "He's a friend of Dorland's."

Kidder did not sugar the pill. "From here on, Walter, Dorland's going to be a lot choosier about its friends."

This was one area, Neil Conroy said to Earl Mohr, that he did not have to worry about.

". . . so, you see, I've got the right friends and, from my point of view, they're in the right places."

The steaks were long since finished, and now so was Neil's narrative.

"I just don't know," Earl Mohr said sadly. "You'll probably still end up with your butt in a sling."

"Maybe. But this way I'm shortening the odds."

Mohr knew better than to go on arguing. Neil was not accepting any under-the-table exoneration, and that was that. "A near miss doesn't sound like much to go on," Earl said instead. "There must be ways to explain it."

"I know." Neil was perfunctory. "I may come up with another one any day."

Mohr was in the habit of checking off all possibilities. "And maybe you won't."

Nothing further was said for several moments. Both men sat, silently reviewing Neil's plans.

"And there's always the Paris Air Show," Conroy said finally. "You can't tell what that will flush."

9

Congressman Safford, meanwhile, was taking an evening off from Neil Conroy and all other constituents. Dinner was at 8 Plainfield Road, not at the Veterans of Foreign Wars Hall. Ben was grateful for Janet's pot roast, and the breathing space. Veterans, like the League of Women Voters and the Elks, are good people, good friends and hard work.

Conversation over the dinner table had ranged from family (the far-flung Lundgren brood was flourishing) to business (anti-Japanese sentiment in Newburg was reaching Pearl Harbor heights) and, finally, to a rundown of what everybody had been doing.

This interval of peace and quiet was satisfying but brief. Inevitably, the outside world intruded.

"Who can that be?" Janet murmured, bustling off to answer the phone.

Of all people, it was Congresswoman Elsie Hollenbach.

Ben went to the phone with forebodings that proved fully justified. Twenty minutes later, he returned, dropped into a chair and announced the news in graduated steps.

"I've got to get back to Washington first thing in the morning."

"That's a shame," said Janet. "You'll miss the Kiwanis picnic."

"What's the big rush, Ben?" Fred inquired.

"The rush," Ben explained sourly, "is because I've got to go straight on. Of all the lousy luck!"

"Ben," Janet asked, thrusting the Kiwanis behind her, "where do you have to go?"

"Paris," he growled.

With a twinkle in his eye that belied the gravity of his manner, Fred Lundgren sympathized: "Gee, Ben, that's too bad."

April in Paris appealed to Fred and millions of others. Ben Safford was not one of them. Either Washington or Newburg was where he wanted to be. Only fund raisers, committee hearings or funerals tempted him farther afield.

So Paris held little appeal for him, and the Paris Air Show still less. A trade show is a trade show, wherever you put it. Boredom, aching feet and commercial hospitality are no better on the banks of the Seine than they are on the banks of the Ohio River or, for that matter, the Illinois Drainage Canal.

Nevertheless, Ben was slated to depart for Le Bourget, within twenty-four hours, as part of a delegation representing the Joint Committee on Uniform Weaponry at the Paris Air Show. Despite appearances, this was not a plum. During economic downturns, sensible congressmen do not clamor for junkets. Far better to appear at local shopping malls deploring unemployment. Ben got landed with the baby because he was not in Washington to defend himself.

Elsie had not phrased it in those terms.

". . . as a fact-finding mission, in view of the recommendations that the committee will be making about coordinating U.S. and NATO aircraft."

"You make it sound as if we're going over so we can report back," Ben had countered. "You know better than that, Elsie. They want us to shill for the American defense contractors—including Dorland. And I've got serious reservations about doing that. I'll explain when I see you, but as of now—"

Elsie deplored his negative attitude. "Of course, I don't know what the administration has in mind extending this invitation to Congress. *But*, whatever their motives, this gives us a unique opportunity. No one—including the Air Force or Dorland—can set this stage."

"Gaping at a whole lot of planes isn't going to solve my problems," he retorted.

58

"Planes are not the only things that will be on display in Paris," she said. "There will also be people."

Mrs. Hollenbach's scheme of priorities was not to be sneezed at. People, not planes, could provide the information Ben needed. But he was too disgruntled to indicate enthusiasm.

"Who else got stuck with this assignment?"

Elsie, public-spirited to a fault, had volunteered. Congressman Oakes, occupant of one of the safest seats in Congress, had not put up much of a fight. Filling the third slot had created such a ruckus that the chairman had fallen back on an ancient ploy, appointing Congressman B. Safford in absentia.

"When do we leave?" Ben asked, bowing to fate.

They were emplaning for Paris at dawn, Monday morning.

This exchange recurred to him Sunday afternoon, when he found himself at the luggage carousel of Dulles Airport outside Washington. As usual, his bag was one of the last to appear. Stylish, floppy duffle rolls and carry-ons drifted past for minutes until he sighted the two-suiter. Reaching forward, he collided with another overeager grasper.

"Why, Ben!" said an unwelcome voice.

"Hello, Atamian."

By rights, that should have ended their encounter. Given the number of congressmen taking to the air over weekends, they are bound to bump into each other at one airport or another.

But this Sunday, Mike Atamian was in no hurry to detach himself and neither was the man beside him.

"Ben, do you know General Khalid?" Atamian said proudly. "The general's with the Saudi Arabian buying mission. He's been out in California, talking to George. That's George Kidder, you know, the new president at Dorland."

"How do you do," said Ben, carefully masking the thoughts that leaped to mind.

"Mr. Safford," Khalid remarked pleasantly, "my limousine is waiting. Possibly I can offer you a ride into town."

"Thank you, I'd appreciate that," said Ben, curious to see how Khalid planned to handle Atamian.

The Saudi's methods were simplicity itself. "I am sorry you are not going our way, Congressman Atamian," he said, extending his hand. "I have enjoyed our discussion, and I look forward to continuing it in the future."

Atamian had not expected to be cast adrift in the middle of Dulles. But after a quick look from Khalid to Ben, he accepted the dismissal. "Anytime I can be of help, General Khalid," he said jauntily. "Good to see you, Ben, but I've got to run."

The sight of Atamian making the best of things did not occupy Ben for long.

Khalid began operations as they approached the limousine. "I understand, Mr. Congressman, that you have been concerning yourself with the inquiry into the VX-92 crash that took the life of my unfortunate countryman."

Not to be be outdone, Ben replied with stately condolences on the death of Ibn Billeni.

"Yes, a tragedy," said Khalid. "But, of course, accidents and other consequences are perhaps to be expected in this sort of situation."

Ben did not propose to beat around the bush indefinitely.

"Among those consequences, there's a real possibility that the board of inquiry will be reconvening."

Khalid inclined his head gravely. "How interesting! And suggestive, too, although you understand that we in the purchasing mission are far removed from all these events."

Ben understood no such thing. "You mean that the normal channel of communication between your government and ours is the Embassy?" he said. "The purchasing mission has other fish to fry?"

"Exactly," said Khalid, pleased. "The requirements of diplomacy, the intricacies of one nation dealing with another—no doubt they seem wasteful to young men full of zeal. But experience proves they are necessary, as we all know."

Ben could only guess at a translation. The young men with

zeal were, presumably, the ones who had bribed Captain Perini. Wiser heads, like his and Khalid's, would never engage in such behavior.

"Yes, indeed," he said meaninglessly.

Khalid narrowed his eyes. "No doubt, all will come out well in the end," he said. "Saudi Arabia is established as a firm friend of the United States. The strands of the relationship between us are many and varied. For both of us, it is vitally important that nothing be allowed to imperil that special relationship."

This time, Ben let silence give his consent. As nearly as he could make out, Khalid was saying that small incidents, like bribing a military official, should be overlooked in view of the larger consideration. Ben was not quite ready to go along.

A quick change of subject got him off the hook.

"I understand you will be attending the Paris Air Show," said Khalid.

"I just heard about it last night," Ben admitted unguardedly.

Khalid did not bother to name his sources. "Then I shall see you there myself. I, too, am attending," he said as they pulled up before the Carlton.

"Fine," said Ben, recalling Elsie on the subject of people versus planes.

"Like you," said Khalid, with a gleaming smile, "I have many excellent reasons for curiosity about Dorland Aircraft. Their displays, I am sure, will attract much attention."

Then, in case Ben had not followed him, he added: "Especially the VX-92."

10

Paris in the spring! For ninety-nine percent of the world's population, this means lovers strolling through the twilight, misty rain blurring the street lamps, and the Seine flowing past ancient stone piers. For the remaining one percent, there is the Paris Air Show. Every two years, specialists from all corners of the globe converge to buy, to sell, to scrutinize the competition, to keep up with the latest hardware.

The lobby of the Paris Hilton, when the congressional delegation checked in, provided a glimpse of things to come. There were white skins, and black and yellow and brown. There were military uniforms from every country with any claim to an air force. There was a grand confusion of languages ringing from the rafters.

Mrs. Hollenbach was refreshed by the scene.

"Splendid!" she said approvingly. "We'll have no problem obtaining a substantial NATO input on unification matters. And I see they've prepared our schedule for tomorrow."

She flourished three sheets of tightly spaced itinerary and began to read highlights. By the time she reached guidance systems, Val Oakes was groaning.

"I think I'll sleep late," he muttered.

"Nonsense, Val," said Elsie, at her most militant. "I expect us to make an early start tomorrow."

The stumbling block to this program was provided not by Val but by Ben. At first, all went well the next morning. Congressman Oakes, while unenthusiastic, did materialize in the dining room.

And just as the last drop of coffee was poured, the fresh-faced young man who was to be their guide appeared. Elsie was gathering her belongings when the hitch developed.

"Why, it's Ben. Ben Safford! Talk about your small world!"

There, resplendent in a sports shirt and dangling camera, was Bryan Faul, with Mrs. Faul beside him. As Ben did not have to explain to his tablemates, the Fauls hailed from Newburg.

". . . Stratford-on-Avon. Then we took the Hovercraft. We've got three whole days in Paris. Then we're renting a car to do the châteaux country. . . ."

While Mrs. Faul chattered happily, Bryan Faul produced a much-folded paper listing twenty-seven castles, thirteen museums and virtually all the cathedrals of Western Europe. In spite of these rival attractions, meeting Congressman Safford in Paris was obviously going to rank right up there with the great experiences of life.

Mrs. Hollenbach took this in at a glance. "Why don't you join the Fauls, Ben?" she said, quelling the guide, who was becoming restive. "You can catch up with us at the Dorland exhibit."

Smiling graciously, she swept her companions to the door.

A full hour passed before Ben parted company with the Fauls. It was time well spent. Faul's support for Ben had always been lukewarm. Now, Ben suspected, he had the Faul vote nailed for life. He was filled with satisfaction as he set forth.

The United States Pavilion brought him back to his senses in short order. It was a vast and echoing cavern, jammed with engines, instrumentation and computers. As Ben went from guidance systems to air traffic control devices, he realized he was incapable of appreciating the simplest gadget. Moreover, he was jostled at every turn by men, many of them in strange uniform, who looked like experts.

As an additional irritant, he could not locate the Dorland area. Past Rockwell turboprops and Beech scanners, past General Dynamic fuselages and Raytheon radar, he trudged fruitlessly.

He did, however, come across the fresh-faced guide.

"There you are, Congressman! I said you'd probably gone off to look at that new helicopter. Almost everybody does."

Ben did not disillusion him. "Well, now I'm ready for the Dorland exhibit," he said.

"Good! The car's right outside."

"The car? Isn't it here?"

The guide shook his head as he propelled Ben toward the exit. "There's no way Dorland could fit into the American building. They've got their own pavilion, and it's the biggest one at the show."

Once they were in the car, cruising at a snail's pace through the mob of rubbernecking pedestrians, the guide remembered his script.

". . . twenty-six countries and nearly eight hundred companies are represented this year," he said impressively.

As Ben had already discovered, there was more to see than airplanes.

". . . three hundred chalets where they'll have audiovisual presentations, as well as lectures. You can learn an awful lot from them."

"I'll bet."

"Of course, the presentations are mostly for the professionals. The crowds come to see the aerial displays. Every morning, a different country does the program."

Overhead, there was the scream and whine of today's jets.

"The Soviet Union's using the new MIGs up there," the guide announced with a jerk of his chin. "But tomorrow is Dorland's turn. Their crack precision team is going to be showcasing the VX-92. You won't want to miss that."

Ben doubted very much if he would be allowed to. But when they entered the Dorland Pavilion, he realized instantly that the hard sell on land featured a giant transport plane. Every single aspect of the Sky Freighter seemed to have a display of its own. The onlookers listening to the sales pitch were just as cosmopolitan as the crowd in the lobby of the Hilton. Whatever the virtues of the

Sky Freighter, they spoke to West Germans and Venezuelans and Pakistanis.

And Saudi Arabians, too. Ben was not surprised to find Val and Elsie talking to the president of Dorland. He had not expected General Khalid.

Mrs. Hollenbach, as a California Republican, did the honors. "You may not have met Congressman Safford, Mr. Kidder, but I'm sure you know that he's a member of the Uniform Weaponry Committee."

"It's a great pleasure, Congressman," said Kidder. "And I'd like to introduce—"

"Mr. Safford and I have already met," Khalid interrupted.

For a moment, Kidder's smile froze, but without difficulty he recovered his stride.

"Then you know that General Khalid is head of Saudi Arabia's purchasing mission. His country is looking for some heavy transports and I know the Sky Freighter is just what they want. All I have to do is convince him. And here comes one of our people to help me do it."

Val Oakes made no attempt to conceal his alarm when the horn-rimmed engineer began to brandish a sheaf of specifications, but he had no reason to fear. George Kidder simply moved slightly to one side, splitting the party into two groups.

"I'll let Rogers do this alone," he explained. "We're pulling out all the stops, trying to sell the Saudis. If we can close with them, we'll have a tremendous potential throughout the whole Third World."

Before Elsie could ask any intelligent questions, they were interrupted.

"Hello, everybody," caroled Congressman Michael Atamian. "Boy, isn't this show something! And, George, they tell me Dorland's got the best time slot for the precision flying. The VX-92 is going to knock their eyes out, isn't it?"

His face tightening, Kidder said, "Yes."

Snubs could not halt Atamian. "That's the way to do it! Show them by flying! Not that I'm an expert, but these ground displays don't really—"

"Dorland isn't selling the VX-92 this year, Congressman," Kidder broke in. "We're pushing the Sky Freighter. The commitment for the aerial display was made before we decided that this was the logical time to concentrate on the Sky Freighter. And, Congressman, we've got an important customer right here!"

"I see," said Atamian, reddening. Then, with a shrug, he flicked his hand to his colleagues and strolled away.

Tactfully, Elsie handled the ensuing awkwardness. "I see the Embassy reception for the American exhibitors is this evening, Mr. Kidder. We have to be moving on now, but I'm sure we'll see you there."

Kidder, who was still staring after Atamian, roused himself. "I'm only putting in a token appearance before I go on to the Saudi Embassy."

Then, as if afraid he had been too abrupt, he offered Dorland hospitality in the dining room upstairs. "I'm afraid I can't join you, but why don't you take a break? Doing an Air Show is hard work."

Upon emerging from the elevator, the three legislators discovered that Dorland Aircraft was making no attempt to vie with the Continental cuisine being offered elsewhere. Dorland was reminding everybody that it came from the great American West. An enormous barbecue contained sizzling steaks and hamburgers and chicken. Smoking tureens of chili marched down one table while luxuriant California salads were ranged along another. Even the wine bottles, as Elsie was quick to note, boasted labels from the Napa and Sonoma valleys.

"I'll have a Coors," said Val, entering into the spirit of the occasion.

After they made their selections, they left the menial details to the guide and were thankful to collapse at a table.

"Well, Kidder was right about one thing," Val grunted. "Hard labor would be easier than doing the Air Show."

Elsie had no time for physical weakness. "Did you notice how Mike Atamian was rubbing George Kidder the wrong way?"

"If Mike doesn't mend that particular fence," Val predicted, "he's going to have to find himself a new meal ticket."

Ben Safford was more bothered by Dorland than by its tame congressman. "I know giant companies aren't like the rest of us, but there are limits. Dorland doesn't exhibit in the American Pavilion, they've got to have one of their own. When the Soviet Union has the air demo today, tomorrow isn't for the United States—it's for Dorland. And tonight, Kidder can't be just another American exhibitor at the United States Embassy, he's got to negotiate with Saudia Arabia. Have I missed something? When did Dorland become a sovereign state?"

Ben never found out what his companions would have answered because the guide reappeared, shepherding a busboy rolling a cart.

As he seated himself, the guide remembered Elsie's remark to George Kidder.

"So you're going to the Embassy tonight. I only wish I was," he burbled innocently. "It's all over town that the Wellenmeisters are throwing a real bash, with no expense spared. You know, they've even flown in a planeload of their friends from California. When you come to think of it, it's really quite a coincidence, isn't it? I mean, that the new American Ambassador right at this moment should be the president of Dorland."

Ben was still feeling sour.

"I only hope he remembers which country he's working for these days," he murmured.

11

As far as the décor that greeted Ben at nine o'clock went, Walter Wellenmeister could have been working for Louis XV. Everything that was not mirrored or gilded was covered in white satin. Resolutely, he tried being fair-minded.

"I suppose if Mrs. Wellenmeister has spent thirty years at barbecues and pool parties, this is a natural reaction."

Mrs. Hollenbach shook her head. "It is far more likely to be her idea of a stately background. In any event, it hasn't been paid for by the taxpayer."

"Well, it's a hell of a background for me," grumbled Val Oakes as he assimilated the full magnificence of the receiving line.

Ambassador Wellenmeister, poised strategically on the landing, was fairly bursting with gratification. The deficiencies of his short, tubby frame were emphasized by white tie and tails. Not that this mattered, since he was eclipsed by his consort. Deedee Wellenmeister was encased in the intricate draping of a white Grecian gown knotted high on one shoulder. Against this classic field, she had dumped the contents of her jewelry chest.

"A grand occasion," the Ambassador trumpeted.

"And isn't it wonderful so many of our closest friends are here!" cried Deedee without referring to private jets. "I'm so glad you could come."

Her jeweled hand was held suggestively high, but Ben had no intention of making a fool of himself.

"My pleasure," he replied with a sturdy handshake.

Deedee then made the mistake of trying to strike a woman-to-woman note with Elsie.

"First impressions in a new place are so important, but I just know tonight's going to be a big success," she gushed.

Elsie observed in measured tones that Ambassador Wellenmeister's familiarity with heavy industry would be particularly valuable during the current restructuring of the French economy.

Heavy industry, however, was exactly what Deedee planned to leave behind.

"There must be a lot of people who can do that. Our goal is to show that Americans know about culture and elegance, too." Drawing a deep breath, she threw out her clincher. "And I have gotten us the most marvelous French chef."

"Well now, that's something we'll all appreciate tonight," said Val Oakes soothingly as he urged his companions forward. "C'mon now, we can't hold up the line."

Under his guidance, they were soon clear of the danger zone. Only then did he allow himself a mild expostulation.

"Now, Elsie, you ought to know better than try and talk sense to a birdbrain like that."

But Elsie's entire career was proof that she did not know better. One of life's instructors, she indefatigably lectured them where she found them. Fortunately, before she could start in on Val, she spotted a worthier target. The two men were able to drift away from the high-level dialogue that followed.

"Thank God," said Val.

"You want to try the buffet this wonderful French chef has put together?" Ben asked idly.

"Ben, you know I fortify myself before venturing on these foreign kickshaws," said Val.

He had to do without both for a while.

"Hello, Congressman Safford. I'm glad to see that the committee is getting the opportunity to see the Air Show."

It took Ben a minute to place Brigadier General Reynold Farrington, who was impressive in full-dress uniform.

"And what do you gentlemen think of the Air Show so far?" Farrington continued.

Ben said it seemed worth the time and effort involved. Looking more walruslike than ever, Val did not bother to answer. Clearly, General Farrington wanted to tell them what he thought.

"A very impressive American presence," he began.

"I hope you're including Dorland, Reynold," said Walter Wellenmeister, who was now free to circulate among his guests.

"Yes, indeed," said Farrington promptly.

Val smiled so benevolently that Ben knew he was thinking about the well-worn track that leads so many retired generals to highly paid positions in private industry.

"Glad to hear you say so," said the Ambassador graciously. "Reynold, and gentlemen, I'd like you to meet General Van Leeuwen of the Dutch Air Force." Barely pausing for the acknowledgments, he swept on: "And if you think today was good, just wait until tomorrow. Then you'll really see something!"

"Tomorrow?" asked the Dutchman.

"Tomorrow Dorland is flying the finest fighter plane in the world, the VX-92. We're putting on a demonstration of capability that will knock your eyes out."

Somewhere along the line, he had stopped being Ambassador.

"Just this morning, George Kidder was saying that Dorland isn't selling VX-92 this year," said Ben with malice. "As I understand it, Dorland is putting its best efforts behind their cargo plane. Sky Freighter it's called, isn't it?"

Wellenmeister laughed unconvincingly. "You've caught me out, Congressman Safford. I was president of Dorland so long that I forget I'm not anymore. You're right. George decided this is the year for Sky Freighter. And I don't deny it's an outstanding plane, but you wait until you see the VX-92 tomorrow!"

Then, recalling other people General Van Leeuwen should meet, he led his guest away.

As soon as they were out of earshot, Farrington shared an opinion. "There's a man who understands airplanes—and the Air Force," he said. "One of the few civilians in the government who does."

"Speaking as a civilian in government myself, I'm interested to hear you say that, General," said Val with deceptive mildness.

Farrington hastened to make himself clear. "What I meant is

that I don't understand why they made him Ambassador to France. You see, we could use him over in Defense. You should see some of the people we have to work with!"

"I have," said Ben.

With a forced smile, Farrington excused himself and departed.

Ben was about to congratulate Val on routing General Farrington when he realized that the credit lay elsewhere. Wending his way toward them, as Farrington had seen and they had not, was Undersecretary Preston Goodrich.

"Some bash," he remarked when he joined them.

Goodrich looked tired. Being the right kind of old friend, Ben did not say so. Instead, he asked after Mrs. Goodrich.

"No, Zinka didn't come over," Goodrich replied. "She wanted to take the kids back to Cleveland. Tell me, was that General Farrington?"

"You just missed him," Val Oakes said, sounding as if he could have been sympathizing.

Goodrich corrected him. "You mean he missed me. He's part of the old-boy network here. I'm not."

Whether you call it the old-boy network or the military-industrial complex, Congress knew all about it. But Val thought he had spotted an anomaly. "I can see why you're odd man out," he said gravely. "Undersecretaries usually are. But what about George Kidder? Why is he ducking these generals tonight?"

"Not to speak of ambassadors," Ben added.

Goodrich lowered his voice. "Because there's been a major confrontation about which plane to showcase here. All the Toms and Dicks and Reynolds have been calling around and leaning on each other. The result has been a compromise. Kidder is pushing ahead, trying to sell his Sky Freighter. But tomorrow Dorland's putting on a big demonstration of Wellenmeister's VX-92—which isn't for sale. Nobody's really satisfied."

During the long trip to Paris, Ben Safford had tried to make up his mind what to do. Neil Conroy claimed that the Utah crash was caused by the VX-92. General Khalid was half admitting it was caused by the co-pilot. After consulting his colleagues, Ben decided he did not have the expertise required to make any kind of judgment. As a congressman, he should confine his role to safeguarding Conroy's right to present evidence.

Technical training, however, was not necessary to hear alarm bells now.

"What started this confrontation? Was it the Conroy case?"

"I thought so at first," Goodrich said reflectively. "But they tell me the squabble began before that. I know for a fact that it was already boiling when I got to Washington."

Val Oakes was a born skeptic. "To those of us who rely on appearances, it still looks as if Dorland switched horses in midstream, right after young Conroy's troubles began."

Goodrich grinned. "Mr. Congressman, those horses were named Walter Wellenmeister and George Kidder, and the switch came before Neil Conroy, not after."

"That certainly is a possibility," said Oakes blandly. "And I'm still in need of refreshment."

Turning, he tried to attract a waiter. His vigorous waving produced nothing more sustaining than other guests.

"Hello, Congressman Safford. Say, isn't this place something!"

Unlike General Farrington, Lieutenant Colonel Lawrence Yates looked just as he had looked in Washington, only happier. A dazzling redhead in green taffeta was hooked onto his arm.

"Miss Ursula Richmond," he announced with pardonable pride.

Miss Richmond's eyes were large, hazel and observant. She could scarcely miss the universal masculine admiration she was drawing. Nevertheless, the poise with which she met two congressmen and an undersecretary was notable.

"And I'll bet this young man hasn't managed to supply you with a drink," said Val unscrupulously.

"He hasn't had a chance yet, Mr. Congressman," she said, taking his measure.

"Well, why don't we see if we can do something about that?"

Colonel Yates stepped in. "You know," he said with nice timing, "Ursula here is a captain in the Air Force."

As might be expected, this threw Val off stride.

"I'd still like that drink, Mr. Congressman," said Miss Richmond, twinkling shamelessly.

"And you shall have it," said Val gallantly, preparing to show them all that the Brave New World held no terrors for an old master.

Fortunately, a waiter with a tray finally materialized.

"A captain in the Air Force, eh?" said Preston Goodrich. Undersecretary or not, he straightened his tie. "Are you on assignment to the Air Show?"

"No," she replied after a sip of champagne. "I'm a flight instructor in Germany—Wiesbaden. I had some leave so I thought I'd take in the Air Show—"

"And I'm the lucky guy she happened to meet this morning," finished Yates triumphantly.

"Ursula!" The exclamation came from a youthful officer just edging past them. Halting unceremoniously, he went on: "What are you doing here?"

"Pete!" she replied, turning to him enthusiastically. "I thought you were in Texas."

"I was, but now I'm on my way to Naples. Say, you know who else is here? Chip!"

"Chip Olson?"

"That's right. C'mon over—"

"I think your girl's just been stolen," Ben remarked as Ursula Richmond was led off.

"She'll be back," said Yates confidently. "And if she isn't, I'll go after her."

"Don't blame you," said Val Oakes. "A captain in the Air Force. Seems a waste, doesn't it?"

No sooner had he made this sexist remark than Elsie, glass in hand, emerged from the crowd. "What seems to be a waste, Val?" Happily, she did not wait for the answer no one was courageous enough to provide. "Good evening, Mr. Undersecretary. Are you talking about the VX-92 demonstration tomorrow?"

"Yes," said Val Oakes. "That's exactly what we were discussing with Colonel Yates here."

Naturally, Yates did not contradict him, but his attention was roaming. After a few proper, if desultory exchanges, he excused himself and departed, no doubt in search of Miss Richmond.

"A fine young officer," said Val, in effect complimenting the Undersecretary.

Elsie's dispassionate spirit of accuracy never rested. "He's not so young, Val."

"Neither am I, Mrs. Hollenbach," said Goodrich, amused. "But, if you'll excuse me, I'd better do some more circulating, too."

The others decided to follow his example. In the succeeding hour, Ben chatted with a California matron who told him how thrilling it was to be the personal guest of the Ambassador, to the sad-faced Dutch general once again, to three African air ministers and to the managing directors of SAS, Qantas and Air Caledonia. Pointed out to him with varying degrees of accuracy were several Hollywood stars, a French novelist and many Russians identified as spies.

"Elsie," he complained when he encountered her again. "How much more time do we have to put in?"

Mrs. Hollenbach, showing no sign of wear or tear, thought briefly before replying. "Val and I had better stay for another hour. You can go anytime, Ben. So could Mike Atamian, if anybody could tear him away."

The afterthought was prompted by a sudden glimpse of Congressman Atamian eagerly buttonholing anybody he could while staying close to the lavish buffet.

"As long as the food and drink last, Mike will hang in," Ben agreed. "Are you and Val really stuck?"

"Well," she calculated, "Ambassador Wellenmeister is a prominent and influential Republican and a close political and personal ally of the President of the United States, who is also a Republican."

"Elsie," Ben said, "I'd be willing to bet you've just put your finger on something so obvious that it's easy to overlook."

12

At the time, Ben Safford was grateful for release.

Second thoughts, as usual, came the morning after. After a good night's sleep, Ben was up and virtuously breakfasting long before Val and Elsie.

"Oh, good!" said an Embassy aide, halting by Ben's table. "I didn't expect you down until much later, Congressman Safford."

Ben did not like the sound of that, and what followed was worse.

"Ambassador Wellenmeister has arranged it all, Mr. Safford," the aide explained, going on to outline a major production. Convoys of transport were arriving at the Hilton and other hotels to whisk distinguished guests to Le Bourget. Their destination was the VIP grandstand, from which they would view the precision flying demonstration of the Dorland VX-92.

"Very kind of Ambassador Wellenmeister," said Ben. "What's Dorland doing along these lines?"

"I don't know," said the aide vaguely. "Now, I have you down for car sixteen at ten o'clock. If you wouldn't mind going in car seven—that's at nine-thirty . . ."

The net result was that Ben was booked to lose today whatever he had gained last night. It never occurred to him that the countdown to the Dorland presentation might prove more enlightening than the tag end of an Embassy gala.

At first, Le Bourget looked like a total washout. It still lacked a full hour until the Dorland Diamonds took to the air, and the grandstand was half-empty.

"Your seat is here, Mr. Congressman," said the usher, leading Ben to a center section carefully ribboned off.

"I didn't realize that watching a flying demonstration was so organized," he observed.

"Usually it isn't," said the young woman. "But Ambassador Wellenmeister insisted—"

She broke off in some embarrassment, but not before Ben got the picture. Ambassador Wellenmeister had been throwing his weight around at the Air Show, as well as at the Embassy.

"And speak of the devil," said Ben amiably.

Three rows down, another usher was showing Ambassador and Mrs. Wellenmeister to the place of honor. Deedee, apparently anticipating a change in the weather, was swathed in fur. The Ambassador was smiling and nodding to everyone within sight.

"Morning, Ben," said a voice in his ear.

Preston Goodrich was sitting next to him.

"Don't get me wrong, Pres. I'm always glad to see you. But are we an official reviewing party or something?"

"Off the record, yes," said the Undersecretary. After a pause, he added: "Wellenmeister likes to get his way, as you may have noticed."

"Yes, I have," said Ben.

"Look!" Goodrich directed.

Just arriving was George Kidder. He was quite alone.

"Dorland Aircraft isn't putting in much of an appearance, is it? Where are the rest of the boys?"

"Where do you think?" said Goodrich. "They're back at the Dorland Pavilion, hustling the Sky Freighter."

"Kidder likes to get his own way, too," commented Ben, watching the encounter below. What went on between Kidder and Ambassador Wellenmeister was there for all to see. Kidder shook hands with his former chief, then took his seat beside Deedee. He neither waved at acquaintances nor called greetings. He was dissociating himself both from the Ambassador and the Ambassador's plane.

A tap on the shoulder made Ben swerve around. There were

Elsie and Val Oakes and, with them, Mike Atamian. Everybody looked uncomfortable.

At least part of the problem was physical.

By some oversight, a seat had not been assigned to Congressman Atamian. Rather than retreating to the unreserved section, he had decided to squeeze in with his colleagues. Minute adjustments all along the row finally produced breathing space.

"That's better," said Atamian. "Say, Ben, you should have hung around last night. The party didn't get going until after midnight, did it, Elsie?"

"I think," said Mrs. Hollenbach above the sudden roar of engines, "I think they must be ready to begin."

Turning back to the field, Ben was in time to see four sleek planes take off. After that, he was mesmerized. It was impossible to do anything but gape as the planes, in tight diamond formation, spun through the heavens as if gravity did not exist.

"Magnificent, aren't they?" Preston Goodrich bellowed at him minutes later.

"They sure are," Ben yelled back.

There was no other word for it. Dorland's VX-92s and the men who flew them were magnificent.

The four streaked past, barely a hundred feet above the airstrip. Wingtip to wingtip, their sheer beauty was literally breathtaking. Ben and Goodrich, like the whole crowd, were spellbound until the quartet abruptly pulled skyward. Then, with an awesome roar, the planes looped into a great arc still within heartbeats of each other.

Some spectators cheered involuntarily as the VX-92s quartered the sky with lazy grace, then reformed and sideslipped across each other's line of trajectory.

Ben could hear buzzing appreciation in many languages. The pure drama of Dorland's flight demonstration was irresistible.

The sky was a clear, cloudless blue. Near the spectator area, flags and banners from all participating nations crackled in the stiff breeze. A scant five hundred yards from the airstrip, the men and women looking on followed the VX-92s through one intricate maneuver after another.

Excitement gripped the entire audience, and Ben was not the only American to feel a prickling of the eyes. These were American planes and American pilots. Somehow, the sun glinting on these extraordinary planes triggered a surge of patriotism.

The VX-92s picked up speed and began their synchronized dives. Closer, closer to earth—then, almost too late, the lead plane leveled out. Then came the left wing, with the same split-second timing. Then the right wing . . .

But, so fast it could not register, the fourth plane continued its screaming descent and slammed nose-down into the ground, disappearing instantly into a billowing pillar of thick black smoke.

Almost immediately, Ben heard sirens, shouts, engines starting, but through sudden blinding tears, all he could see was the column of smoke with obscene flickers of orange flame licking its base.

Though Ben and Val and Elsie were over two hours making their way back to the Hilton, it was not long enough for the nightmare to dissipate. They were still shaken when they arrived to find the lobby crowded with witnesses of the crash, all talking compulsively.

Brigadier General Farrington and Lieutenant Colonel Yates were the first to notice them.

"Did you see that?" Normally, Yates had a deep, even voice, but emotion betrayed him, and his question came out falsetto. He had to repeat it to find his usual register. "Did you see that? The poor bugger never had a chance. This is going to mean the biggest Air Force investigation ever."

Elsie Hollenbach was also distressed, but she could no more help raising rational objections than she could help breathing. "But that was Dorland's precision team."

"And Dorland planes," Yates grated. "Which we happen to be using."

"So what?" Ben was betrayed into snarling. "I thought when these little incidents happened, you just blamed the pilot and went about your business."

"You don't understand." Shock was having a different effect on General Farrington's voice. It had sunk so far that it emerged as a basso growl. "This is different."

Now Ben had himself under control. "How?" he asked on a less belligerent note.

"For God's sake!" Yates exploded. "This was no trainee-pilot. That team has been practicing exactly these maneuvers in exactly these planes for months."

"And three of them are still here. They must know what happened," Farrington added. "Besides, they managed to retrieve the recorder this time. Did I tell you that, Larry?"

But Yates only produced a thin, bitter smile. "And there's no point pretending that having it happen in front of the whole world doesn't make a difference. Just listen to what they're saying here."

His wave around the lobby was unnecessary. They had all been conscious of the frenzied conversations. In every corner, people struggled past the language barrier to describe what they had seen. Even as he looked, Ben saw one Frenchman move his hand in a gesture that was a ghoulish parody of the fatal dive.

"Yes," Ben said temperately. "I can see how, this time, there isn't going to be any room for pressure about moving right along and avoiding adverse publicity."

Elsie took a larger view. "It is certainly not the moment to recommend the VX-92 to our NATO allies. I came here to collect their views, and they are certainly airing them."

"Oh, my God," Farrington groaned. "If there really is something wrong with that plane, this could be the end of my career."

Until now, Neil Conroy had been a constituent problem peculiar to Ben Safford. In little more than two hours, he had suddenly become the property of the entire Joint Committee on Uniform Weaponry. This was made abundantly clear when Congresswoman Hollenbach voiced the very remark that Ben had been stifling.

"Exactly as with Captain Conroy," she said with regal assurance.

"It's not going to do any of us a hell of a lot of good," Larry

Yates remarked in a return to his usual manner. "I know I could use a drink right now. What about the rest of you?"

Eugene Valingham Oakes demonstrated solidarity with his colleagues in his own way.

"I don't believe we'll join you just now," he said blandly.

"Oh, my God," Farrington groaned again. "Do you suppose there really is something fundamentally wrong with that plane?"

Larry Yates was recovering faster.

"Well, that's what Neil Conroy was trying to tell us all along," he drawled.

13

Neil Conroy, of course, made the connection instantly. No sooner had he received word of the crash than he was furiously dialing the local airport.

"I don't care whether it's smoking or nonsmoking," he snapped. "Just get me a seat on the first plane to Washington!"

As a military flier, he was always irritated by the amount of red tape required to board a commercial airliner. Today, it made him lose his temper altogether. Even when he learned that he had over an hour till flight time, he attacked his packing as if there were not a moment to lose.

By the time Peg Conroy and Earl Mohr returned home, the living room had been transformed. An open suitcase was on the sofa, two pairs of shoes were on the floor and a uniform jacket lay across the wingback chair.

"Now what?" exclaimed Peg Conroy, halting on the threshold.

Upstairs a drawer slammed shut.

"It looks to me as if Neil is going somewhere," Earl Mohr observed.

"I can see that," she said tartly as her son strode into the living room, sweater in hand. "Neil, what are you doing? I thought you were going to wait here until—"

Mohr ignored the nonessentials. He took one look at Conroy, then demanded, "What happened?"

Neil did not pause. "Just what I said could happen, Earl," he said, packing with swift, practiced efficiency. "Another VX-92 went down at the Paris Air Show a couple of hours ago."

Glancing over his shoulder, he saw his mother's hand go to her lips in the age-old response to tragedy. "That's right," he said fiercely. "Another pilot's been killed, just like Billy!"

Deliberately, Mohr went over to the easy chair, moved the jacket to one side and sat down. "You think this might give you more ammunition?" he suggested. "To prove that there really is something wrong with the VX-92?"

He could have been talking about a faulty carburetor on the family car.

"It's not a question of might, Earl," Conroy replied less intensely. "This is going to prove it. Nobody can cover up what happened at Paris, or blame it on the pilot. Hell, they'll be forced to ground the VX-92 even before they investigate."

"That's what you want," Mohr said, keeping his eyes on Neil.

"That and a few other things," said the younger man, bending for his shoes.

His mother was not really interested in airplanes. "But, Neil, what are you doing? Where are you going?"

He kept his attention fixed on the suitcase. "Washington, Mom," he said briefly.

"What good—"

"Look, I've got to hurry. The plane will be leaving. I'll explain it all to you later."

Whirlwind departures are a convenient way to avoid saying what you do not want to say. But after the dust settles, the gaping holes sometimes show up more clearly than before.

"Earl," said Peg after her son had disappeared into Newburg Airport on the run, "I'm worried."

He did not start the car.

"Did it . . . I mean . . ." Finally, she managed to get it out. "Did you get the idea that Neil was—oh, I don't know—somehow pinning too much hope on this crash?"

"Well, he wouldn't be human if he wasn't excited. This crash fits in with what he's been saying all along."

"I suppose so," she said, still unsatisfied.

Although he did not say so, Mohr had a worry of his own.

When would Peg realize that Neil had heard about the crash long before he should have?

In California, the waiting was over. The office of the Chief of Design at Dorland Aircraft was funereal.

"Straight down," said one engineer, tapping a pencil with mindless regularity.

"For Christ's sake, Phil, will you stop that!"

Phil stopped, although he knew it was not the tapping that was making their nerves ragged. It was the VX-92 that had gone straight down. First Utah, now Paris.

"No indication of any response at all," he repeated dully.

"It could be that the pilot blacked out," said his chief.

No one in the crowded room bothered to reply. The list of possibilities was drearily long. But Dorland's engineers had been shortening that list for too many months. A terrible certainty was beginning to emerge.

"You know what we've got to do, Phil, don't you?" said the chief bleakly. "We've got to put the whole thing in front of George Kidder as fast as we can."

Phil was not arguing when he replied. "Yeah. Except I think we left it too late. We should have done it right off the bat."

Everybody present knew what *right off the bat* at Dorland meant.

Sergeant Dunnet of the Fairfax police caught the flash on his car radio and frowned. The Air Force had been very guarded with him about the activities of Captain Julian Perini. Now he was finally able to read between the lines.

"So that's what they've been sitting on," he muttered to himself.

"What's that?" his wife asked suspiciously over the announcer's shift to baseball scores.

Sergeant Dunnet was not on duty. He was in his own station wagon, with his wife, three children, two dogs and several large picnic baskets, on the way to a state park. One look at his wife's expression, and he chose the course of prudence.

"I was wondering when to start the coals," he improvised. "Do you want to go to the lake first?"

Even as he spoke, he was agreeing with what his wife would have said, if he had given her the chance.

The Air Force had wanted to keep this one to themselves. Now they were stuck with it, and good luck to them!

It was not a day off for the two air police who had been assigned to investigate the background of Julian Perini's death.

"You think this is going to make a difference?" one of them asked as they crossed the parking lot.

His companion squinted into the sun.

"Probably. We already know it was a lot nastier than they were making out. Now it turns out it's a lot bigger, too. But one thing's for sure," he added cautiously. "It's not going to be our problem much longer. They'll throw in more manpower now."

"So what do we do in the meantime?"

"Exactly what we planned. Have a nicy cozy talk with General Farrington and Colonel Yates as soon as they're back from Paris."

General Khalid was one of the few interested parties in Paris who had not actually seen the VX-92 crash. A man whose shopping list stretched from single-engine crop dusters to sleek airliners had no time to watch flying demonstrations. He had been engaged in discussion with a French manufacturer of executive jets when the news reached him.

At first, the two men had confined themselves to expressions of genuine horror. But business is business. The Frenchman soon modulated into an attack on a heavyweight competitor.

"It is to be hoped that this appalling tragedy is due to the requirements of precision flying and not to some engineering failure on the part of Dorland."

Ordinarily, Khalid would have been grimly amused. Now he scarcely heard his host.

"You must forgive me if I shorten our very interesting discussion," he replied. "I regret that the demands of my schedule do not permit me to remain as long as I had originally planned. I trust I have not inconvenienced you."

He had cut the Frenchman off in the middle of his presentation, but until Khalid actually took his munificient order elsewhere, he could do no wrong.

"I place myself entirely at your disposal."

Not much later, Khalid was on the long-distance line to Saudi Arabia, feeling all the inconvenience of his location. His intelligence staff was some three thousand miles away to the west, in Washington. His superiors were some three thousand miles to the east. It was not the ideal spot from which to report.

"No, Excellence, I have no further information. The crash itself occurred only a short time ago."

The minister wanted to know if this called for action.

"It is impossible to tell. We have taken certain things for granted, and so have the Americans. It has been to our mutual advantage. This may no longer be the case."

Somewhat impatiently, the minister chided him for his circumlocutions. "It is not necessary to impress *me* with the subtle indirections of the Arab mind. You are probably stroking your beard."

Guiltily, Khalid snatched his hand down. He had been away from home too long, he decided. Nowadays, he spent so much time in ceremonial robes that he tended to forget his minister wore business suits and bifocals.

"Yes, Excellence," he said, rebuked. "By the time I arrive in Washington, my aide will be able to brief me. But the Americans revel in their scandals. I fear they will indulge their curious taste for publicity."

"Not at our expense! An isolated situation, handled discreetly, was permissible. It is out of the question that we should be involved in one of their circuses."

Khalid smiled as he struck a blow for Arab indirection. "No formal admission was ever made. It will be simplicity itself to gently recede from our previous position."

"See to it!"

14

Forty-eight hours later, Congressman Eugene Valingham Oakes delivered a statement. "I'm beginning to feel like the last rose of summer."

The coffee shop at the American Pavilion was filled to overflowing. Outside, there were still crowds eddying along the main concourse of Le Bourget. Even the Dorland Pavilion was still carrying heavy Air Show traffic.

Nevertheless, Val's companions knew exactly what he meant.

"George Kidder headed for California before they recovered the body," said Ben Safford somberly.

"Now that you mention it, so did Mike Atamian," Elsie said. "No doubt he felt Dorland requires defending up on the Hill."

"I wonder what George Kidder thinks," Ben replied.

Kidder and Atamian were not the only notable absentees. A large part of the official American presence at the Air Show had left Paris in a hurry. But the Committee on Uniform Weaponry was not alone in being forced to remain behind, under the shadow of the VX-92 tragedy.

Undersecretary Goodrich put down his cup of cooling coffee. "Mr. Oakes," he said, reverting to Val's lament, "if you want cheerful company, you can go over to the Embassy. Wellenmeister's there, big as life—pretending that nothing has happened."

"God forbid," said Val.

"What do you mean, pretending nothing's happened?" Mrs. Hollenbach demanded.

Undersecretary Goodrich had spent two hard days bouncing

between the Embassy and Le Bourget, fending off reporters, answering urgent inquiries from the Pentagon. By now, he did not look tired, he looked battered.

"The Ambassador is concentrating on Franco-American relations. That VX-92 crash is somebody else's accident. If anyone's tactless enough to mention it, he shakes his head and says we mustn't judge too hastily, at least not until we hear what Dorland has to say."

Val Oakes, himself a master tactician, disapproved. "Playing ostrich won't work this time. Wellenmeister should be planning his defense. There's going to be hell to pay in Washington, and soon."

"I know it," said Goodrich. "The investigating team we jetted over has packed up every splinter of debris. Now that they're done, I'm taking off, and I don't look forward to getting back to Washington."

"Do you expect a major battle over grounding the VX-92?" Elsie asked sharply.

Rising to leave, Goodrich shook his head. "No, that battle's over. The VX-92 is grounded until we get some preliminary findings. But—and I'm quoting directly—after the immediate emergency is past, important long-range decisions will have to be made."

"Should I ask who you're quoting, Pres?" Ben inquired.

"Better not. But I'll tell you one thing. Cleveland is looking better and better. Well, I'll see you in Washington, if not before."

"Speaking of Ohio," said Ben after Goodrich had departed, "one of the first things I'm going to do when I get back is contact Neil Conroy. He's going to be champing at the bit."

To his surprise, Elsie took issue with him. "Neil Conroy is the least of your problems."

"Now hold it," he protested. "In the first place, I thought we all agreed that my major contribution is to help him make his case."

"That," Mrs. Hollenbach replied, "was before this horrible crash."

Ben was not altogether sure where she was heading. "I know that, Elsie. But Neil wanted to ground every VX-92 in the world.

And what happened here in Paris has done just that. That puts him front and center—"

"No," she said firmly.

"What Elsie means," Val helped out, "is that taking care of one of the folks back home—wise as it is under most circumstances—is not your top priority right now. We've got something to tell the Uniformity Committee. When it comes to NATO, the VX-92 is out."

"Precisely," said Elsie, with rare approval. "While any formal decision must wait, common sense tells us that. And, apart from NATO, there is also the United States Air Force to consider."

In other words, it was time for Congressman Safford to change hats. He should be thinking about national defense, not individual rights.

It was a transformation that implied heavy responsibilities, as Elsie demonstrated.

"And since we are leaving for Brussels tomorrow morning, I am meeting with General Van Leeuwen for an informal discussion of the entire situation."

"Good for you," said Val Oakes. "Ben and I are going to be doing some research too."

"I see," said Elsie, showing only too well that she knew it was going to be in the bar of the Hilton.

They were not destined to drink alone.

"Care to join us?" Lieutenant Colonel Yates said courteously.

Ben felt no compunction about accepting, even though Ursula Richmond was sitting beside Yates. Smiling faces made a welcome change.

Apparently, Val felt the same. "You're a sight for sore eyes," he remarked genially to Ursula.

Even in linen slacks and a crisp white shirt, Captain Richmond was attracting covert male glances from fifty feet away.

"I thought everybody on duty had gone home," Ben remarked. "Even General Farrington finally went."

"Well, I was sent over on specific assignment," Yates explained. "I'm checking out the new swept-wing designs. Since nobody told me to stop, I've gone right on doing it."

In addition, Lieutenant Colonel Yates had special reasons for hewing to duty.

"What's more, I've done such a thorough job it amounts to overkill," he admitted. "After the way we messed up the Conroy board of inquiry, I figure we'll need all the credit we can get."

There was no such cloud over Ursula Richmond. "The Air Show's been so interesting I decided to stay on and spend the rest of my leave here."

Yates looked smug. "Guess what changed her mind?" he asked softly.

"So you're a bigger attraction than the Mirages?" she challenged.

"I like to think so," he said, sounding pretty sure of himself.

Ursula chuckled. "Different, certainly. Bigger? Maybe you can convince me in Washington."

"What do you mean, maybe?" Yates retorted impudently.

It was standard dialogue—half provocation, half retreat—between two experts. Ben found himself smiling unconsciously for the first time in days, grateful just to be sitting there, a relaxed spectator of the world's oldest game. He was also learning a lesson. A woman like Ursula could be a career officer in the Air Force and still be feminine to her fingertips.

"You're going to be stationed in Washington?" he asked her.

"Starting next week. That's why General Farrington collected me for his list."

Ben was baffled. "His list?"

"Yes. General Farrington was assigned to compile the names of service witnesses to the crash. He was particularly interested in those qualified on fighters who'd be available back home." Ursula grimaced wryly. "As I was right up there on both counts, I thought I'd better bring myself to his attention before someone did it for me."

"Yates here told me that none of you like to serve on boards," Ben remarked. "I didn't realize that testifying was so bad."

Ursula was forthright. "It's the timing that's bad for me," she confided. "Starting a new assignment always means putting in longer hours and getting the feel of a new unit. That's hard enough without having a full-scale inquiry thrown into the works. But I'm not going to spoil my last fling in Europe thinking about it."

"For your last fling, I thought we'd make it special," Yates suggested. "How does dinner at the Tour d'Argent grab you?"

At these words, Val was ready to leave, but he was forestalled by Ursula. Casting a dismayed glance at her slacks, she bounded to her feet.

"Now don't worry, I won't be more than twenty minutes," she said, with a hand on Yates' shoulder to prevent his rising. "But I never realized we were going to be so fancy tonight. You'll just have time for another drink."

With a hasty wave to the congressmen, she was off, speeding toward the elevator. Larry Yates looked after her, a smile lingering on his face.

"In spite of everything," he said, "this Air Show's got one thing going for it. I sure hit it lucky when I picked up Ursula."

Val shook his head as he contemplated these newfangled ways. "There's got to be something wrong with your generation," he observed. "In my time, you couldn't pick up a girl like Ursula because whenever she came out, she had a cloud of men with her. Nowadays, things are different."

Yates raised his glass. "*Vive la différence!*" he toasted.

Fifteen minutes later, Ben and Val scrupulously left the scene. Even with the safety margin, they still glimpsed a vision in black chiffon sweeping into the bar, her dark eyes sparkling with anticipation.

"I'm glad we bumped into those two," Ben said as they crossed the lobby. "I admit they make me feel a little old, but it's nice to know that Paris in the spring still means more than selling cargo planes to Saudi Arabia."

As usual, Val had a quotation at the ready.

"To every thing, there is a season," he intoned, "and a time to every purpose under the heaven."

*   *   *

90

The Committee on Uniform Weaponry got back to Washington a week later. Like everyone else returning from Paris, they had assumed that the action would begin when they arrived.

Within half an hour, Ben Safford knew this was a mistake. Washington, or at least the Washington press corps, was way ahead of them. From the pile of clippings stacked on his desk, Ben learned that the *Washington Post* had not only resurrected the Conroy crash, it had also unearthed a near miss by another VX-92.

"Have they zeroed in on Perini's suicide?" Ben asked as he riffled through photostats.

"Not yet," said Madge in high spirits. "They're having too much fun with the big names to bother with the little fish. George Kidder has been on television three times this week, explaining how he just took over Dorland and how he fears that certain elements in the company may not have been candid with him."

Ben frowned. This sounded perilously close to an admission. "I thought he came racing back to fight for the VX-92."

"That's probably what he intended to do. But on Wednesday, the Air Force investigators announced they'd recovered the flight instrumentation intact and," Madge continued merrily, "by Thursday, George Kidder was taking to the airwaves."

Slowly, Ben began putting two and two together. If Dorland had abandoned its defense of the VX-92, then presumably the company's camp followers had also been called off. And that meant . . .

But, as so often happened in the nation's capital, two and two could come up any number except four. As Ben pondered, the lights on his phone sprang to life. Madge, perched on the corner of his desk, leaned across him to deal with it.

"It's Congressman Atamian on line one and Undersecretary Goodrich on line three," she announced.

"Line three," said Ben instantly.

Goodrich wasted no time on small talk. "Neil Conroy," he said bluntly.

"Do you want to amplify that, Pres?" said Ben, although he had a pretty good notion of what was coming.

Goodrich amplified in bitter detail. Captain Conroy had come storming into Washington. He was buttonholing Air Force person-nel for eyewitness descriptions of what had happened in Paris. He was even threatening to talk to civilians.

"In fact," Goodrich declared, "he's hell-bent on making a bad situation worse. We've got our hands full over here, Ben."

"I know you do," Ben temporized. He valued and trusted Goodrich but not to the extent of forgetting that he was the man in the middle.

Any undersecretary would be getting flak from all directions, as this one demonstrated.

"Look, Ben, we've launched an investigation that's going to make Watergate look like small potatoes. If Conroy will just sit still, he'll float home free and clear. Somebody should talk to him—"

Ben did not pretend to misunderstand. "Not me, Pres," he said firmly. "I wasn't the one who shafted him."

"The Air Force is taking the position that it's still an open question," Goodrich replied carefully.

"The Air Force—and who else?" Ben retorted crudely.

Silence.

"Getting back to the immediate question at hand, Ben, we all admit Conroy got a raw deal. That's what I want to get through to him."

"How fair is everybody else going to be?" Ben insisted.

Goodrich groaned.

"Well, I'll tell you what I will do," said Ben. "I will see if I can get Conroy together with you, personally. How much good this will do I can't tell, but I suppose there's an outside chance."

"An outside chance," said Goodrich dourly, "is better than no chance at all. Thanks, Ben."

"Don't mention it," said Ben with a slight inward grin. "By the way, how's the investigation going?"

"Slowly," said the Undersecretary just as Madge appeared in Safford's doorway, semaphoring urgently.

"Slow and sure or just slow? Okay, Pres, don't answer that. I'll track Conroy down and get back to you." Ringing off, Ben turned to Madge inquiringly.

"You've got a call—"

"Atamian?" he interrupted incredulously. "For God's sake, Madge!"

She continued as if he had not spoken. "From the Saudi Arabian Embassy. Do you want to take it?"

"No," he said frankly. "But I guess I'd better."

He recognized the fluent accents even before their owner identified himself.

"Congressman Safford, this is General Khalid. Perhaps you recall that we have met several times during the past few weeks."

"Of course I remember, General Khalid."

"I apologize for calling so soon after your return from Paris. But as Captain Conroy has chosen this time to visit us, it seemed to me desirable to clear up certain matters at once."

A premonition seized Ben. "Captain Conroy's at the Saudi Arabian Embassy now?"

Khalid's voice was as uninformative as a human voice can be. "Yes, he arrived about an hour ago. And while I regret asking you to join us so precipitately, I really think it might be to everyone's best interests."

"I'll get a taxi right away," Ben said.

At the Embassy, he was led to a small sitting room where Khalid and Conroy had drawn up their chairs to a low table holding a brass pot and a tray with three thimble-sized cups.

"I'd never had it before I was in Turkey," Neil was saying, "but I got to really like it while I was there."

"How pleasant. Ah, Congressman Safford."

After the bustle of securing another chair, Khalid held the messenger with an uplifted finger while he turned to Safford.

"Captain Conroy tells me that he finds our coffee palatable, but it would be a matter of moments to secure a pot of American coffee for you."

"No, this will be fine," said Ben in the interests of fellowship.

"Billy used to make a pot for the two of us all the time," Conroy remarked as their host carefully poured.

Khalid might not have heard the comment. "Did you know that Captain Conroy was stationed near Ankara for almost two years? And he seems to have developed a taste for the cuisine."

"There are lots of Near Eastern restaurants in Washington these days, and they're very popular," said Ben, automatically matching courtesies.

Not until the last drop of coffee was gone did Khalid permit anything of substance to be raised. Then, wiping his lips appreciatively, he addressed Ben: "Captain Conroy came to us to discuss the late Major Ibn Billeni."

When somebody else has the ball, they should make the moves. Ben merely looked inquiringly at Neil.

"Billy didn't cause that crash in Utah. The whole world knows that now," Conroy explained. "So I figured it was time to ask why there was a cover-up. If he wasn't to blame, there was no point in that bribe."

For a moment, Ben was speechless. It took more gall than he had to invade a foreign embassy and cross-examine them about their bribes.

"The issue might be publicity rather than blame," he said with as much delicacy as he could muster. "His countrymen might not like the fact that a member of his family or of his party was piloting an American fighter in the first place. The bribe could have been to keep his name out of the hearing."

"Billy wasn't important—not that way," Conroy retorted.

Khalid decided to take a hand. "When this matter was first brought to my attention, I had an examination made of Embassy disbursements. There was no such payment. Then my thoughts traveled the same path as yours, Mr. Congressman. A wealthy family does not necessarily move through official channels. So I studied Major Billeni's file. He was no doubt a distinguished and accomplished member of our Air Force. But his importance ended with his technical competence."

"His father is a dentist back home," Neil translated for Ben's benefit.

Ben had no time for Neil's contribution. He was staring at the Saudi Arabian.

"Now wait a minute, I'd like to get this absolutely clear. Are you saying now that you didn't bribe Perini?"

"It is what I have been saying all along." Khalid coughed diplomatically. "I do not know if you recall our conversation at the airport. As I look back, I begin to think we were talking at cross-purposes."

Tact with the representative of a foreign power is normally desirable. But not when it sacrifices clarity of communication.

"Then let me put it in other words. I was saying that it was an embarrassment to find out that Saudi Arabia was bribing an American officer," Ben said baldly. "But nobody wanted to rock the boat between our two countries, so we were going to keep quiet about it."

Khalid nodded as if all his doubts were confirmed. "It is as I feared. I, on the other hand, was saying to you that we had not bribed your Captain Perini, but we were willing to allow you that face-saving explanation if it were too awkward for your government to pursue the real explanation."

"And you thought I was party to this?" Ben asked indignantly.

"It was a mistake," Khalid confessed. "I see that now and I apologize. Naturally, the secret would not have been shared with a partisan of Captain Conroy's. I was misled by your membership on the Uniform Weaponry Committee."

"You assumed a lot of people knew what was going on, like the whole Defense Department."

Khalid shrugged. "The customs of American businessmen are well known in my country."

"Businessmen?" Ben inquired.

Neil Conroy was more specific. "Dorland," he snapped. "Who else?"

But Ben was unwilling to pursue this part of the conversation on foreign soil.

"You have certainly given me plenty to think about, General Khalid, and I appreciate your frankness," he said, beginning his farewells. "You were absolutely right about our talking at cross-purposes at the airport, and I'm glad to get it straightened out."

"In view of the crash in Paris," Khalid said smoothly, "it seems to me essential to dissipate any misunderstanding."

"Do you think he was telling the truth?" Conroy asked when they were in a taxi heading away from Embassy Row.

"I'm glad you admit it's up for grabs. I was beginning to wonder if you automatically accept anything said by a Saudi," Ben replied.

Neil was persistent if nothing else. "Anybody can be lying. Do you think he was?"

"No, I don't."

Safford would have been hard put to explain why. Partly, it was Khalid's expression when he said it was well known that bribery was a standard element in the American way of doing business. Ben had seen exactly the same expression on witnesses explaining to committees the need for certain corporate payments abroad. Ben could not tell whether Khalid's statement reflected a general debasement of America's image or, more simply, an Arab distrust of foreigners.

"But that doesn't mean you're right, assuming it was Dorland," he went on.

"Name me somebody else who had the same reason," Neil said calmly, obviously pleased with the results of his foray.

"I hope you're satisfied enough to sit still for a while," Ben said as the cab pulled up in front of Conroy's hotel.

Conroy did not answer until he was on the sidewalk. Then he leaned in the window, grinning. "Sitting still hasn't gotten me anywhere," he reminded Ben. "Moving around seems to be a lot more productive."

Ben could not find a word to reply as he watched Neil saunter away.

They were not the only ones putting in time on the VX-92 crashes. In the Pentagon, Reynold Farrington had just finished presenting some unpleasant facts.

96

"Thanks for telling us, sir," said Captain Edward Severance. "I don't understand it, but I suppose it was inevitable that the Provost Marshal would get involved."

"And naturally we'll make ourselves available, just as you ordered," chimed in Major Carl Kruger. "Will that be all, sir?"

Farrington watched them depart before turning to the last occupant of his office.

"I get the feeling they want to stay as far away from us as possible."

"You can't blame them," Larry Yates drawled. "If I'd had the good luck to vote the other way, I'd be making tracks, too. And Paris hasn't helped."

Farrington sighed. "I know, I know. They're already saying that if we'd handled the Conroy case right, the Paris crash never would have happened."

Larry Yates agreed, but without undue emotion. "We goofed. It's only natural somebody's going to want our hides for it. At least with the air police in charge, the whole thing will be straightened out once and for all."

"I suppose so. Anyway, thanks again, Larry, for telling me what's going on."

In his heart, General Farrington was not looking forward to the general clarification that Larry Yates found so inevitable.

15

Besides Captain Neil Conroy, the Air Provost Marshal and General Farrington, George Kidder was working on the VX-92 problem.

The first fruits of Kidder's industry took the form of a short, gossipy paragraph in the Washington dailies.

> Ducking into town unannounced today were two of the President's oldest and dearest friends. Query: Who's taking care of the Embassy?

"Who else but Wellenmeister?" said Tony Martinelli after one quick look.

"The President's put old buddies into every embassy we've got—except Beirut, of course," Ben protested.

"Yeah, but how many of them sold a lemon to the Air Force?"

The question was laid to rest at noon when the State Department released a terse announcement that Ambassador and Mrs. Wellenmeister were in the United States on a private visit.

"One thing I'll say for the Republicans," Tony said across the lunch table. "They never learn."

"Do you have anything specific in mind?" Mrs. Hollenbach inquired frostily.

"Wellenmeister," Tony shot back. "They're making things worse by pretending nothing's up."

He was right, if the next day's papers were anything to go by. Ambassador Wellenmeister had declined comment on the VX-92 crash. The White House had declined comment on Wellenmeister. The Pentagon was not scheduling a briefing for two weeks. The iron wall of silence had driven the press into a frenzy of suspicion.

Signs of real erosion began to appear in the afternoon. As the Committee on Uniform Weaponry ended its daily struggle with military carbines, a staff member brought in the latest news report.

"Gallivan has just told NBC that there is absolutely no truth to the rumors that Wellenmeister has been recalled," he announced.

"You were right, Tony," Elsie Hollenbach said handsomely. She knew that when White House aides start denying rumors, the rest of the scenario is cut and dried.

By five-thirty, the pressure had increased to the point where an army of cameras was lying in wait outside the Wellenmeister house in Virginia. Viewers of the six-o'clock news were treated to clips of Wellenmeister, golf bag slung to the rear, shouldering his way from car to door.

"I can only tell you, gentlemen—and ladies—that I have no statement to make at the moment."

Naturally, this produced a volley of hysterical questions.

"When will you have a statement?"

"Mr. Ambassador, is it true that you have been aware of a design flaw in the VX-92 for over six months?"

"Mr. Ambassador, is it true that Dorland didn't want to fly the VX-92 in Paris?"

But Wellenmeister shook his head and continued to stride to the house, merely saying to an unseen reporter: "Sam, you'll have to ask the White House about that."

Following hard on the heels of these clips was a scene of the President and the First Lady returning from two days at Camp David. As the President smiled and waved to the usual reception team, he said a few words. "Walter is an old friend, and Sally and I have complete faith in him."

After this kiss of death, seasoned observers were in no doubt about forthcoming events. There should have been a graceful period of growing doubts, a frowning President slowly backing off from his expressions of confidence, and White House aides stepping in to pinch-hit when the doubts were resolved.

These careful orchestrations, however, are possible only when outsiders stay off the stage. If Walter Wellenmeister and the President were unwilling to discuss sensitive issues, George Kidder was seizing every available forum.

Ben Safford saw this at first hand the next morning. Kidder had only seven minutes on the talk show, but he managed to pack everything into that time slot. The two VX-92 incidents were the tip of the iceberg. Dorland pilots had been having trouble with the plane from the beginning. A deliberate campaign had been waged—even before the sales effort to Congress and the Pentagon—to isolate each complaint. As the secret file at Dorland had grown thicker in spite of attempts to debug the plane, the security measures tightened. In a final desperate maneuver, assistance from high levels in Washington had been obtained to persuade the Air Force and George Kidder to showcase the plane in Paris.

"And you consider these pressures to be directly responsible for the tragic consequences at the Air Show?" his host obligingly asked.

George Kidder was very grave. "I am afraid so."

"And you, personally, are convinced that the design of the VX-92 is defective?"

"I no longer have any doubts."

There was general agreement in the House lounge that George Kidder knew what he was doing.

"You've got to hand it to him," Tony Martinelli conceded. "The way he tells it, he didn't have anything to do with Paris. It was all decided by Wellenmeister—and his powerful buddies in Washington."

Everyone agreed that there would be no further references from the White House to ancient ties with good old Walt and Deedee.

Ben went one step further. "Do you think it was the President himself who twisted Kidder's arm?"

Tony believed in going to the horse's mouth whenever possible. Turning in his chair, he called to a nearby group: "Hey, Mike, is it true that Wellenmeister got the White House to push for the Paris display?"

Congressman Atamian was rising. Somehow Ben got the impression that his departure was being forced.

"How would I know?" he asked coolly as he passed Martinelli. "I can't keep up with all their tricky steps."

This silenced speculation for a full minute.

"Well, that gives me all I need," Oakes said at last.

Even Elsie was reduced to marveling. "I didn't think anything could make Mike put distance between himself and Dorland."

"Wellenmeister must be closer to burial than I thought," Ben said.

"And Kidder's doing a good job of nailing the coffin shut," Val observed. "The thing I particularly admired about his spiel was the way he lumped himself together with the Air Force. Just two innocent lambs being set on by a ravening beast. And if you can't blame the Air Force for being deceived, then you can't blame him."

In her own way, Elsie was as big a realist as Oakes. "Don't forget his reference to Congress. By casting us as innocent victims, too, he makes it worth our while to go along with him."

Her analysis received more and more confirmation in the next few hours. Anybody on the Hill who had the misfortune to have pushed for the VX-92 system was eager to accept Kidder's reading.

". . . a deliberate policy of misrepresentation to us . . ."

". . . significant facts kept from the legislature . . ."

". . . we have to rely on experts and they were brainwashed."

Even more significant, colleagues who had heard briefly of Ben Safford's efforts in behalf of Captain Neil Conroy suddenly saw his actions in a new light.

"Say, Ben," said the Democratic whip, stopping in the corridor. "They tell me you started your own investigation into the VX-92 before the Air Show. It might not be a bad idea to get out a press release on that. I'll have Irving give you a ring."

Without waiting for a reply, he rushed off. Ben was still digesting this approach when he arrived at his office, in time to take a call from the Democratic caucus. They, too, sensed the value of a vigilant congressman protecting the taxpayer from the avarice of the military-industrial complex.

"We'll get you on a talk show this weekend."

"But I didn't . . ." Ben protested before he realized he was talking to a dial tone.

Before the day was out, the plan to elevate Ben into a congressional commando was well under way, culminating in a call from *Time* magazine, which was itching to reveal Congressman Safford's role in halting the sale of VX-92 to NATO.

"Nobody will listen," Ben snarled. "I was doing a courtesy for a constituent, that's all. Even if *Time* magazine doesn't know anything about me, everybody in the House should realize I'm no expert on jet engines."

"Don't fight it, Ben," Val advised lazily. "This week you're getting some kudos you don't deserve. Next week you'll get some kicks. The good Lord will see that it all evens out."

Still disgruntled, Ben continued his list. "The leadership has booked me for every single talk show this weekend. According to them, I blew the whistle on the VX-92 single-handed."

Nothing surprised Val Oakes anymore. "The House appropriated a lot of money for the VX-92. Now we need a hero."

"If this goes on, I'll leave town," Ben threatened.

By its very nature, it could not go on. The White House, after feeling the ground swell of support for George Kidder, after reading the first snippets of Ben Safford's publicity and, most of all, after holding a final interview with His Excellency the Ambassador to France, decided to scrap its dignified, stately tempo.

The press corps was duly notified that Walter Wellenmeister would give a televised news conference that afternoon. It was not taking place at the State Department, the White House or any other public location. So, even before the man began to speak, knowledgeable viewers—and the group with Ben in the House TV room was as knowledgeable as they come—knew that it was ex-Ambassador Wellenmeister who was taking to the public confessional.

102

Wellenmeister, in sweater and slacks, was reading a prepared statement on the front steps of his house.

"This morning, I tendered to the President of the United States my resignation as Ambassador to France. My reason is simple. I do not wish to embarrass this great country or its great President because of an error in judgment."

Wellenmeister paused to take a breath, and so did his audience. Deedee, standing at her husband's side, smiled mechanically.

The Ambassador continued: "The error in judgment was made before I assumed the responsibility of representing our nation abroad, and I wish to emphasize that it was a personal mistake on my part while I was still employed in the private sector. First, let me review some important chronology connected with our vital national defense policies . . ."

There followed a full page of self-serving justification.

Then it came.

"Six months ago, after becoming convinced that competitors were exploiting certain minor technical difficulties in the VX-92, I decided to fight fire with fire and intensify Dorland's public-relations campaign in Washington. To that end, in February I transferred twenty-five thousand dollars of VX-92 funds to a friendly legislator, Congressman Michael Atamian of California."

"The bastard," said someone near Ben.

It was not clear whether he was referring to Wellenmeister or Atamian.

Ben himself had involuntarily whipped around to scan the room. Even as he did so, he knew he was wasting his time. This was one day when Congressman Atamian would not be joining his colleagues.

Meanwhile, Wellenmeister was finishing his own peculiar rendition of the past. "At that time, I had no doubt that the flaw in the VX-92 could be readily corrected. I was wrong and, accordingly, I am stepping down. In justice to myself, however . . ."

But nobody was listening any longer. They had too much to say themselves.

"You notice he's apologizing for being wrong about the VX-92. He's not apologizing for bribing a congressman."

"And what about the funds?" queried a legal precisionist. "If they were appropriated, it's a crime to lobby with them."

"Who cares about that?" demanded someone more down to earth. "That minor technical difficulty he's talking about is a plane smashing into a schoolyard full of kids."

There were ringing indictments of Wellenmeister on every side. Nonetheless, there was still a lonely voice for the defense. A senator who had dropped by and stayed for the telecast could not believe that Walter would do anything really criminal or underhanded.

"Misguided, yes," he admitted. "Ill-advised, yes. But really crooked? I can't believe that about Walter . . . not without a lot of hard evidence."

"Careful, Lucius," Val Oakes warned him. "In this town, when you ask for a smoking pistol, somebody hauls one out."

It took less than twenty-four hours. The television news, with its capacity for instant response, was in full swing that evening, analyzing the Wellenmeister confession from every angle. Television, however, suffers from an ingrained bias in favor of things it can take pictures of. Facts cannot be photographed but people can. Therefore, television's analysis rested heavily on personal impressions. But the basic question was virtually untouched. Walter Wellenmeister had told the world he paid twenty-five thousand dollars to relieve Dorland of any awkwardness about the VX-92 crash in Utah. What exactly had he bought with his money?

The Washington *Post* did much better simply because of its bias in favor of the printed word. Somebody went to the files downstairs. Somebody did a little cross-referencing. At long last, somebody went out to Fairfax, Virginia. As a result of these pedestrian employments, the next morning's headlines outstripped all the fuzzy theorizing on the airwaves.

SUICIDE OF AIR FORCE OFFICER TIED TO VX-92 BRIBE

The ensuing story gave Ben Safford all the publicity he had been so thankful to avoid immediately after Julian Perini's death.

> Police theorize that Congressman Benton Safford's investigation of the inquiry following the VX-92 crash in Utah led to Captain Perini's suicide. Perini, who served on the board of inquiry and voted for pilot error, was found dead with $15,000 by his side. Many independent witnesses have reported that Captain Perini was in normal spirits on the last day of his life until the Pentagon arranged for him to be cross-examined by Congressman Safford.
>
> Ironically, Perini would have been safely on the West Coast if Congressman Safford had delayed his questioning by only a few hours. In fact, the body was discovered by Safford, who had gone to Virginia to catch Perini before his departure.

Ben was becoming accustomed to his new image as crusading investigator. The suggestion that Perini had been contemplating a secret flight and that the ever-vigilant Safford had cut him off at the pass was not what was raising the frown on his face. The *Post* had reminded him too graphically of the scene with Perini's body.

Val Oakes' reaction to the story was different. He pointed to the lines at the bottom.

> Mr. Walter Wellenmeister admitted yesterday that he had paid Congressman Michael Atamian $25,000 after the Utah crash in order to minimize adverse publicity for Dorland Aircraft. There has been considerable speculation in the media as to precisely how these funds were disbursed.

"Well, Lucius wanted a smoking pistol," Val murmured. "Now he's got one."

16

The aftershock of the *Post*'s story started at the top and rumbled downward to jolt almost everyone involved with the VX-92.

General Farrington, who was watching his carefully programmed retirement go down the drain, could no longer keep his worries to himself. Instinctively, he turned to an old friend who, like him, had thirty years in the Air Force under his belt. By inches, he began unburdening himself.

"It's been one thing after another, Mitch."

"Come on, Reynold, most of this isn't new. You've already ridden out the worst of it."

Farrington shook his head. "You know damn well it makes a difference being in the headlines. When we first hit the mess about Perini, it was confined. The air police were working on it, and it could have been straightened out quietly. Then we had the crash in Paris. There was no way in the world we weren't going to look like boobs, letting Dorland foist that plane on us. But now! Bribery, rigged boards, a career officer with his brains blown out. All on the front page. That's a major stink in anybody's book."

His friend was too experienced to pretend that publicity did not, of itself, make things worse. "Sure, when the axe falls, it's going to fall harder than it would have without the big headlines. But let's take it piece by piece. First, Dorland suckered everybody— DOD, the service, even the pols on the Hill—into backing the VX-92. What's more, it turns out they were conning us from the start. But you didn't have anything to do with the basic decision—

106

that was made by the top brass. So they can't blame you for that, can they?"

"I was all for it when it was on the drawing board, and I said so."

"For Christ's sake, so did I, so did everybody! That's what I mean. A one-star general is peanuts in a deal like that. The four-star ones are going to be so busy tying the can to Dorland's tail they're not going to bother about us." Mitch searched for the perfect summary and finally discovered the phrase that was already resounding throughout Washington. "If everybody else got sold a bill of goods, it's not our fault that we did, too."

Farrington kept returning to his sores like a dog with an itch. "That's the least of it. But there's the Conroy board, too. You know what everybody is saying. If I'd run that board right, we'd have grounded every VX-92 before the Paris Air Show."

"Maybe if the board had been on the up-and-up, that would have been the result. But how could you know one of your technical experts had sold out? Since when is that the kind of thing they tell you to watch for?"

"They'll say I should have smelled it," Farrington insisted stubbornly.

"An Academy graduate? A career man? Hell no! They're the sort we're supposed to trust. I don't say anybody is going to pat you on the back. But this investigating congressman may be a help to you. You know what I mean —you thought everything was aboveboard, you cooperated, you set up the appointment with Perini. In a way, you blew the thing apart as much as he did."

The pep talk was well intentioned, but Mitch could see it wasn't working. And he thought he knew why.

"Unless there's something else you're worried about," he suggested, trying to be as offhand as possible.

Farrington was not ready for the homestretch.

"There was a lot of pressure to rush the board through. They'd gotten lucky with that assassination attempt on the Queen," he reminded his friend. "They didn't want to blow it with an extended hearing. Having a Saudi involved was no help, either."

Mitch was eager to agree. "Of course everybody's edgy when outsiders come trooping in," he said with sturdy service loyalty. "But the Air Force wanted the lid clamped on, too. That's why they went along with the State Department and DOD, and whoever else got into the act."

"They told me to move right along, so I did," Farrington stalled. "With unanimity from the officers who'd qualified on the plane, I just closed it out and didn't let Conroy introduce his technical evidence."

"And from here it looks like a big mistake. But my God, Reynold, we all know how easy it is to be a Monday-morning quarterback. It's like I said, it's going to be a black mark. It's unfair, but that's life, and it isn't going to be a big deal. You were only following orders."

Farrington was studying the damp circles left by his glass on the table as if they held the secrets of the future. As Mitch watched him, he had a sinking sensation he knew what was coming.

Finally, the dam burst.

"The pressure wasn't just down the chain of command. I was getting it from every direction."

In a half whisper, Mitch took them over the last hurdle. "Dorland?"

"That's it," Farrington admitted miserably. "You know how it is, Mitch. They wine and dine you, and you don't pay much attention at first. But after a couple of years, you're all buddy-buddy. Then, when they want something that everybody else wants, it seems reasonable enough. Particularly when your retirement is just around the corner and you suddenly need all the friends out there you can get."

Mitch sighed. "Yes, I know how it is. Everybody in the service does."

Lieutenant Colonel Lawrence Yates was also confiding to a fellow member of the armed forces. But in addition to professional

108

solidarity, he was getting feminine sympathy as well. Ursula Richmond was dining with him at a famous Chinese restaurant in Georgetown.

She was as spellbound by the latest disclosures as he was.

"Julian Perini!" she was saying. "But I knew him, we were stationed in Germany together."

"Then you know what I mean. It never occurred to Farrington and me that he was on the take."

"I still can't believe it."

Yates grinned at her. "It's easy explaining this to you. The air police are something else again."

Ursula pushed her soup plate aside and said warmly, "Then I'm the right person for you to practice on."

"You may be right. The way this mess is developing, I don't want to say anything that can be taken the wrong way."

"Is it that tricky?"

Yates snorted. "I ask you!"

The waiter removed the first course and began to set out dishes. While he hovered, Yates outlined the many complications that had attended Neil Conroy's board of inquiry.

"But we managed to wrap it all up," he concluded. "Then, before we know it, Perini puts a bullet in his head and they tell us that the Saudis were buying him. Well, you know how the service acts when a piece of dirt like that hits the fan. Everybody concentrated on Perini and lost sight of the plane entirely."

Ursula had plunged a serving spoon into the shrimp mai pei and was gesturing for Yates' plate. "If the Air Force finds garbage in its own backyard, it has to clean it up," she said indignantly. "What's wrong with that?"

"At the time, nothing. But it turns out we were looking in the wrong direction. Wellenmeister says he's the one who did the bribing. Hey, watch it! That's one of the hot dishes, it'll take the skin off the inside of your mouth."

Ursula moderated her lavish technique absently. "It's funny how these congressmen keep popping up. Actually, Wellenmeister says he gave the money to Atamian. And the *Post* says Congressman Safford was onto the VX-92 right from the start."

"I read that, too. He never let on to me that he was an expert. Did he say anything to you that night at the Embassy?"

Ursula corrected him. "Safford wasn't the one I talked to. It was Congressman Oakes." She thought back to her encounters with Val. *"He* certainly didn't strike me as big on jets, but I suppose you never can tell."

"I don't know a hell of a lot about the undercover business, but I'm beginning to learn."

"Now that everything's out in the open, there can't be any more of that," Ursula reasoned. "We all know that Dorland was trying a cover-up. Wellenmeister's admitted it, Kidder's admitted it. What more can you ask for?"

Yates shrugged. "On this deal, anything can come out of the woodwork, and some of it already has."

Ursula's dark eyes were bright with interest. "Tell me all about it."

Like Farrington, Yates had come off duty that day with a knot in his stomach. But two drinks before dinner, a plate of Szechuan cooking and Ursula's wholehearted attention were beginning to produce a sense of well-being.

"You know what?" he discovered. "Talking to you is different. I don't have to stop and describe how things happen in the service."

Ursula paused in her steady attack on a mountain of food that should have left her gasping. "Of course it is," she said, surprised that he did not already understand this. "That's why I'm going to marry somebody in the Air Force. I figure, over my lifetime, it will save several solid years of explanation."

"Oh?" said Yates in mock alarm. "And when did you reach this decision?"

"Back in my second year at the Academy," she replied crisply. "I realized then that ninety-five percent of the men I was going to meet would be in the service. Why fight the odds?"

"I see," said Yates, deflated.

She laughed outright. "That's your male ego groaning," she

charged. "You don't intend to marry me any more than I intend to marry you."

This was perfectly true. Larry Yates was very happy with the life he had been leading since his divorce. But he also liked being pursued by the attractive girls he squired to the beach at Hilton Head, to the ski slopes at Aspen, to a weekend on Maui. They wanted to marry him. Why didn't Ursula? Of course, any woman who spent her days in a cockpit was not going to be wide-eyed at meeting a glamorous pilot. And travel was no good either. You weren't going to get anywhere with Ursula by starting a sentence: "A funny thing happened when I was in Hong Kong . . ."

Almost automatically, Larry Yates came to a decision. At the moment, Ursula was just what he needed. But once the pressure was off, it was back to essentials.

Ursula's personal concerns were narrower.

"Well, I'm sorrier than ever that I've got to be one of General Farrington's witnesses for the Paris crash. From what you say, it would be best for my career to stay as far away from him as possible."

"Farrington's assignment probably begins and ends with collecting names."

"You're right. His aide told me the list was being forwarded to General MacInerney's office for further action."

Colonel Yates prided himself on facing facts. "And I'll tell you something else. Farrington and I are so tainted that we'll be pruned from that list before long."

"Not just you," Ursula told him. "Tom said they'd been asked to strike everybody who was on the Conroy board."

"Tom? You put in some fast work with Farrington's aide by just giving him your local address."

Ursula grinned unashamedly. "It so happens we had lunch together. I think some of the things they do in that office are fascinating, and I was glad to have Tom tell me about it."

Yates was more and more convinced that Ursula and he were not ideal playmates. On the other hand, he rather enjoyed having other men envy him his women and Tom was a notorious envier.

"While he was telling you how fascinating he is, did he find time to mention he has a wife and three children?" he asked mischievously.

"If it comes to that, so do you," she retorted.

"Not anymore!"

Ursula, catching the mingled triumph and relief in his voice, smothered a giggle.

Only then did Yates realize how much he had betrayed himself.

Half smiling, he reverted to business. "Anyway, I don't think being a simple witness can land you in any trouble, particularly now that Dorland has come clean."

"Doesn't that mean the worst is over for you, too? Before, everybody lost sight of the plane when they got jolted by the Perini scandal. . . . Everybody in the Air Force, that is," she added. "Won't the reverse happen now? Won't they forget the Conroy hearing in the flap about the sale of the VX-92 to DOD?"

Yates sighed. "They would except for this latest wrinkle the air police have come up with. Wait until you hear this one."

And in spite of all sorts of resolutions, Colonel Yates spent the greater part of the evening pouring his troubles into Ursula Richmond's receptive ear.

Captain Neil Conroy was also dealing with a woman who purported to have his best interests at heart, but his conversation was not going as smoothly.

"Look, Mom, you have to be in the service to understand these things," he said to the phone for the fourth time.

"I'm tired of hearing that," she told him. "Just because you're in the Air Force doesn't mean you're not in the same solar system as the rest of us."

Neil groaned. "I'm not saying that. But they're used to doing things in a certain way and that's what they like."

Peg Conroy was exasperated by the eternal male reluctance to face the issue. "Who cares what they want? If everybody went by their wonderful procedures, you'd probably be out on your ear by now. I was the one who got Ben Safford working for you."

"I know his intentions are good—"

"Intentions! The Cincinnati *Inquirer* says he's the first one who had the sense to investigate that plane. And you've been saying all along that's what the Air Force should be doing."

She had caught him on both flanks. That *was* what Neil had been saying, and he, too, had read the publicity about Congressman Safford. Peg was clever enough to realize she had gained the advantage, so she swept on.

"Why won't you stop being so pigheaded? Now that everyone admits you were right all along, it's time to force the issue. Once you've got a public exoneration, you can get on with your career. And the rest of us can get back to business as usual."

"There's nothing stopping you. I wish you and Earl would set a date and march down the aisle. Why don't you?"

"How can I order flowers and champagne when your future— a future you've sweated blood for—is going up in smoke?"

Neil Conroy knew perfectly well that he was not the only one who had sweated blood. Like the children of devoted mothers everywhere, he felt a wave of ingratitude at the reminder of her sacrifice. To his eternal credit, he banished the irritation, although not the impatience, from his voice.

"Mom, I'm grateful for all you've done and for the way you've stood by me. And I realize this hasn't been any picnic for Earl, either. But my career's safe now. It's just a question of deciding exactly how and when to take care of the loose ends. You and Earl have your own lives to lead. Go ahead! I can handle this myself."

He should have realized these were the last words his mother wanted to hear.

"The way you've handled things so far!"

Like everybody else, George Kidder was learning that the service is a world apart.

"I don't like the smell of this. Not one single bit," he snarled to the executives gathered around the table.

The strategy session at Dorland was not going the way its president had intended. And for one very good reason.

"We can't decide on a program until we get some information," somebody objected. "And all our communication sources have dried up. The Air Force isn't telling us a thing."

The public-relations man did not see the problem. "But that's not important anymore," he said, flashing his usual smile. "You've forgotten that our campaign was designed to take the heat off, and it has. Of course, George put it across brilliantly, but the upshot is that Wellenmeister and Atamian are the ones who're going to be tarred and feathered. Dorland is clean."

"You damned fool!" Kidder growled. "The whole point of that campaign was to make it possible for us to work with the Air Force. But they're freezing us out."

"They sure are." The man at the bottom of the table was prepared to itemize. "They're cross-examining Wellenmeister and Atamian. They're going through the files of every VX-92 crash. They're reopening the Conroy hearing. They're putting the flight instrumentation from Paris under a microscope. And we don't know what they're finding out. Hell, with Atamian on the most-wanted list, we don't even have a man on the Hill."

"Sooner or later, they've got to make that report public," a vice-president said. "Eventually we'll know what's in it."

This was not what the president of Dorland wanted to hear.

"Eventually!" Kidder snapped. "Do you know what our competition is doing in the meantime? There are two senators from Seattle working night and day to grab our contracts." He made one last appeal to the detail man. "What did General MacInerney say?"

The voice of doom answered.

"He says that the VX-92 is now an internal service question."

17

The House Ethics Committee would have been happy to have the Honorable Michael Atamian declared an internal service question, too.

"In fact," said Tony Martinelli, "what they'd really like is for the Air Force to take Mike out and shoot him."

"It's an awkward position for the leadership," said Mrs. Hollenbach, displaying the bipartisanship she so often advocated. "Since Walter Wellenmeister's resignation, the press has been demanding action, but the House doesn't have any of the details."

Val Oakes was not given to impetuous demands for speed, but he knew when the time for delay was over. "Then we'd better get them!"

"Well, if you think Mike is going to help cut his own throat, Val, you're living in a fool's paradise," Ben rejoined.

Two days later, Ben's remark was proving prophetic. The chairman of the Ethics Committee was not mincing his words.

"Did Walter Wellenmeister pay you twenty-five thousand dollars, or didn't he?"

This was not the way Atamian cared to put it. Because of the intimacy between himself and Wellenmeister, he explained, they occasionally did small favors for each other. This time, when Wellenmeister had been unable to come to Washington, he had asked Atamian to procure some public-relations services.

"It was no big deal," he said, reverting to his native idiom. "Walter could just as well have asked me to get some painters into his house while he was out of town."

115

The homey touch was a mistake.

"Then why," rasped Chairman Savard, "did Wellenmeister make the check for twenty-five thousand payable to the construction company owned by your brother?"

Atamian had been reaching for an ashtray and only a slight interruption in this movement betrayed his shock.

"Son of a gun!" breathed Val from his spectator's seat. "So Wellenmeister's decided to come clean."

But Atamian refused to admit that this was a damning piece of evidence. "It was simply more convenient that way. I'm not used to dealing with that kind of money."

"You've had plenty of opportunity to learn." Savard was now consulting a folder. "Dorland's records show one large check after another to your brother's account."

By now, Atamian's lawyer was plucking at his sleeve, only to be shaken off.

"So?" Atamian challenged. "Just because he's my brother doesn't mean he can't do work for the biggest customer in the district."

They were the last words he managed to fire off before being forcibly hauled into a huddle with his legal adviser. When he was once again upright, he was more prudent. All general accusations of wrongdoing Atamian countered by referring to normal congressional courtesies for major employers. Specific questions he referred back to Walter Wellenmeister. Even a thinly veiled threat to subpoena his bank records failed to budge him.

"Figures he laundered the money enough so that it can't be traced," Tony Martinelli whispered informatively.

"He may think so," Ben whispered back. "But given his track record, he could be wrong."

At the end of two hours, Congressman Savard conceded defeat. "I am afraid we will have to resort to an extended list of witnesses and documentary evidence." His glance fell significantly on the folder. "In the meantime, we stand adjourned for the day."

During the disorderly scramble for the door, Ben lost sight of

116

his colleagues. When he finally made it to the corridor, he was not surprised to find them lurking by the elevator.

"Who have you decided to sandbag?" he asked, proving he knew what they were doing.

"Hal Torance, Savard's legislative assistant," Tony said shrewdly. "He's bound to know what's going on."

Others had not bothered to wait for Torance to reach the corridor. When he appeared, his jacket was rumpled and he was wiping his face. He broke into speech before they could put their questions. "Wellenmeister showed up in the committee office an hour before the hearing. The White House finally twisted his arm and made him produce records."

"What kind of details did you get from him?" Ben asked.

"Almost none. His story is that he gave Atamian twenty-five grand to quash publicity about the VX-92 crash in Utah. He didn't ask him how he was going to do the job because he didn't want to know."

Tony was deeply suspicious. "And that's all he said?"

"Apart from wanting to know if he could leave for the Bahamas now. It seems Deedee needs a good rest," Torance said dryly.

With the White House, Congress and the armed services all swirling busily around the Wellenmeister disclosures, Ben thought that every conceivable arm of government had been heard from. He had forgotten all about local municipalities.

"Sergeant Dunnet on the phone," Madge announced briskly.

Lately, Ben's world had been filled with generals, colonels, captains. How had a lowly sergeant gotten into the act?

"Who?"

Madge was already busy pushing buttons and extending the receiver to him. "Of the Fairfax police," she breathed.

Enlightenment dawned without a second to spare. "Hello, Sergeant, it's been a long time."

Dunnet was in no hurry to come to the point. "I caught you on

Meet the Press the other day, Congressman. You sounded real good."

Warily, Ben thanked him.

"The newsboys finally got your name as the one who discovered Perini's body," Dunnet rolled on, "but now it doesn't seem to be doing you any harm."

No situation is more familiar to a politician than being reminded of his IOUs. "Yes," Ben agreed. "I do appreciate the way you soft-pedaled my involvement two weeks back."

"I'm hoping you appreciate it enough to do me a favor," Dunnet said frankly. "I'd be much obliged if you could come out to Fairfax this afternoon."

"Where in Fairfax?"

"To the same house. It's a long shot, but you might be able to help us."

Ben decided there was no way to figure out what was going on. "When would you like to meet?"

"Right now would be best" was the blunt response.

Something about the air in Fairfax, Ben decided, encouraged residents to summon busy people from Washington at an instant's notice. What's more, they shared an instinct for the right leverage. With Perini, it had been a congressman's duty to his constituent. With Dunnet, it was a man's obligation to pay his debts. Either way, they had you.

"I should be able to leave here in about ten minutes," he said, resigned.

During the final moments of his ride, Ben had unpleasant recollections of his last visit. He arrived to find that some of the details were the same, but the atmosphere was entirely different. The same beagle was in evidence, but today he was chasing a Frisbee tossed by a coltish young girl in a ponytail and shorts. Furthermore, Ben's ring at the front door produced a very pretty young matron.

Before Ben could explain himself, Sergeant Dunnet loomed in the background.

118

"This is Congressman Safford, Mrs. Hanna." Turning to Ben, he continued: "This is Mrs. Carolyn Hanna, Captain Perini was her brother."

The three of them trailed down the hallway toward that ominous room in the rear. Ben was still digesting Dunnet's information when he received his first major jolt.

Sitting in a large armchair, completely at ease, was Captain Neil Conroy.

"You show up in some unexpected places, Neil," Ben observed.

"And I turn up some unexpected facts," Conroy retorted.

Cautiously settling himself, Ben remembered that Conroy's trip to the Saudi Embassy had overturned one preconceived notion. What in the world had he come up with this time?

"You'll find this interesting, Congressman," Sergeant Dunnet began without further preliminaries. "Mrs. Hanna doesn't think her brother committed suicide."

Ben knew better than to reply directly. Devoted relatives rarely believe their loved ones have ended their own lives. No policeman had dragged him to the outer suburbs for a mere expression of faith.

"It must have been a great shock to you, Mrs. Hanna," he said instead. "I suppose you're here, settling his affairs."

Mrs. Hanna blinked, then realized her position had not been adequately explained. "This is our house," she said in a soft Charleston drawl. "That's the whole point. We simply lent it to Julian while Gerry was on temporary assignment in London. My husband works for the World Bank."

A great clarification was dawning on Ben Safford. He had been far too disturbed after stumbling on Perini's body to consider domestic detail, but unconsciously he must have absorbed a general impression. The nagging conviction of something wrong that had persisted for weeks was not caused by the jarring note of a Saudi payoff. It was the house itself, which reeked of family living from the yard to the kitchen to the hallway.

"I came back as soon as I could," Mrs. Hanna was prattling on. "When they sent me the telegram about Julian, I was shocked, of course. But as soon as I returned, I realized that the Air Force was talking nonsense."

Ben braced himself for a declaration about Julian Perini's honesty, his dedication to his career, his unimpeachable integrity.

"Bourbon!" Mrs. Hanna snorted.

"Wh-what's that?" Ben stammered.

"They claimed that Julian got up his nerve with bourbon before shooting himself. Of all the silly notions! Julian never touched the stuff. I suppose you couldn't expect them to know that, but they could have checked."

Ben tried to be tactful. "Even if a man isn't normally a drinker, he might break with his habits at a moment like that. After all—"

"Vodka!"

With difficulty, Ben repressed another stammered response. He was beginning to take the measure of Mrs. Hanna's discourse. As long as she was delivering an unchallenged narrative, she favored a dithering, feminine style that accorded with her filmy dress and softly waved hair. At the first hint of opposition, she cut the cackle with a vengeance.

"Vodka?" he asked politely.

"Julian drank vodka or gin. He never could abide the taste of bourbon. Gerry and I drink it all the time, which is why there's so much in the liquor cabinet. Naturally that must have misled whoever killed Julian." She went on as calmly as if they were all in perfect agreement. "If he thought this was Julian's house and found more bourbon than anything else, he'd decide that was Julian's drink."

Ben Safford had been so busy wrestling with the need ro reconsider Captain Perini's suicide he had not considered the inexorable progression to murder. As Mrs. Hanna dropped her blockbuster, he looked up in startled acknowledgment. The first thing he saw was Captain Neil Conroy nodding to himself with somber satisfaction.

Still struggling, Ben registered a protest. "You can't assume murder on the basis of one glass of bourbon."

Sergeant Dunnet stirred in his chair. "Actually, Mrs. Hanna has a number of other discrepancies."

120

"I certainly do. That's why I had you all sit in this room. Take a look at it. This is Lois's room. This is where she has her friends and does her homework. Gerry and I use the living room or the study. Anybody can see that."

As he obediently inspected his surroundings, Ben wondered how he could have been so blind. The bright colors, the posters on the wall, the stereo set with its cassettes and records—they all pointed to a teenager.

"Is that Lois I saw on the lawn, playing with the dog?"

"Of course it is. Julian was her godfather and devoted to her. If he *had* been going to shoot himself, this is the last place he would have chosen. Would anybody decent go into a child's room to blow his brains out?"

Her appeal received one instant response.

"That's enough to convince me," Neil Conroy said stolidly. "In fact, I don't think he would have used your house at all."

Carolyn Hanna smiled mistily at him. "You're absolutely right. Really, there's so much it's hard to remember it all. For example, you mentioned the dog, Congressman. Pepper was Julian's Christmas present to Lois, and he helped her train him. The two of them taught Pepper to sit and stay and heel. It was wonderful to watch, they were both so serious."

As Carolyn Hanna showed signs of drifting into the past, Sergeant Dunnet took over. "What Mrs. Hanna means is that Captain Perini had already made reservations at the kennel. She says he would never have left the pup locked up in a house with a dead body. He would have put him in the kennel first."

"I realize you don't understand how wrapped up a child gets in her dog," Lois's mother said loftily, "but Julian did. And I know he would have acted accordingly."

For once she was wrong. Ben Safford was remembering the Dalmation puppy he had given to his own nieces many years ago. He would never forget how the whole household had immediately begun to revolve around that dog, and had continued to do so for many years.

"Your brother might not have had time," he said without much conviction.

Captain Conroy intended to stamp out even token resistance. "Tell them about the picture, Mrs. Hanna," he urged.

"That was so silly I'd forgotten it. They had some absurd rigmarole about Julian taking a last look at his girl friend. That picture is Lois's drama teacher. She was in some summer stock production and gave Lois a publicity shot. It's usually over on that shelf by the guitar."

By now, Ben had no further objections to produce. Every indication that had seemed to point so conclusively to suicide had been explained away by Mrs. Hanna. Dimly, Ben was beginning to see that her casual observation, almost upon introduction, was completely apposite. Some unknown had put a bullet into Captain Perini and then set the scene to look like suicide. But in assuming that this house belonged to Perini, the unknown had plunged into one pitfall after another. The preponderance of bourbon had suggested it was the right drink to put in the glass. The photograph of a pretty young woman had suggested a romantic attachment. And the room?

Mrs. Hanna had an explanation for that, too.

"It's clear as a bell what happened," she was summarizing. "They told me Julian was loading his car. Naturally he was doing it through this room, and when somebody showed up, he brought them in here and sat down at that desk. Oh, dear!" For the first time that afternoon, Mrs. Hanna was brought to a halt by emotion.

Sergeant Dunnet took up where she had left off. "And after he finished setting the scene with that Saudi envelope, the murderer skedaddled. You can see why I wanted to talk to you on the spot, Congressman. You must have arrived within minutes. Anything you can remember might be a help. I know it's been a long time, but there's always a chance."

Curiously, this impelled Mrs. Hanna into apology. "It's my fault so much time has gone by. I should have contacted Sergeant Dunnet right away. But it was the air police who came to talk to me, and I just exploded to them about how wrong they were. I never thought of going to anybody else, not until that nice Miss Richmond came."

Ben stared incredulously. "Do you mean Ursula Richmond?"

"Yes, do you know her, too? Well, actually she's Captain Richmond, but that doesn't seem right to me. Lord, I don't know how I'd feel if Lois wanted to do something like that. It doesn't seem natural, somehow, but I know a lot of young women do it these days. What my father would have said . . ."

Ben, in an effort to halt this digression, almost bellowed: "What was Ursula Richmond doing here?"

Mrs. Hanna was reproving. "Why, she paid a condolence call. She and Julian were stationed together in Europe. So naturally when she heard, she dropped by." All the melodrama of rigged inquiries, bribes, public scandal evaporated before the social conviction of the proper way to behave to the bereaved. "As a matter of fact, she was the first one who advised me to contact the local police. She said the Air Force can only do so much in a civilian crime. I suppose it's silly of me not to have thought of that myself, but it's because of the way I was raised. You know my father was an admiral before he retired to write naval history. And with a brother who was a career officer, too, I just naturally took my troubles to the service."

"I'm sure we all understand that," Dunnet murmured soothingly.

"But I blame myself for not acting promptly on her advice. It wasn't until today, when Captain Conroy absolutely insisted, that I finally did something."

Involuntarily, Safford's glance flicked to Neil Conroy, who grinned back defiantly.

"I wouldn't worry too much about the delay, Mrs. Hanna," the sergeant said reassuringly. "By the time Miss Richmond got to you, the trail was already cold."

"That's true. She came even though she'd been overseas until a couple of weeks after his death. And I can't tell you how much I appreciated her visit. You see, she really knew Julian. She didn't believe this nonsense about him any more than I did. And the way she spoke about him—she brought him back to me. He was such a dear!"

Inevitably, Mrs. Hanna had to break off and wipe her eyes.

It gave Ben a chance to put the burning question: "And what exactly are you doing here, Neil?"

"I suppose you could say that I'm paying a condolence call, too," the captain said ironically.

Ben almost gasped. Did Mrs. Hanna realize that Neil Conroy had a justifiable grievance against her late brother?

Apparently not.

"And I can never be grateful enough to you, Captain Conroy. Do you know," she said, turning to the others artlessly, "that he stood over me and practically willed me to put in that call to the police department?"

"I'll bet he did," Ben grunted.

Dunnet had no time for side issues: "Well, Congressman, what about it? Do you remember seeing or hearing anything the day you came?"

But no matter how he cudgeled his memory, Ben could not produce one scrap of information. Certainly he had not been conscious of another presence in the house, or even in the yard. As for cars on the street, he could only explain that when he was not driving, he was not watching the traffic.

"That's okay, we'll ask your cabby. His name's in the file."

"But—" Ben broke off as the implications became clear.

Dunnet smiled grimly. "Oh, yes, we checked your story, Congressman. It was just a matter of routine with a suicide, but it may pay off now."

The sergeant then continued the process of calling a spade a spade by addressing Mrs. Hanna. "You know, Mrs. Hanna, all I'm concerned with is your brother's death. Just because this is a murder case doesn't mean that the Air Force won't go on investigating the bribe he took. And the Justice Department and the Ethics Committee, too, if the papers are right."

The explosion that Ben expected did not come. Mrs. Hanna smiled pityingly. "You're as bad as the air police. Julian take a bribe for fifteen thousand dollars? Don't be ridiculous," she told him with gentle certainty.

This seemed like a wonderful time to leave as far as Ben was concerned. He was pleased to see that Neil Conroy had enough decency to add his own farewells.

The minute the front door closed behind them, Conroy went into action.

"Satisfied, Ben?"

"Satisfied!" Ben almost choked. "You stood over that poor woman and forced her to call the police to make as big a stink as possible."

"The stink's been there all along, Ben. I'm just trying to let a little sunlight in. That's the way to disinfect a stink."

Ben knew there was a good deal of sense in Captain Conroy's position, but any congressman towed by his constituent into one morass after another has a right to vent steam.

"You call changing a nice clean suicide into a murder disinfecting?"

The captain smiled. Ben was beginning to notice that the stronger Neil's position was, the more tolerant he became. So the answer, when it came, was no big surprise.

"It wasn't as clean as you think. They tell me the air police have been going the rounds at the Pentagon, collecting alibis. I guess Mrs. Hanna got through to them."

"Then, if there was already an investigation, what were you gaining by dragging Dunnet into it?"

Neil's voice hardened. "Come off it, Ben. You know the score as well as I do. The more agencies running around, the harder it is to pull a whitewash."

"And who's going to fix the Justice boys and the Air Force? You think your murderer has that much clout?"

"I sure do! It's pretty plain what happened. Dorland bribed Perini. Then you started to apply pressure, they were afraid he'd crack and they killed him."

As Ben's own thoughts had been following the same path, all he could produce was a counsel of prudence. "If you're going to say

125

that sort of thing, say it to me. But don't go off half cocked in public."

"Is that what I've been doing?" Neil asked coolly. "From the results I've been getting, I'd say I must be doing something right."

"Too damned right!" Ben retorted. "You've got an inside source at the Pentagon. How did you know this was the right time to lean on Mrs. Hanna?"

Neil shook his head in mock disapproval. "You're stalling, Ben. Do you believe the lady or don't you?"

"About what?" snapped Ben. He liked being crowded as little as most men. "She says that her brother was murdered, and she says he didn't take a bribe."

For a moment, Neil hesitated, then: "Forget the business about the bribe. That's what any sister would say. But do you believe that Perini was killed and the scene staged? It explains the Saudi envelope, and that's been fishy since the day I talked to Khalid."

In honesty, Ben could only make one answer. "Let's say that the lady has really shaken me."

And that, he said to himself, applied to Captain Ursula Richmond as well.

18

Like Carolyn Hanna, Congressman Mike Atamian had a brother to whom he was close. His was still very much alive.

"Jesus Christ, Mike, you're supposed to be the smart one," said Frank Atamian, striding restlessly around the living room in Chevy Chase.

Atamian knew this was a lament, not a reproach, but it stung just the same.

"That's a big help," he said sourly.

Halting, Frank protested: "You know what I mean."

"Sure," said Atamian, avoiding eye contact.

"Oh, Mike!" said his wife from the sofa. "Don't take it out on Frank. Not after he's come all the way from California."

"Honey," Atamian suggested, "you know what we could use? A cup of coffee."

Her disappearance into the kitchen was a relief for all of them. Gloria was not at her best playing the loyal little woman. Mike's family always made her so nervous that she overacted disastrously.

And Frank resented her. In his book, she was one of Mike's few serious blunders. Playing games with Gloria was one thing. Marrying her was another.

Mike himself had been feeling the lack of someone he could really talk to.

"It's not as bad as it looks, Frank," he said in a friendlier tone.

Frank was an older, somewhat rougher version of his brother. But the family resemblance ended with looks. Frank was cautious, Mike was not.

"You always say that," he grumbled.

"And it's paid off, hasn't it?" Mike replied.

"Have I ever denied it?" Frank asked plaintively. "But, Mike, this Ethics Committee? God, they got that senator from New Jersey, didn't they? What if you get expelled from Congress? What happens then?"

As they both knew, the Atamian Construction Company was a by-product of that House seat.

For once, Mike did not scoff at his brother's anxieties.

"I'm not saying it's a sure thing," he said, unconscious that he was passing a personal milestone. "Wellenmeister's really done a job on me."

"You know what I'd like to do to Wellenmeister, don't you?" Frank interrupted passionately.

Nodding, Mike continued: "But so far it's under control. I was doing public relations for Dorland, period. They can't tie the can on me for that goddamned bribe—at least not if I hang tough."

More than most brothers, Frank had solid reasons to be encouraging. "You can do it, Mike. You've always been a real fighter."

Despite these words, staking out a position and sticking with it was not the Atamian way. There had to be a second line of defense to fall back on, just in case.

"On the other hand," said Mike, "if they really start digging—"

With sudden alarm, Frank said, "Mike, you got a lawyer?"

"You think I'm a dummy or something?" Mike retorted indignantly. "I don't make a move these days without a lawyer. And I've got one of the best."

Despite everything, Frank laughed at the old joke. Another difference between the brothers was that Mike always went for the best.

"Anyway, there's a chance we can ride it out," Mike said, sounding almost like himself. His chances to show off before an admiring audience had been few and far between lately.

"You mentioned digging," said Frank apologetically.

Atamian's bravado collapsed. "Then I go for the jugular," he said with raw anger. "Frank, nobody's throwing *me* out of Congress! But nobody!"

The growing doubt on Frank's face drove Mike into a frenzy. "If they think they can throw me to the wolves, they can think again. Sure, compared to Dorland and the Air Force and the White House, little Mike Atamian looks expendable. Well, I'll let you in on a secret. They don't know it, but I've got enough information to blow this thing sky-high if I want to."

Frank had no moral objection to using these weapons. But how would they work?

"Plea bargaining, that's how," said Mike viciously. "They're going to guarantee my seat—or else I cause the biggest stink this town has ever seen."

As if regretting the outburst, he retreated. "Not that I want to do that. You know me, Frank. I don't believe in rocking the boat. And I won't unless I absolutely have to. But if they push too hard—well, they'll regret it."

Frank wanted desperately to believe every word. But he was not sure that he did.

"Well," he muttered unhappily, "anything you want from me, you just ask. You can rely on me."

"I know that, Frank," said Mike solemnly.

But Frank was hopeful of other allies. "What about the rest of Congress?" he asked. "Can you count on them?"

"Sure," said Mike Atamian without a flicker. "You know how it is, Frank. They see people trying to shovel the blame on me, and they don't like it. Smearing anyone in Congress hurts the whole gang."

"I suppose so," said Frank dubiously.

Goaded, his brother said, "What do you mean, you suppose so?"

Slowly, Frank Atamian figured it out.

"Couldn't it cut two ways? If they think you're hurting them, what's to keep them from dumping you as fast as they can?"

"Let them try!" said Mike Atamian evenly.

*   *   *

He would have been badly shaken to learn they were already at it.

"We've got to settle Atamian once and for all," said the Speaker. "I don't want things dragging out. Not with Social Security coming up."

Ben Safford and Val Oakes exchanged glances. Although the meeting in Speaker Walter Bullivant's office might be informal, the call for action was nonetheless imperative. With the House heading into the shoals of Social Security, clearing the decks was an absolute necessity.

"Savard's doing his best," Val answered. "But it looks to me as if this thing is mushrooming out of control."

"That," said the Speaker, "is precisely the trouble. I haven't kept up with every wrinkle of this Conroy situation, Ben—"

"I think now we can call it the Wellenmeister situation. Or even the VX-92 situation," Ben replied.

The Speaker had not called them in to bandy words.

"But I get the impression that there are too many investigations and too many agencies. Everybody, including Savard, is going his own way."

Experience had taught Ben to respect the Speaker's instincts.

"You mean that nobody's doing any coordinating, Walter?" he said. "You may have something there."

"You bet your boots I do," said the Speaker forthrightly. "I happen to have heard that the Justice Department is still worried about Wellenmeister."

"The official theory was that Wellenmeister has come clean," Ben reminded him.

"It was," said the Speaker maliciously. "And it made everybody, including the White House, very comfortable. Unfortunately, it didn't stand up."

Ben had to agree. Ambassador Wellenmeister's whole apologia had rung a little hollow. Particularly his contention that he had handed Mike Atamian a bundle without asking any questions.

"Justice isn't the only one," said the Speaker. "The Department of Defense is nosing around Dorland, the Air Force is putting

130

the Conroy board through the wringer and I want to take care of Atamian."

"Too many cooks spoiling the broth?" Val asked.

"It's got to stop," the Speaker replied. "I want them all in the same place, at the same time. Otherwise, Mike Atamian could fall through the cracks—and we'll be stuck with him for God knows how long!"

"Do you think you can manage it, Walter?" Ben asked.

His curiosity was genuine. The powers of the Speaker of the House of Representatives, while great, are not unlimited.

"When it comes to Mike Atamian," said the Speaker, "I'm going to push every button I can. And twist as many arms as I have to."

That was enough for Ben.

"This," he said, "should be something to see."

19

The Speaker was as good as his word. Within hours, Congressmen Oakes and Safford were booked to represent the House at a morning meeting in Undersecretary Preston Goodrich's office.

"To see if we can establish ground rules for subsequent proceedings," said the Speaker with a straight face. "Get every one of the SOBs rattled, with special emphasis on Atamian. Legally, of course."

"I'll leave my rubber hose here," said Ben. "Tell me, Walter, how did you do it?"

"Don't ask," said the Speaker darkly.

As soon as he entered Preston Goodrich's quarters, Ben saw that there had been similar pep talks elsewhere in the federal government. Speaker Bullivant was not the only one getting fed up with the stalemate. In fact, thought Ben, judging from the heap of umbrellas, raincoats and briefcases in the outer office, everybody was.

In the conference room, he encountered row upon row of determined faces.

As usual, the Air Force component looked bandbox fresh. Ben could only assume that there was something about military gear that resisted torrential downpours better than civilian wear. Approaching the long table with Val, he made another discovery. Adversaries had already sorted themselves out and were seated accordingly. But it was not accusers on one side and the accused on the other.

"The Air Force must be taking on all comers," said Val after one glance.

General Farrington, the entire Conroy board and a representative of the Joint Chiefs of Staff had lined up in strict order of precedence. Apart from curt nods, they ignored the rest of the gathering until a White House aide tried to sit in the vacant chair on their side.

"If you don't mind, I'm saving that seat," said the major general leading the team. "We have one more member coming."

The aide withdrew, everybody shuffled into place and Preston Goodrich was about to begin the proceedings when the door opened once again. In marched Captain Neil Conroy, wearing full-dress uniform. Looking straight ahead, he reported to the major general.

"Sorry to be late, sir."

"That's all right, Captain. I should have gotten to you sooner. Just take a seat here."

Everything but trumpets, thought Ben with real appreciation. There were still formalities to go through, but the Joint Chiefs of Staff had decided to make a statement. Conroy was being received back into the fold—with a bang.

What's more, to judge from the expressions displayed by the rest of the military, this was a last-minute call.

Undersecretary Goodrich was taken aback. "We're glad to have Captain Conroy join us," he said.

The major general made his speech anyway. "The Air Force has been the major victim of this whole setup. We've been sold a defective plane, we've had a pilot killed, we've had another pilot railroaded and we've had an officer bribed. Captain Conroy's presence here is because his interests are those of the Air Force."

The Department of Justice was feeling pretty militant, too.

"Good, then we're all interested in the same thing," said one of their tigers resoundingly. "And, Mr. Undersecretary, I'd like to start with a few questions for Mr. Wellenmeister."

He was stealing the spotlight with a vengeance.

"I have no objection," said Goodrich.

"And neither do we," said Wellenmeister's attorney ringingly. "My client will be happy to cooperate."

To Ben, Wellenmeister looked far from happy. Instead of his

133

usual ruddy glow, there was an angry flush on his cheeks. His eyes were narrowed in what looked like permanent rage.

The Department of Justice wasted no time.

"Mr. Wellenmeister, you've told us you gave Congressman Atamian here twenty-five thousand dollars—in connection with that crash in Utah. Is that right?"

Glaring at his tormentor, Wellenmeister said, "That's right."

"What did you think Congressman Atamian was going to do with the money?"

"I didn't think about it at all."

The lawyer from the Justice Department was young and sarcastic. "Do you mean you didn't want to know about the sordid details?"

Ben found himself holding his breath. He would have sworn that Walter Wellenmeister could not stand this kind of baiting. But he had to give the devil his due. There was no explosion.

"Nonsense!" said Wellenmeister firmly. "I wanted to tamp down the publicity. All I needed was discretion. The last thing I expected was that he was going to pass out bribes."

Staring fixedly into space, he ignored the buzz of conversation that ran around the table.

The lawyer scowled. "And when all your problems miraculously disappeared, you never gave it a second thought?"

"Don't forget that assassination attempt on the Queen," Wellenmeister said sharply. "It monopolized the news for weeks. I thought we'd been lucky."

"But the Air Force held a board of inquiry, didn't it? What did you think when they decided it was pilot error—without even touching the technical material about the VX-92?"

Wellenmeister's explanation was pat. "I wasn't president of Dorland then. I'd been appointed Ambassador to France. It wasn't my pigeon anymore."

"You're not seriously asking us to believe that you didn't follow the results of the board?"

"Yes, I am," said Wellenmeister. If he had left it at that, the

134

honors would have been evenly divided. But something prompted him to add: "I had a lot of other things to think about."

This revealing statement brought a pleased smile to the face of the young attorney. But he was willing to let it speak for itself. Instead of pursuing Wellenmeister further, he shifted course.

"Thank you very much, Mr. Wellenmeister," he said. "Now, I'd like to turn to Representative Atamian."

Atamian and his attorney were sitting down the table from Ben, so Ben did not have an unobstructed view. Whether Atamian was looking cornered or defiant, he could not tell.

"Congressman Atamian. You've heard Mr. Wellenmeister. So you know what the question is. What exactly did you do with the twenty-five thousand dollars he gave you?"

"I spent it on normal public relations," Atamian replied. "On the advice of counsel, I'm not going into details."

The Justice Department had profited from Representative Savard's groundwork.

"The books of the Atamian Construction Company show that the money was given to you in cash."

"That's right," Atamian said, almost cordially. "And I paid for services in cash, too. You can't make anything out of that!"

In Mike's place, Ben would not have been hurling challenges.

Congressman Oakes agreed. "Remind me to tell Tony that Mike didn't bother laundering any money," he murmured to Ben. "His system is a lot simpler."

A similar opinion drove the Department of Justice back to open sarcasm. "And that's what you call normal public-relations services? Handing somebody an envelope of cash?"

"It's a crazy world out there," said Mike Atamian negligently. "If somebody wants to be paid in cash, it's no skin off my nose."

Leaning forward, Ben Safford studied his colleague. Mike was radiating a tight, wary smugness. If it was genuine, possibly this was the time to carry out Speaker Bullivant's instructions. One way to rattle this particular SOB, Ben was pretty sure, was to raise the sticky

135

question of tax evasion. But before he could speak, Preston Goodrich forestalled him.

"I have a few questions I'd like to ask, too," he said mildly, in effect flicking control of the meeting away from the Department of Justice. "I've been thinking that it may be a mistake to confine ourselves to the Utah crash. The fact of the matter is that we seem to be dealing with an ongoing effort to cover up flaws in the VX-92. So I wonder if you'd tell us a few things, Mr. Kidder."

George Kidder must have been expecting to be called. There were lawyers to the right and left of him. Nevertheless, his head went back slightly, as if a blow had landed.

"Certainly, Mr. Undersecretary," he said, his face completely blank.

"Mr. Kidder, you were president of Dorland during the board of inquiry, and during the Paris Air Show as well. What exactly do you know about these payments to Congressman Atamian?"

Kidder took a deep breath. "Not one thing," he said, stressing each word.

Goodrich did not resort to irony. Instead he was reasonable and the impact was much the same.

"But if Mr. Atamian was obtaining public-relations services for Dorland, wouldn't you know about it?"

"No," said Kidder. "Taking over a large company involves hundreds of problems. There isn't time to get down to all the petty details."

"Of course," said Goodrich with grave sympathy.

"Neat," said Val Oakes, in Ben's ear.

Ben agreed. Goodrich's performance was masterful. With minimal effort, he was reminding George Kidder, and everybody else in the conference room, that large companies and the way they work were no secret to this particular undersecretary.

"And you're telling us that Congressman Atamian's activities fall into the category of petty detail? Is that right?"

Belatedly, Kidder realized he had erred and he was stuck.

"That's right," he said doggedly.

"But, Mr. Kidder," Goodrich continued, "the books show payments to Congressman Atamian during your tenure. Are you claiming you didn't know about them?"

Ben could see beads of perspiration on Kidder's brow.

"Such payments had nothing to do with the VX-92," Kidder insisted. "Dorland has many interactions with the federal government. I don't deny that we may have fallen into the habit of expecting Congressman Atamian to smooth the way, to set up appointments with the right people, to help make our point of view on important issues felt."

Abruptly, Preston Goodrich took off the kid gloves.

"But then, Mr. Kidder, you're saying you had time to keep up with insignificant activities like that—but not to keep abreast of the threat to the VX-92."

"If you mean the Conroy hearing," Kidder shot back, "that's exactly what I'm saying."

This was too much for the Air Force.

"What about the Paris Air Show?" the major general interjected. "Was that too minor for your attention, too?"

Kidder turned to him. "As I think everyone here knows, Dorland was extremely reluctant to put on a VX-92 display in Paris."

"Agreed," said the major general. "But you told us that was because of marketing considerations."

"We felt that we could do a more impressive job next year," said Kidder stubbornly.

"Not that there was a design flaw that you were trying to keep from us?" the general demanded.

"My God," said Kidder, sounding drained. "Those were Dorland planes and Dorland men in Paris. If we'd known, do you think we'd have let them fly?"

Deliberately, the major general stared at him. "I don't know whether you would—or not."

Undersecretary Goodrich waited to see how Kidder would respond. When nothing came, he said, "As you see, Mr. Kidder, we have a serious problem here. If Dorland is counting on a continuing relationship with the Department of Defense, you're going to have to convince us that at some point we can expect candor."

The threat to Dorland was as naked as the threat to Mike Atamian.

Walter Wellenmeister was the one who broke.

Rounding on Atamian, he shouted, "You bribed Perini! Why the hell don't you admit it? My God, you can see what everybody else here is thinking, can't you? And you're not doing yourself a damned bit of good!"

"Wellenmeister—"

"Mr. Ambasssador, if you please—"

"Walter, shut up, will you—"

Over the din of conflicting advice, Mike Atamian's voice rang out. "That's your opinion, Walter!"

The Air Force did not give a damn about Walter Wellenmeister and Congressman Atamian, at least not directly.

"Julian Perini," said the major general, dropping the syllables like stones. "He killed himself because of that bribe you two are talking about. Maybe it was the best way for him. But right now, I wish he hadn't. Because if he was here, there wouldn't be any pussyfooting around about refusing to answer. I'd have it out of him—"

"Perini didn't commit suicide."

The new voice seemed to come from nowhere. After a minute of bewilderment, the major general located it.

"Captain Conroy!" he said wrathfully.

It was too late to overawe Neil Conroy. Solid as a rock, and just about as movable, he faced his superior.

"Captain Perini didn't commit suicide," he said deliberately. "He was murdered."

"Conroy, what are you talking about?"

"And," Neil continued implacably, "the police know it, too. They think he was killed because he knew too much."

At the top levels, this came as news, and unwelcome news at that. But Ben Safford was not the only one present who knew Neil was right.

General Reynold Farrington supplied corroboration. "That is

correct, sir," he said colorlessly. "The air police have begun reviewing the Perini case in that light."

"They were doing the rounds at the Pentagon just the other day," Larry Yates joined in.

The uproar that followed was typical of Washington, Ben thought. In the stratosphere of policymaking, other operations were so far away as to be out of sight. Nobody knew exactly what the troops were doing. So the head men in the Department of Justice and the Air Force were the last to realize what was actually happening in the field—and what it meant.

But Mike Atamian made the connection all right, and he made it fast. Springing to his feet, he glared around the table like a trapped animal.

"Murder!" he screeched. "What kind of play is this? You figure to pin a murder rap on me? You're crazy! C'mon, Charlie, we're getting out of here right now."

"Wait a minute, Mike . . ." Ben began.

But Atamian was already at the door.

Ben hurried after him. In the outer office Atamian was furiously tossing coats aside, burrowing down to his own in frantic haste.

"Mike, you're just going to make things worse for yourself by tearing out of here like this," Ben said.

"That's absolutely right," said Val, coming up behind him.

By now, Atamian had shrugged himself into his dripping raincoat. Snatching up an umbrella and a briefcase, he turned on them.

"You think I'm going to sit still while you frame me?" he spat.

"Nobody's framing you," said Ben. "The whole reason for this meeting is to get to the truth—"

"Sure!" Atamian rolled his eyes. "Let's get together and talk about the bribe. And oh, by the way, the guy was murdered! What do you take me for?"

He spun on his heels and stormed out. His lawyer was forced to snatch up an armful of wet belongings and break into a run to keep up with him.

"I'm afraid we've lost an important witness," Ben reported when he returned to the conference table. "Atamian isn't going to be talking to anybody until he's had a long huddle with his lawyer."

In a taxi, speeding back toward Capitol Hill, Mike Atamian's legal huddle was already well under way.

"You know the old saying," said Charlie Crowder. "Tell the truth to your priest, your doctor and your lawyer. It goes double when you're talking about murder."

Atamian sat hunched forward, staring straight ahead. "Murder," he said dully, without bothering to turn.

Unobtrusively, the lawyer studied him. Atamian, white around the mouth, did look shocked. But Charlie Crowder had been in Washington long enough to know how deceiving appearances can be.

"They're trying to pull a fast one on me," Atamian suddenly said.

"I won't give you any argument on that," said Crowder, keeping certain reservations to himself. "But if this guy Perini really was murdered, you and I had better concentrate on starting over from the top."

Just then, the taxi pulled up at the House Office Building. When Atamian did not bolt, Crowder thought he knew why. Lawyers are a lifeline that people sometimes cling to.

Atamian, however, was held fast by outrage. "What the hell are you talking about?"

Repressing a sigh, Crowder said, "I'm talking about taking some precautions. Don't get excited."

"I never killed anybody."

"Okay, you didn't kill anybody," said Crowder smoothly. "But, Mike, this public-relations story of yours isn't going to be good enough. It might work on a bribery charge. Maybe even with the Ethics Committee. But not when they start talking about murder."

Atamian began a protest. Then, shrugging as if it no longer mattered, he made a major concession. "The only thing I did was

140

spread a little money where it would do the most good. That's all. And I'm willing to swear it on my mother's grave."

Unimpressed, Crowder nodded toward the cabby. "Fine, but this isn't the time or the place—"

"That goddamn bastard Wellenmeister must be lying through his teeth," Atamian went on. "That's the only way it makes any sense. But that set them all off in the wrong direction."

"Wellenmeister?" said Crowder, thinking how often schemers like Atamian outsmarted themselves. "He's a long way from this Perini murder. You're the one who's right in the line of fire. Forget Wellenmeister."

"Like hell I will," said Atamian.

Crowder simply looked at him.

"You think that twenty-five thousand ties me in?" Atamian did not bother to lower his voice. "You're all wet. You see, Charlie, Perini wasn't the one I gave it to."

20

As soon as Undersecretary Goodrich had his office to himself, he realized that the highest authority of all in Washington was probably still in the dark.

The White House returned his call in record time.

"Pres? I just got your message. What the hell do you mean, murder?" said the strained voice of Jim Kraus.

Goodrich was grimly amused. After years as a nonentity, Kraus was enjoying the heady power of being a White House aide. One of the games he played was refusing to accept calls. Messages were taken by an underling, and Kraus, in his own sweet time, got back to the supplicant. Goodrich himself had waited as long as forty-eight hours. Today was different in more ways than one.

"That's right, Jim. The air police are satisfied that the Perini suicide was faked."

"Hold it! I don't know whether we can go along with that."

"The Virginia police are working on that theory, too."

As Goodrich had expected, Kraus was baffled by the introduction of a group that did not even appear on his organization chart.

"Christ! That's all we need, a bunch of locals mixing into the act."

This statement was followed by the sound of rapidly drumming fingers. Finally: "Wellenmeister's been a jerk."

Goodrich could think of no useful comment to make and remained silent.

"The trouble is that nobody knows how big a jerk," Kraus confided.

"I see."

In other words, the White House feared that good old Walt might conceivably have added murder to bribery.

"And there's no way we're letting anything like that touch the boss."

Goodrich bit back the temptation to say that it was a little late in the day for that. "What do you want me to do?"

"Stay on top of things. We don't want any more big surprises here. And spread the word to those MPs of yours that Wellenmeister's on his own."

Goodrich was furious. He resented the assumption that if Kraus had wanted to swaddle Wellenmeister in protection, the Undersecretary of Defense would have ordered the air police to lay off. On the other hand, there was no point in locking horns when he was, in fact, being told to do exactly what he was doing.

"The air police and the Department of Justice already know that," he said, keeping himself under control.

"That's the line to take, Pres."

Returning to private life was looking better and better. Gritting his teeth, Goodrich said, "Everybody seems to think it's only a matter of time before Atamian talks."

"So he fingers Wellenmeister, so what?" Kraus said expansively. "We've written them both off."

"And suppose he fingers somebody else?" Goodrich asked with deliberate malice.

"Hey!" It was a squeak of alarm. "That's not in our game plan. We're not playing it that way."

As a White House aide, Jim Kraus was not only offensive, he was also incompetent. In spite of his tough talk, he did not have a game plan, or anything approaching one. As the last two weeks had proven to Goodrich, Kraus was only capable of reacting—feebly and often tardily—to the actions of others.

"I only hope Atamian knows the rules you've laid down," Goodrich replied. "Otherwise, there could be a lot of people embarrassed."

As usual, Kraus was weak on detail. "Run that list by me again, will you?"

With some pleasure, Goodrich rattled off the longest list he could. Inundated by names, every one of which could set off waves, Kraus reached one of the big policy decisions he was so fond of.

"I'll tell you what, Pres. The best thing of all would be to wrap this up." Even to his own ears, this lacked the knockout punch that was supposed to be his trademark. Hastily, he made an addition: "Pronto!"

It might be the best thing for the White House. Goodrich was not certain that it would be the best thing for the United States Air Force. He did not bother to say so.

The minute Goodrich rang off, Jim Kraus dialed his assistant's line.

"Vinny, I want you up here on the double," he ordered.

One reason Kraus was so inept at manipulating official Washington was that he was accustomed to think in terms of Presidential campaigns rather than Presidential incumbencies. The White House was filled with men advocating a specific agricultural program or defense posture because of its intrinsic merit. This always came as a surprise to Kraus, who assumed, as a matter of course, that you said whatever sounded best. He might be ill-equipped to deal with the real problem of the VX-92, but he was temperamentally qualified to insulate the White House from any fallout.

"Now look, Vinny," he announced the moment the door had closed, "the boss is going to be on the Coast next week, and he'll be seeing a lot of old friends."

"I'll get you the list."

"Never mind that. Just make sure that the Wellenmeisters don't show up at these shindigs."

Even as his assistant nodded, Kraus spied another possible threat.

"We've got to think of the missus, too. Check through her charity committees to make certain that Mrs. Wellenmeister isn't into cerebral palsy or anything like that."

The last thing Kraus wanted right now was a picture of the First Lady and Deedee joined in good works.

"No problem," Vinny said crisply. "We can always get her bounced. Anything else?"

"I guess that takes care of— No, wait a minute."

During the ensuing silence, Kraus's expression became almost furtive. There is a fine distinction between ruthless conduct toward those who have lost power forever and those who may rise again.

"Look, I don't want this getting out, but better safe than sorry," he said, lowering his voice instinctively. "As a purely temporary measure, though, let's keep space between us and the Kidders, too."

His lieutenant, who would cheerfully have accepted orders more extreme than these, was a little too eager for Kraus's peace of mind.

"Watch it with the Kidders," Kraus cautioned. "Don't forget the fund raisers start in a couple of months."

Any congressman who really works at his job has very little time to spare. Ben and Val were forced to give Tony Martinelli the juicy details of their meeting as all three hurried off to a committee hearing. Tony was fascinated.

"I'll bet Mike louses it up," he predicted. "He expected pressure, but not this kind."

"Not unless he's the one who shot Perini," Val observed.

"Even then," Tony insisted, "Perini's been dead a couple of weeks now, and it looked as if that suicide setup would hold. Besides, I don't see Mike pulling a gun. If Perini had looked like ratting, Mike would have worked his butt off trying to fix him."

Even Ben, no admirer of Congressman Atamian, had to agree. The murder of Julian Perini was altogether too straightforward a course of action for Atamian. "Then what does he think he's doing? If you're right about this being a big shock to him, he should be falling over himself trying to come clean and pin it all on somebody else."

"Mike's figuring how much to ask for," Tony said instantly.

Val shook his head sorrowfully. "Bad timing."

"That's Mike's trouble. He's crooked, but he's not very smart. He probably thinks that somewhere, somehow, there's got to be something in it for him."

Val had seen countless Mike Atamians come and go in the

halls of Congress. "If he opened up right now, he'd earn a little something from the Justice boys. They might drop the charges against him. But that doesn't satisfy him. So he'll hold out for a big payoff and miss the boat entirely."

Ben was genuinely curious. "Just how big a payoff does he think he can get?"

"With Mike, the sky's the limit. He's up to his ears in a big mess. I see it, you see it. Even he sees it, but not the right way up. In Mike's book, if this is such a big mess to a lot of important people, then they ought to be willing to shell out to get his cooperation. He probably thinks he can stay out of jail, hold his seat and fatten his bank account."

"Don't forget the obvious thing he may have in mind," Val cautioned. "Whatever he's got to say is bound to be a big embarrassment to Wellenmeister and Dorland. So it's plain as daylight to him that his silence should be worth so much to them that they'll take care of him."

Ben had no problem putting his finger on the flaw in this reasoning. "The White House has already started tossing Wellenmeister overboard. If things get much worse, they'll be willing to jettison Dorland, too. Those people aren't in a position to take care of themselves any longer. How could they possibly take care of Mike?"

"That's why he's going to fall flat on his face," Tony said triumphantly. "Mike's big trouble is that he doesn't understand luck."

Ben and Val both groaned. Like Napoleon, Tony was a great believer in luck. Unfortunately, he had developed an elaborate theory which he was fond of expounding. Luck could come or go, anywhere, anytime. According to Tony, this was something all serious students of poker, politics and life should keep in mind.

"Sure, it's smart to play the odds," he began as they turned in to the corridor leading to Committee Room B. "But first you've got to know there *are* odds."

Val had an older and grander formulation of this truth.

"God moves in a mysterious way His wonders to perform."

Tony managed to smile at a passing columnist and simultaneously shake his head. "Take Wellenmeister," he said. "A week ago, he was sitting on top of the world. Today, he's a disaster area."

Ben was willing to give Tony just so much rope. "What do you mean, disaster area?" he countered. "So they've taken away his latest toy, and he's suffered a little mortification. He's still got more money than he can use and fancy homes all over the place."

"What about his good name?" asked Tony, leering ironically.

"His name was never as good as he thought," Ben grunted. "And if you're going to tell me that he's in any danger of going to jail—"

Martinelli was deeply offended. "What do you take me for? A simp? The only way our Walter goes up the river is if he strangles Deedee. And even then his chances are pretty good."

They were digressing from the great theory.

"You're simply saying that nobody could have predicted what's been happening," Ben argued. "But luck had nothing to do with what's happened to Wellenmeister. Committing a crime did."

Val was always the spokesman for hardheaded realism. "A lot of people who give—and take—bribes don't get caught, Ben."

Tony was in a playful mood. "Besides, Wellenmeister didn't get caught. He confessed. Remember?"

Val took this correction in the spirit intended. "He got caught all right. They just haven't got around to telling him. But there's still a lot to come out in the wash."

"Like whether Mike Atamian was acting on his own or whether someone was holding his hand all the way," said Tony, not bothering to lower his voice although they were trotting directly past Congressman Atamian's office. "Say what you like, Ben, there's a guy whose luck has run out in a big way."

Ben opened his mouth to reply but the words never emerged. There was a distant background thump following hard upon Tony's words, and the oak door to Atamian's quarters was buckling outward. Then a violent, invisible wave hit them, and Congressman Safford was slammed off his feet into the base of one of the stately marble columns of the House of Representatives.

Even as he lost consciousness, he heard a voice screaming.

"My God! It's a bomb!"

147

21

There were hands gently exploring Ben's head. Opening his eyes, he looked up into the concerned faces of Tony Martinelli and a strange medic.

"Ben! You had me scared, boy!"

"What happened?" he asked groggily. As his vision cleared, Ben was slowly absorbing the fact that the dapper Mr. Martinelli was covered with plaster dust and one side of his face was rapidly discoloring.

"Somebody blew up Mike Atamian with a bomb," Tony replied grimly. "We got the tail end of the blast."

It was coming back to Ben now. Tony had been arguing with Val and him—

"Val! Tony, have you seen Val?"

A reassuring voice spoke from several paces away. "Spared to fight again another day," said Congressman Oakes, making his way through the crowd to their side.

As Ben began struggling to his feet, his field of view enlarged, and what he saw was enough to take his mind off his throbbing headache. Half the Capitol security police seemed to be in the corridor, some of them clearing a path for a stretcher. There was a lot of confused shouting near the gaping hole that had been Congressman Atamian's door, and, closer to Ben, a group of secretaries tried to comfort a woman who was weeping, her face hidden by arms that showed long ragged gashes.

"You've all got to be checked out," the medic insisted. "I'll take you downstairs."

Martinelli was not leaving without some facts.

"What's the bad news?" he asked, jerking his head incautiously toward the hole, then wincing.

Congressman Atamian had been killed instantly. That was all the medic knew.

It took Elsie Hollenbach a full hour to fight her way into Val Oakes' office. This was one measure of the convulsions gripping Capitol Hill, Washington and the nation.

Another was provided by one of Val's staffers. "All network programming has been scrapped," he said, depositing a bucket of ice.

"I wonder what it was like around here when those Puerto Ricans let loose with guns from the Visitors' Gallery?" observed Val, reaching back into history. "Hello there, Elsie."

From the doorway, she surveyed Ben and Val by the desk, then saw the recumbent figure. "Is Tony all right?" she cried.

Touched by her concern, Tony forced a jaunty smile. "Right as rain, Elsie. Grab a chair, and tell us what's going on out there."

He was lying on Val's ancient leather couch with an ice bag over his rapidly maturing black eye. Either his cheerfulness or the bottle at his elbow reassured Elsie. She turned to Ben.

"And you, Ben?"

"No lasting damage," he replied with a grin, "although this suit is never going to be the same. And Val's okay, too."

The only bruises Congressman Oakes had sustained were to his dignity. Some freak of the explosion had sent him sliding down the halls of Congress like a bowling ball.

With these preliminaries over, Elsie sank into a seat and gratefully accepted the martini Val mixed for her.

"They told us Mike was killed outright. Did anybody else die?" Ben did not want to ask, but somebody had to.

"By some miracle, no. The only one who was close to him was his legislative assistant and he, mercifully, had just dropped his pen. When the blast came, he was virtually inside the kneehole of the desk. They say that's what saved him. He's been taken to the hospital with a broken ankle. And the two girls were on the other side of the filing cabinet. They have some minor injuries from the flying debris. All in all, it's a good thing Mike was by the door so that some of the force went outward."

"I suppose so," said Ben, trying to be selfless about it.

Tony was more interested in the breakdown of protection. "What the hell were the police doing, letting some bozo waltz in here with a bomb?" he demanded indignantly.

Contrary to general appearances, Capitol Hill is not wide open. There are over a thousand security personnel patrolling the area and a significant number of detection devices. Planting a bomb is not as easy as it may look.

"Apparently, Mike Atamian carried it in with him, in his briefcase," Elsie explained. "The explosion was triggered when he opened his case to get something."

There was a sober silence. Everybody in the room regularly performed that very same act.

"Makes you pause for thought, doesn't it?" mused Val Oakes, so shaken he did not produce a Scriptural comment.

"It sure does," agreed Ben. "A letter bomb could get slipped into my case about five times a day."

But Elsie Hollenbach was shaking her head. "No, not a letter bomb. The latch itself was booby-trapped, and the police are fairly sure what happened."

It had not been easy to establish the facts with one witness on a stretcher and two others in hysterics. But, thanks to patient determination, the relevant details had slowly been extracted. Atamian's secretary had personally prepared his briefcase for the meeting in Undersecretary Goodrich's office. She had not only opened it, she had inserted several bright green folders. There were no bright green fragments in the debris. When Atamian returned from the meeting, he had put the case down in full view of his staff and left it untouched until he was again preparing to depart. As a final point, the case had been an over-the-counter item, except for his monogram.

"So their theory is that there was a switch of briefcases," Elsie concluded, "with the deadly one substituted for the harmless one."

She paused and looked almost pityingly at Ben and Val before adding her final sentence. "The only place this could have happened is at your meeting this morning."

Ben gulped. "Well, Val, you said Mike should have opened up on the spot, instead of holding out for a big payoff. You were more right than you knew."

"Somebody certainly didn't intend to let him have second thoughts," Val reasoned.

Ben and Val had concentrated on the victim. Tony was looking elsewhere.

"Do you realize what this means?" he demanded, jerking himself upright with one hand clapped to the ice bag. "The big boys are so rattled they're doing their own dirty work!"

In essence, Tony Martinelli was saying that the protection usually afforded by a network of hired hands had just evaporated. The minute the words were out of his mouth, Ben and Val and Elsie recognized that it was a new ball game.

Walter Wellenmeister did not.

"I don't know why you're wasting your time here, Phelan," he complained to the man from the Department of Justice the next day. "We've been over that business of the payment to Atamian. You should be out looking for his murderer."

Mindful of orders from above, Phelan decided to do some straight talking.

"That's what I am doing," he said quietly.

Still, Wellenmeister did not understand.

"Well, all this harping on a measly twenty-five thousand isn't going to get you anywhere. I'd like to help you out," he said, mildly regretful, "but there's just no way I can."

He half rose, signaling the end of the interview. It was as if Mr. Phelan had asked him for a job, and he had announced that he knew of no openings.

"Let's go over it again," Phelan suggested, settling himself more firmly.

Wellenmeister was annoyed. "What in God's name do you

people want from me? I've cooperated to the hilt. Hell, I took the heat. I stood up in front of the whole country and said everything was my fault. There wasn't one thing more anyone could do. In fact," he added judiciously, "I'm beginning to think I was a little too hasty letting them sell me the theory that a press conference would settle things! It hasn't, and I took a lot of knocks for nothing."

Like everybody in the Justice Department, Phelan knew exactly how much pressure it had taken to make Wellenmeister accept even minimal responsibility for his own actions. Wellenmeister had known about the inadequacy of the VX-92 and, instead of pulling the plane from production, he had proceeded to sell it. When the Utah crash had threatened adverse publicity, he had resorted to bribery. Then, in a final act of callous disregard, he had pushed for the fatal demonstration in Paris. Nonetheless, he saw himself as some kind of Horatius at the bridge. Thanks to him, the White House and its friends had gotten safely across the river.

Ignoring the self-justification, Phelan said, "I suppose you saw a fair amount of Congressman Atamian when you were still with Dorland."

"Whenever it was useful." Wellenmeister puffed out his chest. "Of course, I had a great many demands on my time. Running a show like Dorland isn't a nine-to-five business. It takes real dedication. But, given the company's stake in Washington, I needed congressional inputs on a regular basis."

"Did he usually carry a briefcase at your meetings?"

Incredibly, Wellenmeister did not sense danger. "Maybe," he said indifferently. "I wouldn't notice something like that."

"Let's see if we can jog your memory. Did you ever give Atamian cash?"

Wellenmeister did not like the question. "Our regular procedure involved an accounting transfer to the credit of Atamian Construction Company," he said, trying to wrap bribery in a cocoon of respectability.

"We know that," Phelan said unkindly. "But were there exceptions to the regular procedure?"

"Occasionally, Mike preferred cash."

152

"And how did you get the cash to pay him?"

This intrusion into the mysteries of his corporate household offended Wellenmeister. "I sent my secretary to the cashier's office," he said shortly.

"And then?"

"She brought it to me, and I handed it to Mike," Wellenmeister said with exaggerated patience.

"And where did Atamian put it?"

The tempo of question and answer had slowed so that Wellenmeister's next answer had an almost ritual finality.

"In his briefcase."

Phelan nodded in satisfaction. The police laboratory had already determined that the initials on the deathtrap had been applied with a simple craft punch. But how many people knew Atamian used the initials M.G.A.?

"So you had ample opportunity to observe Congressman Atamian's briefcase?"

At last, the warning bells were sounding.

"That's as good as asking me if I killed him!" Wellenmeister roared in horrified protest.

Phelan was stolid. "We're asking everybody the same questions," he replied, sinking the fact that they were starting with the ex-Ambassador.

"Why should I kill him? I didn't do anything. All he could say was what he did with the money."

"Well, we'll never know what he would have said now, will we?"

Wellenmeister's eyes were almost popping out of his rapidly reddening face. Phelan watched the phenomenon with interest. In spite of his record, in spite of the fact that he was, at this very moment, being interrogated as a murder suspect, Wellenmeister was still dumbfounded that his word should be openly questioned.

Phelan was shrewd enough to realize that it was the last fact that was the shock. Probably Wellenmeister knew he was surrounded by people well aware of his capacity for deceit. But he expected them to put a good face on it. The fact that Phelan, whom

153

Wellenmeister regarded as an employee of his important friends, was willing to abandon convention was a very ominous sign.

"You're looking in the wrong place. So maybe I did have a pretty good notion what Mike was going to do with the money, so what?" asked Wellenmeister, admitting more than he intended. "Who'd kill to hide that?"

"Probably nobody." Then, because part of Phelan's assignment was to make it crystal clear to Wellenmeister that he could no longer rely on special treatment, he went further. "But there's one thing you left out, Mr. Wellenmeister."

"What's that?"

"Captain Perini wasn't just bribed. He was murdered, too. And I guess almost anybody would want to keep that quiet."

Wellenmeister stared back, his whole face drained by alarm.

George Kidder's follies were less evident than Walter Wellenmeister's these days. But, as Ben Safford had discovered in Paris, the very size of Dorland Aircraft encouraged its president to feel that he was at the helm of a ship of state. When Mr. Phelan arrived at the reception desk, Kidder was closeted with two of his lawyers trying to decide whether to send in the Marines.

"The papers can't write this sort of story and get away with it," he insisted.

One of the many things shaken loose by the bomb in Mike Atamian's office had been official reticence about the death of Julian Perini. To the incredulous delight of the press, they had been handed not one murder, but two. Nor were they experiencing any difficulty in knitting together the two incidents. As clearly as the law allowed, they told the world their conclusions. Dorland had hired Atamian to bribe Perini. When pressure was about to go on Perini, Dorland killed him. Then, when the pressure shifted to Atamian, Dorland killed him, too.

"Actually, all the *Post* did is draw attention to the sequence of events," the younger lawyer remarked. "They haven't actually said Dorland murdered anybody."

"Not yet," the older one interjected.

George Kidder was not interested in hairsplitting. "Whatever they say, they've got to stop. You know the size of our government contracts. There's too much at stake to take risks."

The lawyers were quite happy to be interrupted by the news of Mr. Phelan's arrival.

George Kidder was not.

"I can't give you much of my time," he announced, coming out to the anteroom to indicate how brief their discussion would be.

Blandly, Phelan launched into his work, knowing that he had just been handed another card. Sooner or later, Kidder would be unnerved by the public nature of their encounter. The receptionist was already having a hard time pretending to be occupied by her filing. Phelan began by asking if Kidder had had many contacts with Congressman Atamian.

"Barely met the man," Kidder snapped. "He came to see me once at headquarters."

Only when his memory was prodded did he admit to other meetings.

"That's right," he agreed impatiently. "I ran into him at a couple of parties, both at Dorland and at the Air Show."

"Was he carrying a briefcase at headquarters?"

George Kidder stared back arrogantly. "How the hell would I know?"

The message was clear. Congressman Michael Atamian had been too insignificant to occupy the head of Dorland. And so was Mr. Phelan.

Undisturbed, Phelan continued his questions. George Kidder realized their tenor much sooner than Walter Wellenmeister had.

"You're as bad as those reporters," he charged angrily. "Somebody's death was convenient for Dorland, so that means Dorland went out and murdered him. Dorland is not John Doe running around with a Saturday-night special. We run a business here. But this kind of crazy talk could do a lot of damage."

"Mr. Kidder, if we find that someone at Dorland shot Captain Perini or planted a bomb in Mr. Atamian's briefcase, it's not going to be a question of a bad PR image, it's going to be Murder One."

As Phelan looked sternly at the president of Dorland, he spotted the spellbound receptionist now avidly listening for all she was worth.

"Corporations don't commit murder," Kidder said stolidly.

"They certainly shouldn't," Phelan agreed. "But I'm beginning to wonder how far you'd go to protect Dorland's image."

"Don't be absurd. The engineers didn't come clean to me until after the Paris crash. When Perini was killed, I didn't even know about the VX-92."

"Then you don't have any objections to telling me where you were when he was shot."

Kidder blinked, and for the first time surveyed the reception room with disapproval. Phelan thought the unnerving process had set in, but Kidder's next words disabused him.

"No, I don't have any objection. But it's just occurred to me that the lawyers sitting in my office might be interested in our discussion. I think it's time we joined them."

It was all very well for George Kidder to act as if Dorland's lawyers might have some academic interest in the latest views of the Justice Department. But Phelan had reached this point in other interrogations. In some circles, it was known as yelling for a mouthpiece.

"Neither of them has an alibi worth two cents," Phelan reported to his superior later in the day. "And they're both worried about something."

"You mean they were both in Washington?"

"That's right. Wellenmeister was introducing Kidder around town, but they split early in the afternoon. Dorland keeps a place out on the Chesapeake to entertain VIPs. Kidder went there for the weekend, and he says he was alone on the grounds from four to six."

"Great!" Phelan's superior snorted sarcastically. "Just communing with nature?"

"He claims he wanted to do some thinking before the guests arrived and he started hustling people over drinks."

"And Wellenmeister?"

Phelan laughed shortly. "That's better yet. He was due at Camp David for the weekend for a State Department briefing. His story is that he spent a couple of hours alone in his hotel room before the limousine came at six-thirty. You'll never guess what he says he was doing."

"What?"

"Studying a history of France."

There was a limit to the amusement the Justice Department could derive from Dorland's executives.

"All right, let's get to the nitty-gritty. What do you think they're worried about?"

"Wellenmeister's so shook up he let slip that he had a damned good idea what Atamian was going to do about the Conroy hearing. They must have talked it over. If he was that dumb, he may have even gone with Atamian to grease Perini. And you wouldn't believe how much Wellenmeister wanted that ambassadorship. I think he might have killed to stop Perini from queering that pitch."

Over the last ten years, the Justice Department had experienced almost every form of aberration.

"Crazier things have happened. Okay, Phelan, what goody are you saving about Kidder?"

"He didn't run for his lawyers until I asked for his alibi on the Perini job. He didn't like that question at all."

"In his shoes, who would?"

"That wasn't it. It smelled to me as if he didn't want to say who was with him. And if that information is more sensitive than a murder alibi, it kind of makes you think, doesn't it?"

22

For Ben Safford, the next day was an unmitigated disaster. It began, as the House infirmary had predicted, with only mild discomfort. Twenty-four hours' experience had taught him that he would be in the grip of a raging headache by quitting time.

As soon as he arrived on the Hill, he discovered that his schedule, already sagging under postponed matters, would have to be stretched to bursting point.

The first extraneous item demanding attention was, infuriatingly, the funeral of Congressman Atamian.

"You can't be serious," he told the Speaker.

"I got you and Elsie in here because we've got to be prepared to send a delegation," Bullivant replied. "You know what the boys are like."

Ben could not deny that the House was perfectly capable of tying itself into knots debating Atamian's obsequies. For some reason, the question of funeral procedure always sparked passion in the most unexpected quarters, and members who had sat mute for six years would wax eloquent about the respect due a fallen comrade.

It was no accident that the senior Democrat of the California delegation was sitting at Bullivant's elbow.

"But, Walter," Ben said, "this is no time for us to be pushing the fact that Mike was a colleague. He was a disgrace and an embarrassment to us. We should be grateful he can't do us any more harm."

Ben then sat back and waited for support. Elsie, both as a Californian and as the House's acknowledged arbiter of moral stan-

158

dards, was in a stronger position than he was to make the case for nonattendance.

Instead, her words were no comfort at all.

"What has to be, has to be," she said, in about as spineless a statement as he had ever heard from her. "But I must refuse utterly to participate in the eulogy."

"Then we'll take that as settled," said the Speaker, an expert at seizing even token agreement. "And, Ben, I told the Department of Justice that you'd be available this morning."

"That's all I need."

Once they were outside, Ben rounded on Elsie.

"What's wrong with you, Elsie? You're the last person I expected to back down."

"It was not a question of backing down," she defended herself.

Ben had forgotten that Elsie, in succeeding to the seat of her late husband, had also assumed certain social obligations. As she proceeded to remind him, when Henry Hollenbach had gone to his reward, the House, almost en masse, had trekked out to California. Elsie, who liked to pay her debts tenfold, had long since established herself as ready and willing to show up at any interment.

"Even Mike Atamian's?" Ben asked incredulously.

Elsie was a soldier of the old school. "Even Mike Atamian's," she said, biting the bullet.

Yesterday, the Department of Justice had sent Mr. Phelan to turn the screw on the chief suspects. Today, his mission was to extract information from promising witnesses.

By the time Ben had been over his story for the fifth time, the comfortably remote sensation inside his skull had moved forward and increased its tempo.

"This isn't getting us anywhere," he grumbled, turning restive. "Besides, you can't really be sure the switch took place in Goodrich's office. For God's sake, there were people milling around all over the place. It would have been too risky. It probably happened while Mike was on his way to the meeting."

Phelan decided that the careful release of a few tidbits might juice up his witness's flagging efforts.

"Of course you weren't there for the cough drops," he said brightly.

"What cough drops?" Ben sensed a lure but could not help himself.

"The others had to wait about ten minutes for you and Congressman Oakes. They kept going back and forth between the two rooms, ordering coffee and calling their offices. Atamian himself came out at the beginning and took a pack of cough drops from his case. Two people saw him do it."

As if the discussion had tripped a switch, Ben's headache became stronger. "So maybe it happened afterward."

Phelan was smiling with satisfaction as he shook his head. At last his witness was thinking, and that was what he wanted.

"I guess you haven't heard about our latest find. The real briefcase was stuffed behind a bookcase in the outer office where you all left your coats."

Ben knitted his brows. The sequence was not difficult to follow. "You're saying the murderer removed Atamian's case from the pile, planted the substitute, then had to get rid of the original harmless one."

"Right! Except Mr. Goodrich wasn't so sure it was harmless. When they spotted it behind the bookcase, he evacuated that part of the building and called the bomb squad."

"Then he's behind schedule, too," said Ben with fellow feeling.

How long ago was it that Preston had been comparing Washington unfavorably to Ohio? At this rate, Zinka was going to be returning to Cleveland sooner than she had dared hope.

A sudden difficulty occurred to him. "Wait a minute! How did the killer bring in the rigged case?"

"Under a raincoat draped over his arm" was the prompt reply. "Or even just turned around so the initials didn't show."

"That's right," Ben remembered of his own accord. "Mike had initials twice as big as anyone else's."

Phelan was pleased to see this recollection emerge without

160

prompting. "M.G.A.," he said, rolling each syllable around his tongue. "All enclosed in a big circle."

Ben nodded. "I'd forgotten the circle."

"Did you know the middle initial was G?"

"No, but I'm bad at that sort of thing," Ben said, automatically excusing himself.

"Almost everybody is, unless they've got a reason to notice."

For a moment, Ben was confused. Then he realized the lines along which Phelan must be thinking, and a picture formed in his mind's eye. How often had some accountant at Atamian Construction watched—perhaps enviously?—as thousands of dollars disappeared into that wide-open leather maw? And there was the reverse situation as well. Given the nature of Atamian's services to Dorland, Julian Perini might not have been alone in following eagerly as Mike's hand went in empty and emerged with a thick wad of bills.

"I guess a lot of people could have noticed that monogram," Ben agreed, "and the order of arrival at the meeting doesn't help you at all."

"No. In addition to everything else, Goodrich sent his girl to get coffee, so she wasn't sitting in the outer office. Anybody could have done it," he said in a congratulatory spirit, "not just the people who arrived after Atamian."

Ben did not care for the wording. "Congressman Oakes and I did not leave each other's side," he said stiffly.

Phelan had the grace to look shocked. "That never crossed my mind," he protested.

"Well, it should have."

With a mechanical smile, Phelan moved on. "On the other hand, you had a real good view of Mr. Atamian's departure."

"Yes, I did." Ben was not likely to forget. "You already know how the news of Perini's murder was broken. Mike was in a panic. He couldn't get out of there fast enough. I followed him and tried to persuade him to stay, but I wasn't getting through. He didn't hear what I was saying, and I doubt if he really saw what he was picking up. He just grabbed his raincoat and the case that was lying by it.

161

Whoever planted it was lucky that Mike wasn't in the mood to examine anything."

"So were you. If he'd been in any doubt, Mr. Atamian probably would have opened the case."

Until now, Ben had been preoccupied with his near miss by Atamian's doorway. This was a new thought, and it sent cold chills down his spine.

"Anything I can do to help," he offered with real vigor, "don't hesitate to ask."

Phelan was sympathetic. "It kind of clarifies your thinking, doesn't it? Mr. Crowder felt the same way when I pointed out that the case could have been opened in the taxi."

Clarify was exactly the right word. From now on, Atamian's killer was the enemy.

As an active participant in the discussion, instead of a wet sponge that Phelan was supposed to wring dry, Ben did some thinking.

"You haven't asked me about Neil Conroy," he remarked. "How come? I can't believe the people you've talked to haven't made a big point of his coming late and alone."

"There's no need to worry about your constituent on this one," Phelan reassured him. "Captain Conroy was lucky. Goodrich's girl was back from the cafeteria by then. She took his coat and led him to the conference room. Besides, as Conroy himself told me, he's not the one with a motive. It's the people at Dorland."

Ben could imagine. Neil had already been singing that song when they left Mrs. Hanna's house. Everything that happened subsequently would be seen by him as confirmation. And now that the press was on his side and the Air Force had received him back into the fold, he would be airing his opinions with even more assurance.

"I know his thinking," Ben said repressively. "Is there anything else I can do for you?"

"No, I've got what I came for," Phelan said, rising and glancing at his watch. "And I expect it's past your lunch hour. I hope I haven't taken up too much of your time, Mr. Congressman."

One committee meeting and two roll calls were already down the drain.

"Not at all," said Ben politely.

But before he was able to get away to eat, Janet called with a report on public reaction back home.

"Here in Newburg, they're saying it was all part of the Dorland cover-up," she said. "So I suppose nobody will ever be arrested."

Ben was in no mood for cynicism.

"Don't bet on it. The people from the Justice Department were just here asking a lot of questions."

"That's because you got so much publicity as the congressman who broke open the VX-92 scandal," she said smugly. "But do you really think they're going to dig very hard?"

She had succeeded in rocking him.

"What do you mean by that?" he demanded.

"Well, Atamian isn't very much of a loss, is he?"

"Janet!" he yelled, glad to be able to take it out on someone. "It wasn't an act of patriotism to get rid of Atamian. Somebody just as corrupt was afraid he'd talk!"

During his long tenure in Congress, Ben had fallen into the habit of expecting the Lundgrens to keep him on the right track. And here was Janet practically condoning murder!

"All I said was that the chances are against it," Janet continued, unruffled. "I certainly agree it would be a good thing if they catch this man. You don't have to get so excited."

Throwing caution to the winds, Ben exploded. "Like hell I don't! It's only a stroke of luck that the bomb didn't get me."

"*What?*"

He was in for it now. Janet proceeded to cross-examine him on the state of his health with a thoroughness that the infirmary had come nowhere near matching.

"Headaches?" she cried in alarm. "Oh, Ben, why don't you come home for a week and get a good rest?"

"Because I've got too much to do."

This earned him a lecture on the theme that nobody is as indispensable as he thinks he is. On the other hand, Janet was now second to none in her vindictiveness toward *that dangerous lunatic running around with bombs*.

As Ben hung up, he reflected sourly on the narrowness of Janet's civic concern, conveniently forgetting his own performance along these lines.

Lunch, far from providing a peaceful respite, simply re-awakened a nagging doubt that Ben had previously managed to put to sleep.

It did not help to encounter the Speaker on his way back to the office.

"Frank Atamian has decided that the funeral should be private," Bullivant announced. "Guess he's got his hands full trying to stay out of jail. Up till now, Mike took care of things like that."

"Wonderful," said Ben ungratefully. "An hour wasted this morning for nothing."

"It beats going out to California."

Even Ben's modest plan to seek the advice of his colleagues had to be put on the back burner.

"Do you know if Val and Elsie are back yet?" he asked as soon as he reached his own quarters.

Two days ago, Madge had burst into tears at Ben's first post-explosion appearance in the office. Since then, however, she had fended off reporters and borne the brunt of Ben's irritability. Her own fuse had shortened considerably.

"You don't have time for that now. Charlie Crowder's been here for twenty minutes," she said, then added as if speaking to a five-year-old: "He was Congressman Atamian's lawyer, remember?"

Before Ben could think of a crusher, Madge left to escort in his visitor.

In Washington, certain lawyers are not simple officers of the court. They are many-headed beasts—part lobbyists, part politicians, part influence peddlers. Charlie Crowder was one of this

164

breed, and he was not cooling his heels for twenty minutes without a very good reason.

He was also married to a senator's daughter, Ben recalled as Crowder entered with feline neatness of step.

"I've told my story to the Justice boys," he said when the time came to get down to essentials. "But the way things are going, I'd feel happier if someone in Congress knew, too. As you've been spearheading the probe into the VX-92, Ben, I figured you were the one to talk to."

What a tribute to the power of the press, thought Ben, when even the insiders were being misled. Prudently, he held his tongue.

"Of course, this is a gray area in client-attorney privilege," said Charlie, looking steadily out the window where there was absolutely nothing to see.

"What's the scoop, Charlie?" said Ben.

"Something Mike told me when we were leaving Goodrich's office. Oh, he was mad as hell, you saw that. And he was scared. And he was a blowhard. But this sounded straight to me."

"Yes," said Ben, acknowledging that Charlie Crowder had heard enough to be a pretty fair judge.

"He swore up and down that he had never bribed Julian Perini."

When Ben did not respond, Crowder frowned slightly, then said: "His actual words were: *Perini wasn't the one I gave it to.*"

"I don't understand anything anymore," Ben complained when he finally caught up with his friends. "First this business about Ursula Richmond, then Charlie Crowder's fairy tale."

In Washington, influential lawyers get more extended consideration than young women, however attractive.

"Forget the girl," Tony urged. "So she's popped up a few places since you met her. It's just coincidence."

"That's what I convinced myself when it happened three times," Ben said stubbornly. "But four times is too much."

Ben had lunched with a staffer from the Uniform Weaponry Committee who spent his time dodging in and out of the Pentagon.

165

When Ben had recognized Ursula Richmond across the restaurant floor, the staffer had obligingly identified her companion.

"Look," Ben continued, "it's no secret she's seeing Larry Yates. Then she turns out to be an old chum of Julian Perini's. Okay, I said, she's got a lot of friends in the Air Force, as we saw at the Paris Embassy. But now she's snuggling up to General Farrington's aide."

To Tony it was simple. "She's doing the rounds. God, Ben, even you must know she's not the only one."

Frowning, Ben turned to Congressman Oakes. "You've met her, Val. What do you think?"

"She's not doing the rounds," Oakes said with the assurance of an expert. "Sounds to me as if somebody is trying to get information through her. That's why she's pumping people over restaurant tables."

Mrs. Hollenbach was impatient with male folly. "Because she's a woman, you are overlooking the obvious explanation. She was probably not pumping General Farrington's aide but reporting to him."

Ben was still dissatisfied but, having unburdened himself, he was eager to progress to Charlie Crowder's revelation and its most significant aspect.

Given the value of inside information, why had an old Capitol hand made him a free gift?

"Could be that things have gotten so hot Charlie doesn't want to be the only one sitting on it," Val argued.

Tony nodded wisely. "Sure. Look what happened to poor Mike when he didn't unload fast enough. Clamming up in this Dorland stink hasn't turned out to be healthy."

"I think we can accept that Charlie is telling the truth," Elsie decided, "but what about Mike?"

Tony assumed that he was the ranking expert on Atamian's thought processes. "It explains why Mike acted the way he did. Until you shoved a murder at him, he thought he was in the clear. Even if he had bribed someone on the Conroy board, it wasn't his fault if the Saudis rushed out and bribed Perini. That had nothing to do with his fun and games."

"Are you telling me he thought two people on that board had been bribed, independent of each other?" Ben demanded, outraged.

"Mike thought everybody was on the take. With him, it was just a question of whether there was a slush fund waiting to be tapped."

His head reeling, Ben said, "And when it turned out not to be the Saudis?"

Val was becoming a convert to Tony's reasoning. "Wellenmeister making assurance doubly sure. At least, Atamian would think so, and that's why he was certain there was big money in it for him."

"This is all very well as theory, but there is still the question of probability," Elsie reproved them. She was never one to change course precipitately. "Until now, everybody has agreed that Captain Perini was the rotten apple at the Conroy hearing."

Ben enjoyed the rare moments when Elsie was guilty of inaccuracy. "That's not one hundred percent so, Elsie. Perini's sister said it was ridiculous to think Julian would take a bribe of fifteen thousand dollars."

Elsie waved away sisters, Tony smiled indulgent approval of family loyalty and Val Oakes sat up straight with a bang.

"Wait a minute, Ben. Is that how she put it? Not that it was unthinkable for Julian to be bribed?"

"What difference does it make?"

Val cocked a quizzical eyebrow. "I can think of one. Particularly since you said the little lady was awfully strong on detail. And I'm beginning to remember all that stuff about Perini's father. What does that business about retiring early to write history mean to you?"

Ben looked at him with dawning appreciation.

"The same thing it does to you," he said slowly. "But that's crazy. It would mean Perini was innocent all along, and that the air police have been looking in the wrong direction from the beginning."

When it came to felonies, Tony Martinelli was usually the first one to find his balance.

"Which makes it the best reason for faking Perini's suicide that I've heard so far. And an even better one for blowing up poor Mike."

Ben's headache was now a raging tom-tom that was setting the pace for his impatience.

"If Val is right, and that's a pretty big *if*," he fired back, "who'd be able to tell us for sure?"

Val was a big believer in the direct approach. "Why not ask the little lady herself?"

Ben had to listen to five minutes of outrage at the press coverage before he could bring Carolyn Hanna to the point.

"Mrs. Hanna, when I was at your house, you said it was absurd to think that your brother had taken that bribe. What exactly did you mean?"

"Why in the world should Julian do something like that for fifteen thousand dollars?" the pleasant drawl asked.

"You mean he didn't need the money?"

"Julian lived very simply. I doubt if he spent half his income from the Perini trust. Of course, all that would have changed when he started a family. You know how it is with bachelors, particularly the studious ones." She laughed lightly. "Julian probably didn't know how much a sofa costs. But there was plenty of time for all that."

By now, Ben had recovered his breath. "In other words, he was a rich man?"

Like everybody in her position, Mrs. Hanna shied at this phrasing. "Oh, I wouldn't say that. Not really rich. But you could say that he was comfortably off."

As Ben sighed, fundamental honesty forced her to amend her statement.

"Very comfortably off."

168

23

The air police had already arrived at the same conclusion and were acting accordingly.

"They're late," General Reynold Farrington remarked.

The others all looked at the clock, which registered five minutes after three, chorused assent and then returned to their occupations. Major Carl Kruger and Lieutenant Colonel Larry Yates were discussing sports cars in undertones. General Farrington, behind the desk, turned a page in the file spread open before him. Captain Edward Severance looked stolidly into space.

Actually, General Farrington was reflecting on the change in his circumstances. When Congressman Benton Safford had requested interviews with the members of the Conroy board, every courtesy had been observed. Today it was different. A brusque voice from the Air Provost Marshal's office had directed him to assemble the members of the board for interrogation at three o'clock.

When the door finally opened to admit three men, things got even worse.

"We've brought along Sergeant Dunnet of the Fairfax Police Department. Captain Perini was murdered in his jurisdiction. It's going to save a lot of repetition if he sits in with us," said the officer leading the group.

Grimly nodding, Farrington said only: "And the murder of Congressman Atamian?"

"That is primarily a matter for the federal authorities, but we'll be asking about that, too."

Farrington was noticing the escalation in rank. Last time

around, the Air Force had sent a captain. This time, it was a colonel and a major.

Colonel Bixby continued relentlessly. "Your aide has given us an office across the hall. We'll start with Captain Severance."

Severance rose but hesitated. It was not the general in the crowd who was supposed to wait while junior officers went through the line. Only when there was no objection did he follow his interrogators.

The minute the door closed, Farrington voiced his conclusion. "They're going to do us in reverse order. If they're afraid of my influencing Severance at this point, they must be crazy."

Yates could see another possibility. "Or they're getting the dissenting minority out of the way first, so they can really bear down on you and me. Either way, Carl here will be next."

"I suppose so," Kruger said expressionlessly.

To break the uncomfortable silence, General Farrington recalled a personnel problem.

"They tell me you're asking for reassignment to Washington." Kruger fell on the subject.

"Well, sir, they brought me back from Germany for the board. Then they kept me here for the business about the Perini bribe. And now . . ." His voice trailed away.

Yates came to his rescue. "We've got to face the fact that we're all witnesses. Hell, as far as the Atamian thing goes, we were right on the spot."

He did not have to add that, at best, this would be a matter of months.

"In the meantime, my family's still in Europe. I'd be better off kissing my German assignment goodbye and getting another one here," Carl Kruger said.

The rest of the waiting period was passed in a discussion of ways and means.

Larry Yates was not surprised by Colonel Bixby's opener.

"I see by your record that your explosives training was a good

170

many years ago. Do you still regard yourself as having a basic competence in this area, Colonel Yates?"

"If you mean could I put a simple bomb together, sure. But times have changed. Any civilian can walk into a bookstore and get a how-to-do-it manual. Unless there was something special about this one."

Colonel Bixby ignored the implied question. "When you talk about civilians, are you reminding me that most of the Dorland people started as engineers?"

"Not on your life. My whole point was that the killer didn't need any training at all. In fact," Yates continued blandly, "one of those fat politicians could have done it."

"I see. Well, we'll bear that in mind. Now, I'd like to know what you remember about the scene in the outer office where Atamian left his briefcase."

Yates frowned. "I've been racking my brain ever since we heard the news," he said. "And I don't see how I can help. It was raining buckets that day, you know, and there was a mob scene in the reception area with everybody getting rid of coats and umbrellas."

"Did Atamian arrive before you did?"

"Oh, yes," Yates said readily. "Almost everyone was there, dumping their stuff, except the two congressmen. And Conroy, of course. He was last. In fact, he came in after the meeting had started."

"Did you yourself carry a briefcase to the meeting?"

Yates smiled ruefully. "I did."

"What about the others?"

For the first time, the smooth rhythm of Yates' answers was broken. "I can't honestly remember about the others," he said finally. "In our group, we all had cases except Ed Severance. But a lot of the civilians must have had them, because there was a pile."

Bixby had already heard the same story from Severance and Kruger.

He knew that anybody familiar with the status symbols of

Washington could have relied on those briefcases. Bixby was simply hoping for some fugitive recollection that might be of assistance.

"And did you notice anyone spending an unusual amount of time rummaging around the pile?" he persisted.

"No, I didn't. God knows I'd tell you if I had, but we were all kind of intent on what was going to happen, on how Atamian and Wellenmeister would play off each other," Yates said.

Bixby cleared his throat. "Then we'll drop that and move on to the Conroy inquiry. I'm interested in how you interacted with the other members of the board. We have the record of the formal part, but did you have private discussions with any of the officers?"

"With all of them," Yates said promptly.

"Go on."

"Kruger and Severance thought we didn't have enough information for a decision. General Farrington, Perini and I thought we did."

Bixby shook his head at this bald recapitulation. "Come, come, Colonel Yates. I could get that by reading the record. You'll have to expand."

"There isn't much more to say about Carl Kruger and Severance. As for Perini, he was pretty quiet in the full meetings, like you'd expect from the low man on the totem pole. But he was absolutely confident about his technical judgment. He'd just finished qualifying on the VX-92, and he could give you chapter and verse without a blink."

"That brings us to General Farrington," Bixby pressed.

Yates shifted uneasily, then rubbed the heel of his hand against his close-cropped hair. "Look," he burst out, "we all knew this was a pressure job. It turns out it was more pressured than we realized, but it was a tricky situation. General Farrington made no bones about wanting to push right along with as little mention of Saudi Arabians as possible."

Now that he had rattled his man, Bixby was willing to slow down. "All right," he said soothingly, "so much for what General Farrington told you. What did you tell him?"

"That when I qualified on the VX-92, I had no trouble with it to speak of. Of course, my experience wasn't as current as Perini's, but there was no way I could contradict him."

"No trouble to speak of?" The echo was soft and insinuating.

Yates shook his head irritably. "The plane was brand new when I flew it. There were some minor bugs, and I made some suggestions, but nothing that was going to make it plow into a schoolyard."

"So you felt that it was Perini you weren't contradicting, not General Farrington?"

"That's right," Yates snapped back.

Without a pause, Bixby pressed on to new ground.

"About Perini personally. What did you know?"

"Not a damn thing. I'd never met him or heard of him before the hearing."

"Did he talk about himself at all?"

"I think the only personal reference I ever heard him make was about some course he was going on. He was pleased about that."

Bixby began to shuffle his notes together and then, almost as an afterthought, said, "I think there is a question Sergeant Dunnet would like to ask you."

Dunnet sounded almost fatherly. "I know it's a while back, Colonel Yates, but it would be a big help if you could tell us what you were doing at the time of Captain Perini's death. It may help if you try—"

He was interrupted by a bark of laughter from Yates.

"It may have been a while back, but they kind of fixed it in my memory. I left the office early, and I was getting ready for the weekend, so I was in my apartment."

"Alone?"

"Alone."

"Thank you very much, Colonel Yates."

"No, I didn't go into the office at all that day. I had left early for the weekend," General Farrington was saying a few minutes later.

"You were out of town. Where?"

173

"On the Chesapeake."

Sergeant Dunnet smiled encouragingly. "And where was this place you were staying?"

"As they can't give me much of an alibi, I don't see how they come into it."

Bixby came to the support of his colleague. "I'm afraid we'll have to insist, General. And I expect your aide has the information anyway."

It was probably the last reminder that was effective. General Farrington, a dull red flush rising over his face, capitulated. "I was staying out at the Dorland place," he said defiantly. "But the other guests didn't come until dinnertime. The only one I saw was George Kidder, for a couple of minutes around four o'clock."

"According to the Justice Department," Dunnet replied, studying his notebook, "that isn't what Kidder says."

Farrington was scornful. "Naturally. Ever since the Conroy board hit the headlines, Kidder's been pretending he never heard of me."

There was a long silence before Bixby spoke in a colorless voice. "Thank you, General Farrington. Now let's move on to the hearing itself. You took technical advice from your juniors?"

"I had to. And the ones who had experience with the VX-92 were in complete agreement."

"So I understand. That is to say, they agreed there was nothing wrong with the plane. But were there variations in the vigor with which they supported that theory?"

For the first time, General Farrington had to think about an answer. "Well, there were differences in style. Only what you'd expect, though. Captain Perini buried me under a ton of statistics. Colonel Yates gave me his conclusions. But that's natural. I'd expect a captain to feel his judgment wasn't enough unless he backed it up with some facts. If he didn't, I'd make him. Particularly someone like Perini."

Bixby raised an inquiring eyebrow. "You didn't like him?"

"Oh, he seemed all right. It's his file I didn't like. That leisurely gentleman-officer bit may have been all right fifty years ago. Nowadays, we need serious career men."

"Then you had no personal knowledge of him?"

"None whatsoever."

The three investigators relaxed when they were once again alone.

"I'm glad we got to them before they find out that Atamian fingered somebody on the Conroy board," Bixby remarked.

"I thought the feds had decided to sit on that," Dunnet said.

Bixby looked at him pityingly. "In this town, Sergeant, everything leaks sooner or later. Every man jack of them will know before the week is out. In the meantime, it's not hard to see the lines they're pushing."

The major spoke from the corner where he had been taping the interviews. "Yates thinks it's obvious. Dorland hired Atamian to bribe Perini. When the heat went on the board, they killed Perini. When the heat went on Atamian, they killed him."

"I agree. Otherwise, Yates wouldn't be coming to Farrington's defense."

"He may not know as much about Farrington as we do," Dunnet said mildly. "Such as the fact that he was spending his weekends sitting in Dorland's pocket."

"He'll find that out, too," said Bixby, a man who stuck to his guns.

The major was less interested in generalities. "Then do you think that Colonel Yates' description of the board consultations is accurate?"

"Like hell I do," Bixby snorted. "Look at his record. Yates is up for promotion, and he's ambitious. Under those circumstances, I'd say he was willing, maybe a little too willing, to oblige the senior member of the board. If Farrington wanted technical advice to come out in a certain way, I think Yates would give it to him that way."

"On the other hand," Dunnet said fair-mindedly, "there's that

175

business about Perini's background. If Farrington read the personnel file, would he have tried to fake a Perini bribe?"

Bixby was not impressed. "It worked, didn't it? Until the Paris Air Show?"

"The fact of the matter is that it's a dead heat between Yates and Farrington," the major concluded. "Unless one of them comes up with something new after he finds out about what Atamian said."

Dunnet had no illusions about what would happen. "They'll both come up with something. A lot of recollections about how suspiciously the other one behaved during the Conroy inquiry."

"So where do we go from here?" the major asked.

Bixby was already on the move. "We go to the other person who may be able to help us. Have you forgotten that Captain Conroy was there?"

24

The Washington grapevine was working even faster than Colonel Bixby bargained for. He heard the first news leak on the car radio as he and Dunnet and the major drove into the city.

But Neil Conroy, run to earth at his hotel, had been too occupied to turn on his television set. Looking at him, Colonel Bixby realized how thoroughly the tables had been turned since the inquiry into the Utah crash. Now it was the members of the board who were taut and nervous.

Despite this advantage, Neil Conroy was not a particularly good witness. In deference to Sergeant Dunnet's concerns, the first question involved an alibi for Perini's death. Here, too, the captain was on unassailable ground.

"I was on leave until disciplinary proceedings. So I went back to the base in Utah, packed my things, then flew home to Ohio. Friday at dinnertime, I was clearing out my desk."

Dunnet was nodding, pleased to clear away the underbrush. "Anybody see you?"

"Oh, they saw me all right," Conroy said ironically. "They just weren't talking to me much."

Bixby tried to break through this barrier. "Then you're the only one who has nothing to worry about. You're completely in the clear for both murders."

"Yes, I know," said Conroy without much enthusiasm.

Bixby gave it up and turned to the actual sessions of the board of inquiry.

"I assume you were questioned by all the members?"

Neil frowned. "I think so," he began hesitantly, before his memory produced a firmer impression. "Yes, that's right. Of course, some of them did more talking than others."

"Naturally. Just give us your general recollection."

"Well, the first one to drop out was Major Kruger. It was obvious he wasn't very up to date on fighters—any fighters, not just the VX-92."

The colonel confined himself to encouraging noises.

"General Farrington didn't know much either. Perini and Severance knew a lot, and they harped on the flight conditions at the time of the crash. You know it was snowing, and they wanted to know about wind velocity and visibility and icing on the wings— that sort of thing."

"And Colonel Yates?"

"He's got some bee in his bonnet about trainees. The way he wants you to nursemaid them, nobody would ever learn on these new jobs unless he went up by himself."

Colonel Bixby surveyed his quarry thoughtfully as he chose his tactics. Neil Conroy would not be human if he were not still smarting from the results of that board.

"Then General Farrington and Colonel Yates really contributed nothing to any discussion of the VX-92?"

He had pushed the right button.

"Oh, yes, they did," said Neil implacably. "General Farrington had plenty to say when I tried to introduce the only evidence that counted. And Colonel Yates was baking him every inch of the way. If they'd done their job, the VX-92 would have been grounded that week!"

There would never be a better moment for the key question.

"Of the two of them, who pushed harder?"

But Neil Conroy was too human. Jab his wound, and recollection became vivid, all right. Unfortunately, what he remembered was his own bitterness and not the actions of others. Doggedly, Bixby went down the list. "And Perini?"

"He was a captain. You didn't expect him to say much in the

hearing. Of course, I don't know what they all said to each other outside."

That was the central problem. Because all the important things had been almost certainly said far from the official transcript which Colonel Bixby now knew by heart. His only hope had been to pick up fleeting impressions that were beyond the scope of a stenographic record.

With a sigh, Bixby remembered that he had other obligations as a representative of the Air Force.

"The desk said you're checking out. Going somewhere?"

"I've been called back to active duty, sir." No amount of control could hide the triumph in Neil's voice.

Bixby's congratulations were perfectly sincere.

"I'm glad to hear it. You've had a hard row to hoe, but you've behaved well in a difficult situation."

When Neil's face broke into a radiant smile, Bixby knew there was nothing to be gained by extending his stay. Nobody walking on cloud nine was going to be a big help right now.

Congressmen usually see individual constituents when they are engaged in some kind of confrontation with the federal government. It made a nice change of pace, as Ben was the first to admit, to see beaming happiness across the desk.

Nonetheless, as his interview with Neil Conroy progressed, Ben was aware of a growing dissatisfaction.

"I'm leaving to go back on duty, and I want to thank you for all you've done, Ben. I never dreamed you were going to start a whole campaign because of me."

"It was nothing," said Ben modestly.

Neil intended to make a real production of this. "Like hell it wasn't. It not only got me back my career but, by wrapping the whole thing up, you saved a lot of pilots from ending like that poor guy in Paris."

"Actually, it isn't wrapped up. I don't know if you've heard the latest?"

179

"I caught it on the news coming over here," Neil admitted.

Little knowing that he was treading in Bixby's steps, Ben leaned forward. "Then you realize that it's boiled down to Farrington or Yates."

"Come on, Ben. That's just what they're saying now."

"Maybe you haven't been following the details," Ben suggested, taken aback.

Neil laughed. "Sure I have—all the way."

"I'm not with you."

"Look! First, Perini was supposed to be bribed by the Saudis. Then they said he wasn't bribed by the Saudis but by somebody else. Now, suddenly, the story is that he wasn't bribed at all. It's not hard to figure the reason behind all this," Neil explained. "As usual, Dorland is trying to wriggle off the hook. Whatever is best for the moment is what they say about Perini. After all, they murdered the poor sap to keep their noses clean. Now that everybody's cottoned on to that, they're trying to pretend there wasn't a bribe."

Ben felt as if he were in the path of a steamroller. "But that's not it, Neil. The point is that Farrington or Yates took the bribe. Perini was just a red herring."

"That's what they're saying now, Ben." Neil smiled exasperatingly. "As soon as it's worth their while, they'll switch to something else."

"What is it with you? You're not listening to a word I say."

Insulated by his tremendous sense of well-being, Neil did not wish to give offense. "That's not it, Ben," he hastened to say. "I'm listening but you can't seriously expect me to believe that men like General Farrington and Colonel Yates go in for murder."

"You'll believe anything about this *they* you keep mentioning."

"Well, whoever it is," said Neil, intent on keeping the peace, "they'll probably straighten it out in due time."

Ben had just made a discovery.

"What you're saying is that you don't care."

"Why the hell should I?" Neil exploded. "I've gotten out of this by the skin of my teeth. At the very beginning, when they were offering me that rotten exoneration, you said the odds were all against me. Do you think it was easy to say no and risk everything I've worked for? But I did it, and I pulled it off. Now the important part is over. Are you telling me that I don't have the right to relax?"

Surprised by this storm of self-justification, Ben was ready to agree to anything. "Of course you do, Neil. You've got a right to be proud of yourself. By hanging in there, you kept the VX-92 a live issue. A lot of people have cause to be grateful to you, whether they know it or not."

"So now I'm forgetting all this and going back to my career," Neil announced, still defensive.

"And I wish you all the luck in the world."

It took a while, but they had re-established cordial relations by the time Neil left, once again brimming over with anticipation of a hero's return to the Air Force.

Ben realized that they were now following different roads, and it was not hard to understand why. Neil had not seen Julian Perini's brains spattered all over that desk; Neil had not watched Michael Atamian's door dissolving under the force of bomb blast. Neil had, however, sat and listened to his co-pilot's neck breaking. So Neil wanted safe planes for the Air Force while Ben wanted to see the killer caught before he targeted another victim.

If Ben Safford could have seen Walter Wellenmeister's reaction to the latest news, he would have accorded more respect to Neil Conroy's interpretation of events.

"There!" said Wellenmeister exultantly. "God knows it took them long enough to straighten things out. Some nutboy in the Air Force has been running around killing people who knew he took a bribe. Now that they've finally proven I'm innocent, we'll get some action. I'll talk to Dexter today."

His wife was enthusiastic. Deedee had been a loyal helpmate in sunshine and shadow, partly because that was her nature and partly because she had difficulty distinguishing between the two. She had, however, noticed that the curtailment of Walter's business life meant that he was home all the time. And, somehow, that wasn't working out.

"Do it right away!" she urged.

But Wellenmeister's chat with Dexter took an unexpected turn.

"Now, Dexter, I've been patient, nobody can deny that."

"Believe me, Walter, they appreciate it," said Dexter soothingly.

"But, dammit, there are limits." Wellenmeister was gaining confidence as he recalled the many campaign contributions that had been extracted from him by Dexter. "I was willing to stick it out as long as there was a big question mark. But with everything settled, there's no reason for me to go on being pilloried."

Inspecting carefully manicured nails, Dexter said, "The Justice people have had to go through the motions, Walter. You understand that. Now that they're zeroing in on somebody else, they won't be bothering you anymore."

An earlier Wellenmeister had valued Dexter's air of being close to the hub of decision-making, but times had changed.

"I'm not talking about them. I'm talking about the press and the public. That's where the damage has been done, and I want to see it rectified," he demanded with something of his old arrogance.

Dexter was adept at dealing with recalcitrance. "These things take time, Walter," he murmured, drawing on his long years as a go-between. "Once it's all cleared up—"

"Oh, no, you don't! From what I hear, they could run around this maypole for years. If you can't do anything, then I'll have to talk to Jim. I'll be seeing him next week on the Coast."

"I wouldn't plan on that, Walter."

Dexter said the words so gently that Wellenmeister thought he had misheard.

"What's that?"

Dexter was immeasurably regretful. "In the White House, there are all sorts of overriding duties. You've got to do some things you don't want to do, for the good of the country. Jim Kraus asked me to tell you that, right now, he's putting distance between you and us. So you won't be getting any invitations from the Coast. He knew you'd understand."

182

Jim Kraus would have had to be an arrant optimist if he genuinely thought that.

The next ten minutes were remarkably unproductive. As Wellenmeister moved from blind anger to personal hurt to naked supplication, Dexter simply produced slightly variant phrases to enunciate the same sentiment: like the Swiss Guards, Walter was expected to die at his post in defense of his master.

When Wellenmeister re-entered his house in Virginia, his shoulders were slumped and his steps dragging. He had left with such high hopes, and he was returning in defeat. What's more, Deedee was not the only sufferer during his present isolation. Both at Dorland and at the Embassy, Wellenmeister had been used to a cloud of assistants and secretaries who were alive to every detail of his working life. Deedee would listen endlessly, but you couldn't expect her to understand the basic infighting.

He was proven wrong on the first count the minute he walked into the living room. Deedee did not let him get a word in edgewise. She was holding an open letter in her hand.

"They've thrown me off the Arbor Day Committee. They even had the nerve to send me a resignation letter and tell me to sign it," she said, shaking the offending document at him.

Then she proved that she was not as far from her husband in fundamental comprehension as he had assumed

"When I think of the check I gave them," she raged, "I could just scream!"

The Wellenmeisters were not alone in being discontented with the current situation, as Ben Safford learned late that afternoon.

"Do you know a Captain Ursula Richmond of the Air Force?" Madge asked from the doorway, in uncharacteristic doubt. Usually, Madge was the one who reminded Ben of the identity of strays in his world.

"I met her at the Paris Air Show," Ben explained.

"Well, she's on the phone. Do you want to talk to her?"

Ben stiffened.

"I suppose so," he said slowly.

Without asking why he was so reluctant, Madge made the connection.

"Congressman Safford? We met several times at the Air Show."

The crisp, cool voice came as a mild shock to Ben. You had to see Ursula to get the double-whammy effect. On the other hand, Ursula herself was in no doubt that, once seen, she was forever memorable.

"Of course I remember you," Ben said warily, willing to give her that much.

But Ursula seemed to be concentrating more on her own words than on his response.

"When we met, you hadn't gone public with your probe into the VX-92," she began carefully. "Now, of course, I realize you must be keeping on top of those murders, and you know they've boiled it down to two possibilities."

"So does everybody, since they broadcast Charlie Crowder's testimony," Ben said unhelpfully.

If Ursula Richmond thought she was going to add him to the list of those she was pumping, she had another think coming.

"I just wanted to make sure how much explaining had to be done," she continued, ignoring his remark. "It seems to me that once the field is that narrow, it's an intolerable position for everyone—for the investigators, for the Air Force and, most of all, for the innocent one. Of course, you'll be surprised that I'm taking an interest but—"

"Not really," Ben interrupted curtly. "I've already come across the tracks where you've been nosing around."

There! That should force the issue.

Ursula was undaunted. "I'm not denying it. Everybody in the Air Force has a justifiable reason for concern."

As a matter of fact, Ben had thought of one all-embracing justification. But no arm of the military would approach him in this manner. Now was the moment when a legitimate investigator would have produced credentials.

Instead Ursula pressed on with her persuasion.

184

"It can't be that difficult to prove which one is guilty. Just in the last twenty-four hours, I've gotten something. Did you know that General Farrington was negotiating with Dorland for a vice-presidency? That's how he intends to take care of his retirement."

This was news to Ben, but he was not giving Ursula the satisfaction of admitting it.

"So what?" he said indifferently. "Lots of generals take jobs with defense suppliers after they retire."

"Do they play footsie with them while they're heading a board looking into the supplier's airplane?" Ursula asked indignantly. "Anyway, it's worse than that. Farrington tried to use George Kidder as an alibi for the Perini murder, only Kidder wasn't cooperating."

So much for Elsie's theory that Ursula Richmond was reporting to General Farrington. She had been doing exactly what Ben thought in that restaurant. And Ben had very little doubt on whose behalf she was working.

More in sorrow than anger, he tried to give her some advice. "If you think it's that important, you should tell the air police."

"They already know, but they're not willing to act without something concrete. That's why I'm calling you."

"What makes you think I have different standards?"

He should have known the answer.

"You started a probe into the VX-92 before you had anything concrete," she pointed out.

By now, Ben knew it was impossible to convince anybody in the world that he was not the crusader the newspapers had portrayed.

"You're talking about two totally different courses of action. The House shared the responsibility for the VX-92. Part of our job is deciding on defense systems. Finding murderers is somebody else's job. Leave it to them. They'll get there in the end."

Ursula snorted so richly that for a moment it was like talking to Janet. "And in the meantime? While they're waiting for an apple to fall on their heads? Surely with only two suspects, it should be simple enough for us to rig something . . . some kind of test, say . . ."

"You're talking about entrapment," Ben said baldly.

"I didn't mean it like that."

"It doesn't make any difference," Ben said, finality in his voice. "As far as I'm concerned, you're an unknown quantity. You want to play mysterious games, go ahead. But I like to know who I'm working with."

To himself, he added: And whether they're trying to use me as a patsy.

If nothing else, Ursula was a good loser.

"Well, I always knew you were a long shot," she said with beguiling frankness, "but you were the best I had."

"Thanks a lot," Ben said dryly.

Ursula chuckled. "That's better than it sounds. Anyway, you've reminded me that when you want something done right, you've got to do it yourself."

She rang off so quickly that Ben was caught off guard, and he was sorry. The chuckle at the end had reminded him how engaging she was. But he very much feared that Ursula's emotions were undermining her judgment.

How far would Captain Richmond go to clear the innocent or—even worse—to protect the guilty?

25

Ben Safford, in recognizing the distinction between his own goals and those of Neil Conroy or of Ursula Richmond, honestly thought he was prepared to endure frustrating delays in the investigation of the VX-92 killings. He did not know how close he was to the limits of his patience until a chance encounter provided the final straw.

He had left his office hurriedly for a committee meeting, only to have his progress halted as traffic in the corridor slowed to a crawl. Craning his neck he spotted some protocol-conscious officials escorting a large and colorful delegation of foreign dignitaries. When Ben briskly pulled out to pass, one of the entourage joined him, matching stride for stride.

General Khalid was as gracious as ever.

"The Prince is looking forward to his meeting with your distinguished Speaker," he said after suitable greetings.

"I'm sure the Speaker reciprocates."

"Much has happened since we last met, Mr. Safford," Khalid continued, coming to the point.

Ben raised an eyebrow.

"Since that includes a bomb blast not far from this spot, I'd call that an understatement, General," he replied.

"A most lamentable tragedy," said Khalid. "But these things pass. Time can blessedly veil the deepest pain."

Whether this was intended as the wisdom or the mercy of Allah, Ben wasn't buying it. "On the contrary," he said firmly, "we hope time will do some unveiling."

"Do you?" asked Khalid with more than a hint of skepticism. "I confess, I have wondered. Often energetic endeavors that pro-

187

duce no results are exactly what prudent men are content with. Great upheavals are easy to initiate and difficult to finish. But perhaps I have been wrong. In any event, it has been a pleasure to see you once again."

He drifted down a turning after his Prince.

"Dammit, he practically congratulated me on our common sense in letting a murderer go scot free," Ben fumed when he reached his destination. "On top of that, Pres Goodrich tells me that the air police have just about given up."

Tony Martinelli had sources of his own. "Over at Justice, they've even stopped having conferences."

"Look, you two," the chairman called down the table testily. "I don't care if Dorland and the Air Force both self-destruct. We're going to report this bill out before the recess. Now George here has a report on the Dolphin missile."

But he was not the only one who had overheard them. Throughout the meeting, Mrs. Hollenbach abstained from a single trenchant observation, even when the committee's lightweight tried to drag them all down a blind alley.

"What's eating you, Elsie?" Tony asked as they all straggled into his office for a post-game rehash.

"Walter Wellenmeister," she announced portentously. "His corruption has been the mainspring of this entire affair. And yet, at this very moment, he is probably lying in a hammock in Fairfax waiting for the dust to settle."

Tony was bracing. "Oh, cheer up, Elsie. Sooner or later the IRS will get him. He's sure to have fiddled his tax returns, they all do."

Both frivolity and elevated thinking were grating on Ben today.

"If you want to worry about anyone, Elsie, worry about the guy who blew Julian Perini's brains out, then slipped a bomb into Mike's briefcase. We've lived with moral imbeciles like Wellenmeister for a long time, and I guess we can go on doing it. But let the real Neanderthals run wild, and we're in big trouble."

Elsie was accustomed to friendly jabs from Tony. A volley

from Ben astonished her. Before she could counterattack, Val Oakes began to bank the fires.

"You're both talking about the same thing. Elsie, you're hot and bothered about Wellenmeister because he set everything in motion, and it does you credit. And you, Ben," he continued, giving neither adversary a chance to speak, "you're mad because you saw some of the dirty work. I confess I join you in that. But squabbling doesn't help."

Mrs. Hollenbach stared down her patrician nose, and Ben realized that the first step was up to him.

"I'm sorry for blowing up at you, Elsie, but it gets to me," he apologized. "Everything's bogged down, and there's nothing we can do about it."

"You just have to face it, Ben," Oakes said, continuing his good work. "I don't approve of bombs going off in my vicinity any more than you do, but the air police have given this their best shot, and that's that."

Unexpectedly, it was Tony who rejected this fatalism. "You're all coming at this from the wrong end. Maybe you can't budge the police, but you could do plenty about the killer."

Every now and then, Congressman Martinelli was carried away by flights of fancy, and his colleagues were forced to bring him down to earth. "Tony, we don't even know which one he is," Ben chided.

"But we do know that he's pretty quick on the trigger. Make him think somebody's about to name him, and he'll go into action like gang-busters," Tony argued. "And don't tell me we couldn't do it, because in this town starting a rumor—any rumor—is a lead-pipe cinch."

"You've just overlooked one little difficulty," said Val, humoring him. "There probably isn't anybody who could name the murderer."

Tony's bright glance flickered over Ben, who was losing interest, Val, who was openly dubious, and Elsie, who was still consumed by private outrage.

"Oh yeah?" he said cunningly. "What about Wellenmeister? This joker can't be sure Atamian didn't tell his boss."

His tactics produced immediate results. Elsie rarely allowed herself to feel vengeful, but when she did, she took her inspiration from the Old Testament. After a moment's contemplation, she nodded slowly.

"I believe that Tony's proposal may have some merit. If the murderer believed himself threatened, he would probably make an immediate attempt on Wellenmeister," she said with every evidence of satisfaction.

"Hold it, you two," Ben ordered. "Before you spin out completely, think of the consequences. So we start a rumor and goad a killer into action, then what?"

Tony and Elsie both stared at him resentfully.

"What Ben means," Val said, "is that we could get the killer going with an unofficial rumor, but it wouldn't work with the Justice people. So how do we set a trap?"

Deflated, Tony admitted that Val had put his finger on a snag. It took longer for Mrs. Hollenbach to agree, rather wistfully, that they could not permit Wellenmeister to be endangered.

Ben tried to soothe her.

"I'm sorry, Elsie, but I guess you're going to have to reconcile yourself to the fact that he'll go on lying in his hammock— Did you say Fairfax?" he ended abruptly.

Elsie regarded the site of the hammock as irrelevant. "Yes, the Wellenmeisters rented Simon Arkwright's place in Fairfax Station," she said, referring to an incumbent defeated in the last election.

Nothing could keep Congressman Oakes' attention from politics for long. "You mean Arkwright rented his place, instead of selling it?" he demanded. "There's optimism for you."

But just as the problem seemed to be defused, the odds had become three-to-one.

"I'm not thinking about Arkwright," Ben declared impatiently. "I'm thinking about Sergeant Dunnet. You want to bet he's pretty frustrated about Perini's murder?"

"He may be frustrated, but he still follows the rules," Oakes said. "Dunnet would never go along with this kind of setup."

190

"Not beforehand," Ben agreed. "But after it was in motion?"

The introduction of a police presence, however local, gave a new dimension to the entire proposal. Val cocked his head and studied this latest wrinkle.

"I do believe he'd have to," he said at last, with dawning interest.

Immediately, four agile minds began conning ways and means.

Even Mrs. Hollenbach had grudgingly conceded that Walter Wellenmeister must not only be protected, he must be removed from the scene entirely.

"Whatever crazy idea you've got in mind, Ben, forget it!" the Undersecretary said when he was approached. "In the first place, it's not my kind of party, and in the second place it wouldn't work. Wellenmeister doesn't want to spend a lot of time with me. We're not old buddies or anything. And he knows as well as I do that he's on the administration blacklist."

Preston Goodrich and Ben were having a drink after work at the Watergate. This had the unexpected effect of creating a clandestine atmosphere.

"Suppose I took care of all that?" Ben said, suppressing the instinct to whisper.

"You've got some cockeyed scheme, Ben," Goodrich accused him.

"Okay, okay. But all I'm asking you to do is keep Wellenmeister out of circulation for three hours."

"On a boat, no less!" Goodrich exclaimed sarcastically.

The conspirators had finally realized that Wellenmeister's absence was essential not only for his safety, but also for the success of their plan.

"It's as good a place as any to keep clear of TV and radio," Ben insisted. "And there's no question of your undertaking obligations for the administration."

Goodrich was severe. "There better not be." In spite of himself, he was weakening. "And what in God's name am I supposed to say to him for three hours?"

"Absolutely nothing," Ben said triumphantly. "At considerable length, of course."

Goodrich frowned. "And you think this could clear things up?"

"It's got a chance."

"You realize you're asking me to choose between the Air Force and the administration?"

Ben could scarcely deny it.

"Okay," said Goodrich after a brief pause. "I'll go for the Air Force. What do I do, just call Wellenmeister?"

"In an hour or so. Elsie Hollenbach is softening him up."

In some ways, it was unfortunate that Mrs. Hollenbach's assignment should have involved personal contact with Walter Wellenmeister. But the very distaste with which she performed her duty went a long way toward convincing Wellenmeister that a turning point was at hand.

". . . have agreed to sound you out about some kind of resolution to your current dilemma. It is difficult for you, it is embarrassing for the administration and, most important of all," she said, sounding like a hanging judge, "it is a liability to the entire party."

"Well, what can I do about it?" Wellenmeister asked peevishly.

Elsie was gratified by the results of her tactics. These days, Wellenmeister did not give a damn about the best interests of the administration or the party, if he ever had. But she could hear just how frantic he was to escape his present limbo. Living with disgrace was eating him alive.

"You have already done too much," she replied coldly. "But it is in all our interests to work something out. Naturally there will be a good many conditions and details to be ironed out—if that is possible. At this stage, an informal discussion, completely off the record, is indicated. It may be that the principals are too far apart for any effective compromise."

The more doubtful Mrs. Hollenbach became, the more eager Wellenmeister became. "At least it's a first step," he said. "I don't see why we have to have this fancy runaround, but if that's the way they want it, okay."

"I would not raise your hopes too high, Mr. Wellenmeister. You understand that I am making absolutely no commitments for anyone."

"All right, all right. But why couldn't they tell me themselves? They won't even answer my calls."

"There will be no direct communication unless every single item has been satisfactorily decided."

With grim amusement, Mrs. Hollenbach reflected that only a man as desperate as Walter Wellenmeister could conceive this situation ever existing in Washington, D.C.

In his initial enthusiasm, Tony Martinelli had said that nothing could be easier than starting a rumor. But the introduction of a rigid timetable had imposed certain limitations.

"It's got to be a commentator who goes on the air at a specific time," Val had insisted.

By the next morning, the groundwork had been laid. Oakes had artfully let a few words drop into the ear of an important senator whose wife had been appointed to a desk in the White House. Tony had put the press corps of Washington through a sieve to get the man he wanted.

So at nine o'clock that morning the House dining room saw two hard-working congressmen fighting the good fight at two separate tables. Congressman Oakes was providing scrambled eggs to Norman Persons, a brilliant young economist and the sole native of South Dakota currently on the White House staff.

". . . lowering HUD expenditures by ten percent, which will compensate for the Defense increase . . ."

"Yes, indeed," said Oakes, happy to see that Persons was intoxicated with his own importance and his access to inside information.

Across the room, Tony was dealing with Fullmer Burt, widely respected newsman.

". . . so I said, I don't care how old she is, she doesn't look like your aunt to me, Senator. You should have seen his face, Tony."

"Uh-huh," said Tony, unobtrusively checking his watch. "Gee, I guess it's time to be going."

Wending his way out, Congressman Martinelli recognized a familiar face.

"Val!"

"Well, Tony."

Without waiting for an invitation, Tony joined Val's party, bringing his guest with him.

"Norman Persons," said Val in introduction. "I guess you know that Norman is one of the comers up at the White House these days. And, Norm, you've been seeing Fully Burt on the screen for years."

Persons drew a deep breath of exhilaration.

"Say, Val," said Tony, "what's this I hear about Wellenmeister?"

"Wellenmeister?" Val repeated. "I haven't heard a thing."

Tony ostentatiously prepared to drop the subject. "Well, you'd know."

"I haven't heard anything either," said Fullmer Burt curiously.

Martinelli played his next card. "There's probably nothing to it, but Van Scorsby—you know him, he covers the White House for the Boston *Globe*—was telling me there have been hints from somebody there about Wellenmeister coming clean."

This might be weak on detail, but it was perfection itself on references. Burt was reminded of a rival news medium; Persons was reminded of rival sources.

"There's always talk," Val said contemptuously. "Depend on it, they'd run something like that past the leadership first."

Norman Persons could not resist the temptation so carefully placed in his path. Clearing his throat, he said, "There was some talk about Wellenmeister at the White House yesterday evening."

"What kind of talk?" Burt pounced.

Persons lowered his voice to a confidential level. "They're still deciding how to handle it. But Wellenmeister's going on TV tonight to name names. And then—a Presidential pardon."

"Jee-sus," said Martinelli, supplying the exclamation mark.

Fullmer Burt frowned, and Val deftly weighed in again.

"I don't believe a word of it," he said, deliberately provocative. "They wouldn't do that without letting us know."

Stung, Persons spoke without thinking. "I can't tell you who, but I got it from someone close to the President. And one thing I can say. They've already touched bases with at least some senators."

"Well, I'll be damned," said Val, awestruck.

"I don't think," said Norman Persons virtuously, "that I should say anything more about it."

He had already said quite enough.

Sergeant Dunnet was the toughest nut to crack.

"You've done what?" he roared, downing his coffee cup.

"At one o'clock this afternoon, Fullmer Burt will tell the world that Wellenmeister's going to name names tonight," Ben repeated. "What's so hard to understand about that?"

Like most policemen, Dunnet did not relish amateurs taking the bit between their teeth. "Apart from the danger, it's stupid, that's what. This guy of yours isn't going to walk into a trap like that."

"He walked into an undersecretary's office with a bomb under his arm," Ben retorted.

"I grant you he's willing to take chances."

"And we're not setting Wellenmeister up, no matter how much he deserves it," Ben hastened to add. "From noon until three, he'll be on an Air Force launch, cruising up and down the Potomac. Maybe the trap will be a dud, but I think the killer is desperate."

Dunnet was outraged. "So you've unleashed him on my town! If he sees somebody like Wellenmeister going into a shopping center, he'll probably heave some nitro through the door."

"If he heads anywhere, he'll head for Wellenmeister's house," Ben said persuasively. "And he'll do it fast. It'll probably all be over by the time Wellenmeister gets home."

"And if it isn't?"

"Then Wellenmeister will be inside a protective net."

As the net involved a police stakeout and roadblocks, Ben held his breath.

Then Dunnet looked squarely at him. "Mr. Congressman, you and I are going to have a long talk. But not now. I've got a lot of things to do."

Ben was relieved to hear it.

The best laid plans go awry. Two things happened that Ben and his colleagues did not anticipate. Fullmer Burt made so many waves preparing his newscast that a rival network got word of his plans and jumped the gun. At twelve noon, they stole his thunder, almost word for word. Reaction was immediate.

At the Pentagon, General Reynold Farrington left a meeting to get a file. When he did not return, another officer went in search of him.

"No," said Farrington's aide, "he just stood there listening to the news and then he left."

At a small restaurant near Dupont Circle, Colonel Yates threw a bill on the bar.

"Tell my date something came up," he said, making for the door.

The barman stared after him, bemused, as the television set over his head continued the story of Walter Wellenmeister.

At the White House, the telephone lines began to hum.

"Dexter! What the hell is your boy up to?"

"Now, Jim . . ."

Even more unfortunately, Preston Goodrich was prevented from completing his mission. At twelve-thirty, his monologue came to a sudden stop, and he dashed through the hatchway to the railing.

Walter Wellenmeister turned gravely to the helmsman. "We'd better turn back. The Undersecretary is seasick."

26

Bad as the situation was, worse lay in store. When Ben Safford and Sergeant Dunnet raced out to the Wellenmeister house, their first stop was the communications van parked on the street.

The specialist in charge took a narrow view of his duties. "Wellenmeister? You mean the fat little guy who lives here? He got home in a cab about ten minutes ago," he replied to Dunnet's question. "Stayed just long enough to get out his car."

Relief flooded over Ben, but it was premature.

"They passed right by me," Jerry replied, flicking a switch on and off.

"They?" Dunnet and Safford demanded together.

"He was driving some Air Force guy," said Jerry.

"Christ, the killer was here in the house before Wellenmeister got back." Dunnet was shaken by this catastrophe, but still functioning. "Jerry, find out which way they went."

Jerry might not be interested in the big picture, but he was proud of his technical apparatus.

"They turned onto Route 66, heading west," he announced in an incredibly short time. "Lucky thing Wellenmeister drives a sky-blue BMW."

But he was speaking to air. Dunnet had charged back to his car, snapped an order to the driver and they were taking off, leaving barely enough time for Ben to hurl himself into the rear seat. For the next five minutes, Dunnet concentrated on his transmitter, rapping out instructions to identify the BMW, to alert the state police, to check the whereabouts of Lieutenant Colonel Lawrence Yates and Brigadier General Reynold Farrington.

By the time they were racing along Route 66, the task seemed hopeless to Ben. In the usual expressway traffic, locating one specific car seemed impossible.

Dunnet was more experienced. "Thank God for limited-access roads. We've got the edge if our friend doesn't turn off too early."

"He's got a head start, he can lose himself," Ben objected.

"Just a couple of minutes, according to Jerry. And the further he gets from the city, the more noticeable he becomes. Besides, he won't dare speed and, in case you haven't noticed, we are."

The rate at which they were traveling was one of the things Ben was carefully ignoring. Fortunately, Dunnet's words gave him something else to think about.

"I hadn't realized we were heading out into the country. Where do you figure he's going?"

It was the driver who answered. "To a nice lonely spot with no witnesses," he said calmly.

In a moment the radio seemed to provide confirmation. The first report was relayed from Headquarters. A sky-blue BMW had been seen sweeping past the cutoff to Centreville, before the APB had gone out.

"He must be a fool," Dunnet decided. "The longer he spends on this, the more likely it is that the other guy will have an alibi. He's in a panic, that's the only explanation."

The driver disagreed. "He doesn't know he's being followed, Sarge. Two-to-one he dumps the body close to the city."

Ben groaned. The trap calculated to flush a murderer had worked too well.

"I didn't think anything could make me sorry for Wellenmeister," he said, "but this has."

"We may still be in time," Dunnet replied, "but I'm beginning to wonder what's going on."

His bewilderment lasted until the exit signs for Manassas Battlefield Park, commemorating the battles of Bull Run.

198

"I've got it," he announced suddenly. "The killer's making for Bull Run Mountains."

Ben, who did not believe in divination, opened his mouth to protest before catching the significance of the word *mountains*. "You mean he's going to stage an accident?"

"Sure. He's tried a mock suicide and an outright murder. If there's a chance in hell of covering up Wellenmeister's murder, he'll go for it. That's why they're using Wellenmeister's car, that's why alibis don't matter."

"And it wouldn't be a bad idea," Ben reluctantly agreed. "Everyone knows Wellenmeister has been going to pieces under the pressure. We've set him up for this big public confession scene. When his body is found tomorrow morning, you've got the picture of a distraught man driving in a hurry to get back to Washington."

"Over hilly back roads on mountainous terrain. And Bull Run is the place to stage it, if he doesn't want to drive all the way to the Blue Ridge."

"You know this territory better than I do," Ben conceded.

This was amply proved in the next series of exchanges between Dunnet and his driver. Insofar as Ben could follow at all, they were engaged in a consideration of possible routes. First they discussed the major roads amidst a bewildering array of numbers. Routes 234, 681 and 701 were tossed around, weighed and rejected. Then, from multilane highways, they went on to consider twisting gravel and-dirt alternates. The old Woolsey road, the one that cuts over to Broad Run, the fork at Waterfall—all came in for prolonged evaluation.

To Ben, it seemed hopeless. He had never realized what a seamed and pockmarked countryside lay outside his back door.

Just as confusing were the nonstop argument in the front seat, the endless clack of the radio listing the numerous intersections at which the state police had *not* sighted the BMW, the thickening traffic on Route 66 as some unseen mill let out its workers and, finally, even the clattering of a traffic helicopter.

At last, consensus was reached in the front seat. Before Dunnet could announce their decision, however, the radio produced its second relayed report.

"Headquarters got through to the Pentagon," Dunnet repeated. "They had to use your name to get any action, Congressman."

"If things go wrong, it's the last time my name is going to be worth anything," Ben replied realistically. "What did they have to say?"

"Not much that's any use. Both Farrington and Yates have gone missing."

"That's all we need," said Ben, jolted by this additional bad luck. "We're right back where we were at the beginning. Either one of them could be our man."

Dunnet was not quite so pessimistic. "There's only one Air Force officer in the car with Wellenmeister. That should be enough to pinpoint him."

But Ben was looking farther ahead. "It would satisfy me, but what about hard evidence? If he handed Wellenmeister a line about being concerned for his well-being and knowing a safe place to hide, we won't have any more proof than we have now."

"You're forgetting one thing. The killer thinks Wellenmeister knows who he is. So he didn't waste time spinning yarns. He just shoved a gun at Wellenmeister. He had to. I'm not worried about evidence right now. I'm worried about saving Wellenmeister's life."

Ben did not require repetition on this point. "So what have you decided to do?"

Even as Dunnet explained, they were looping off the express-way and accelerating down a side road.

"It's a calculated risk," he said, swiveling in his seat. "If he's heading for the Bull Run Mountains and if he's going by the map, there's one fork that's the logical place for him to end up at."

"And if he's going all the way to the Blue Ridge?" Ben asked anxiously.

"That doesn't bother me. The state boys will pick him up if he tries to go that far. The kicker could be that he's got peculiar local knowledge and avoids the fork entirely. But neither of these cookies has been spending his time in the mountains, so I'm betting against it. In any event, we'll get to the fork before he does."

"Oh, no, we won't," said the driver.

"What's that?" demanded Dunnet, swinging back to face front.

"Take a look down there when we pass these trees."

They were breasting a fairly significant rise, and when they cleared the copse of woodland obscuring the view, they could see into the valley ahead where a single car was speeding in a cloud of dust along the narrow road. To Ben, it was simply a blob of light blue. But the experts were more enlightened.

"It's a BMW all right," Dunnet grunted.

For the next ten minutes, thanks to the twisting nature of the road and the abundant stands of trees, the chase was a tantalizing peekaboo affair. They would round a corner, strain to see ahead, catch a fleeting glimpse of their quarry, only to have it cut off immediately. As they began to gain elevation, Dunnet and Safford thought for one terrible moment they had lost their man.

"Nope," said the driver calmly. "Look back. This switchback loops a long way around."

And there, not so far beneath them but a significant length in the rear, the sky-blue blob was still in sight.

"So far it's been a piece of cake," said Dunnet, who was studying a large-scale map. "He hasn't had a hell of a lot of choice. But the old hunting trails start soon, and if he knows what he's doing, he could turn off almost anywhere."

"Can't we catch up with him before then?" Ben asked.

"Even if we can't, we don't have to worry," Dunnet said easily. "I've asked the state police to cut him off at the next intersection."

This time it was the state police who were too late. The BMW, for once completely visible over a period of several minutes, swept by the mouth of the debouching town road without encountering any hindrance and disappeared around a distant curve. Only when Dunnet's car had completed its own circular approach did anything appear, and with sufficient suddenness to cause all participants to grind to an emergency stop.

With a few picturesque oaths, the driver once against accelerated through the gears while Dunnet, taking in the nature of the support he had received, did a little cursing of his own. "Great!" he growled. "Two troopers on motorcycles."

"What's wrong with that?" demanded Ben, glad to see any reinforcements.

"They're too damned obvious, that's what. That bozo up ahead hasn't caught on to us yet. We're too far back, and we're unmarked. But let him catch sight of these cowboys, and he'll shoot up a side trail when we can't see him."

The expert in the driver's seat was urgent. "There's a stretch up ahead where he'll have a choice of three turns. After that, there's a two-mile patch where he'll be hemmed in."

Dunnet picked up the handset and barked at their escort to hang back.

Even to Ben's untutored eye, the changing nature of the hills was conveying its own message. Until now, the road had been twisting and narrow as it climbed, but the supporting countryside had not been overly dramatic. The drops by the side were more suggestive of crumpled fenders than fiery explosions. It was all too obvious that things would soon be different. In short order, Wellenmeister's BMW was going to be at the perfect site for a fatal accident.

Within seconds they were passing the driver's side trails. Automatically, they all began counting—one, two, three.

"Now!" said Dunnet.

Simultaneously their own car leaped ahead, Dunnet ordered the motocycles to let loose and a light on the console started winking.

"Headquarters is trying to get through, Sarge."

"Never mind about that now!" Dunnet yelled as the cyclists separated to roar past them. Barely had they regrouped than an additional roar began overtaking them.

"What the hell is that?" asked Dunnet, searching the empty road behind.

202

He was looking in the wrong direction as Ben Safford was able to tell him after leaning out the window. "A helicopter is passing us."

Then deafening bedlam drowned them, making conversation inside the car impossible. The helicopter sturdily chugged its way ahead of them, ahead of the motorcycles and around the next corner.

In the meantime, Dunnet had finally made himself heard over the transmitter, and the answer left him more puzzled than ever.

"Headquarters doesn't know a thing about the chopper," he announced blankly.

A dim suspicion was forming in Ben's mind even before the driver produced the fruit of his own observation.

"It had Air Force markings."

Ben tried to work it all out. Maybe the helicopter had been following them. But maybe it had been following the BMW. In which case, there had been no need to . . .

Before he could proceed, sound effects signaled the conclusion of the chase. The noise of the helicopter came to a sudden end, to be followed almost immediately by a thudding crash. Then a series of squealing slithers announced the halting of the motorcycles, and the police car swept around the corner to see exactly how unnecessary it had become.

The helicopter was sitting firmly astride the road. The BMW was canted broadside with one fender crumpled against a boulder. Several air force police were already at its side.

Dunnet had only one thought in mind as he threw his door open and rushed to the BMW where a familiar tubby figure was slumped over the wheel.

"Is Wellenmeister all right?" he demanded.

"He's fine, he's just fainted," said a cheerful MP, "and we've got our man over here."

Spread-eagled against the other door was Lieutenant Colonel Lawrence Yates.

"And I just took this off him," said a corporal, brandishing an automatic as the cuffs snapped shut.

203

When Yates straightened, he did not look defeated or even concerned. Behind an iron mask of impassivity, he glanced indifferently over the motorcycles, over Sergeant Dunnet, over Ben Safford. Only when his gaze continued to the helicopter and he saw the last passenger alighting did he lose his detachment.

"You!" he blurted.

"That's right," Ursula Richmond responded levelly.

"I thought you were a flight instructor," Yates said bitterly. "I suppose you were air police all along."

Ursula did not reply until she had reached the ground. "Oh, I'm a flight instructor," she said, "but I also happen to be the future Mrs. Neil Conroy."

27

"Do you mean to say that you suspected Larry Yates all along?" Ben Safford asked Ursula a week later.

"Good heavens, no. It didn't cross my mind at the beginning."

Ben was slightly reassured. Every congressman had been lectured to the point of nausea about the new look in women. Ursula was already prettier than he was, younger than he was and far more technically educated. If, in addition to all that, she could unravel military-industrial conspiracies between dabs of lipstick, it was time for him to retire.

Ursula was not quite that smart, but she was smart enough to realize some of the requirements of this dinner party.

"All I wanted to do was have everything settled, so that I could get married on schedule," she announced.

This sentiment produced a gust of sympathy from the head of the table where Zinka Goodrich, dressed in a flowing caftan of some exotic brocade, was presiding over a serving dish. "That is, to me, entirely natural," she cried. "Any woman would feel the same."

Ursula, although grateful for the support, waited in vain for a similar response from the woman at whom her remark had been aimed, the woman who should have understood the desire to keep a wedding on track. But Peg Conroy remained stubbornly silent.

When Preston Goodrich, seeking to atone for various shortcomings, had proposed a victory dinner for Neil Conroy and his congressmen, Ben had half expected Zinka to seize on the suggestion and expand it beyond recognition. The ground rules for a celebration, to her way of thinking, had been long established. You prepared gigantic quantities of strangely spiced food, you summoned all the people your house could hold and then, at the last minute, you rushed out for a pile of throwaway glasses and plates. Usually her slapdash tactics worked wonders, and by the time her husband had pruned George Kidder and General Farrington from her list, the stage was set for another successful evening. Then Peg Conroy and Earl Mohr arrived, Peg grasped the role that Ursula was going to play in the future and the storm flags started flying.

Zinka was willing to hurl herself into the arena, and even Elsie was ready to do her bit, but the men retreated cravenly into a review of the events leading to the capture of Larry Yates.

"Actually, I suppose you could say that I got everybody haring off in the wrong direction," said Neil Conroy, more nervous than Ben had ever seen him.

Preston Goodrich followed this lead. "God knows it was a logical mistake. After that bomb was planted on Atamian, I didn't see what else to think except that Dorland was protecting its interests with every crime in the book."

"You climbed aboard about the same time I began to peel off," Ben remarked.

"But that was before Charlie Crowder spilled the beans," Goodrich objected. "There weren't a whole lot of other possibilities then."

"Think about it for a minute," Ben advised. "You just said Dorland was trying to protect its interests, and the result was that you suspected them of hiring a lot of hit men. What kind of protection job is that?"

Elsie, a Californian, was interested in detail. "The immediate impact of the Atamian murder was a wave of anti-Dorland feeling and a move to drum the company out of the Defense establishment. In other words, it produced exactly the situation Dorland was trying to avoid."

"And the reaction was foreseeable," Ben said, ramming his argument home. "Give the devil his due. George Kidder had done a damned good job of rallying Washington opinion behind him after the Paris crash—and that was because he was pretty shrewd about public indignation. He was willing to give up on the VX-92 in order to have the Pentagon and Congress on his side for the future. Would he have sacrificed all that to prevent Atamian from coming clean?"

This was meat and drink to Tony Martinelli. Still keeping one wary eye on the potential female volcanoes, he could not resist joining in. "Hell, no! Not when it was Wellenmeister who did the bribing. Kidder was already doing his best to get the poor guy tarred and feathered."

"That's another point against the Dorland theory," Ben reminded them. "It assumes a continuity in Dorland policy that simply did not exist."

Some habits die hard. "Come off it, Ben," Neil Conroy said. "You expect me to believe that Wellenmeister was crooked and Kidder was pure as the driven snow?"

"Good God, no!" For a moment Ben was so indignant that he almost committed the error of justifying himself. Instead he took a deep breath and said, "Look, maybe it would be better if we took this from the beginning."

"That would certainly be a big help," Goodrich observed, then softened his criticism by pouring a generous measure of acrid, resinous wine into Ben's glass.

Neil jumped in before anyone else could say a word. "The beginning was a long time before the Utah crash!" he insisted.

Ben decided that, with most of the men unnerved and Neil still harboring old grudges, he would have to take charge.

"Exactly," he agreed. "We now know there was a continuous problem with the VX-92, both in the Air Force and back at the plant. Dorland wanted to cover that up, and they were pretty efficient about it. They managed to contain the knowledge. Right?"

"I suppose so," Neil said.

Ursula stirred, then made her first contribution. "I'd heard about it," she said with a hesitancy totally alien to her usual confident manner.

It took Ben a minute to realize that Ursula was reluctant to remind Peg of her profession. Certainly the dashing green silk she was wearing was about as far from an Air Force uniform as she could get. Oh well, this was one problem that Mrs. Conroy could not ask her congressmen to solve.

"That's what I mean by containment. The information was restricted to a few scattered pilots. Nobody who was in a position to do Dorland damage knew anything about it. Then came the Utah crash, and they got lucky with the news coverage. So Wellenmeister tells Mike Atamian to squash any remaining publicity and gives him a wad of cash to go on with."

This was close enough to the bone to make Peg Conroy forget other preoccupations. "And he didn't care that he was destroying Neil's career while he was at it."

It is difficult to tell a devoted mother that her son is of no importance in the maneuverings for high stakes, but Mrs. Hollenbach was ready to try.

"Perhaps you don't know that Walter Wellenmeister has been more forthcoming since Colonel Yates' arrest. He now says that he never intended that Congressman Atamian suborn your son's board of inquiry, and I believe him." As she heard the echo of her words, Elsie hastened to correct a possible false impression. "Not that I think Wellenmeister has any moral standards. Far from it. But many businessmen prefer to move in a gray area of ethical ambiguity. It's not just a question of defending their probity to others. They like to convince themselves that what they are doing is proper. Wellenmeister was probably hoping for a swift, silent and indeterminate finding."

Peg was indignant at this quibbling. "You mean something like a verdict of not proven? And a big black question mark on Neil's record for life?"

Elsie, who should have known better, acknowledged her mistake by bowing her head and gravely agreeing that it came to much the same thing in the end.

But just as she gave up the battle, reinforcements came rattling in. "Well, I think there's a lot in what you say, Elsie," Preston Goodrich declared. "The Air Force and the State Department and

208

Dorland all sounded the same at my level. They were pressuring to hush things up, not to find a scapegoat."

"That's just the point," Ben argued. "You're talking about institutional forces and they're all alike. Wellenmeister thought he was paying off Atamian to drop the right words in the right ears."

Tony nodded sagely. "And Mike wasn't about to tell his bank account that the right ears had stopped listening to him a long time ago. Instead he decides he'll bribe someone to throw the blame on the pilot. You've got to hand it to Mike for spotting this Larry Yates as a twister."

But, according to Zinka Goodrich, it was instinct, not shrewdness. With a sweep of her flowing sleeves, she intoned richly: "The jackal will smell out his brother when others cannot."

Until now, Val Oakes had been more interested in comparing reactions to the wine and food with Earl Mohr than in the general conversation. The last observation, however, was like a trumpet call to an old war-horse.

"That isn't exactly the way we put it in South Dakota, but by and large, we'd agree with you."

"And Yates earned his money quickly and efficiently," Ben said. "He persuaded Perini it was a question of pilot error, the two of them presented a solid front to Farrington, who was only too glad to accept their technical advice, and the thing was done. I'm surprised it was so simple."

Ben ended by turning inquiringly to Conroy, but Neil had withdrawn into a frowning study. It was Ursula who squared her shoulders and plunged in.

"So long as Julian hadn't had trouble with the VX-92 himself, it would have been easy for Larry. If Julian had heard some scuttlebutt, Larry would have leaned back and in a fatherly way advised him that there were always rumors about bugs in new planes. Larry's relaxed, laid-back style was just a front. Even when he had nothing riding on it, even when he was just taking a woman out to dinner, he never let you forget for a minute his superior rank, his superior experience, his superior achievements."

Dimly, Ben recalled how, at their very first encounter, Colonel Yates had deftly contrasted his own world-weary flexibility with the callow assurance of captains and majors. The performance had been skillful enough to seem like no performance at all.

"And Ursula saw through him just like that!" Earl Mohr marveled.

"When you're a captain in the Air Force, and a flight instructor on new planes to boot, you see a lot of them like that," Ursula said thumpingly. "At least Larry Yates really did have a high degree of technical competence. Some of them don't."

Even a man as unversed in feminine guerrilla conflict as Ben could recognize a major shift when it took place under his nose. It did not need Zinka's enthusiastic nods to tell him that Ursula had abandoned the idea of selling herself to Peg as Miss Sweet Sixteen. Now she was defiantly underlining her contacts with other men, her flight skills, her rank. In other words, she was telling her future mother-in-law: *What you see is what you get.*

Peg's probable reaction was enough to make a peace-loving man blanch. Ben hurriedly turned to the rest of the table.

"There you are," he said. "Yates might be able to get away with his soft sell, but there was no way Perini wouldn't remember as soon as the questions began. When I turned up, Yates figured he had to silence Perini and he had to satisfy my curiosity. Faking a suicide accomplished both his goals."

They were now in Tony Martinelli's area of expertise. He cocked his head for a moment, then spoke judiciously. "Having the money spill out of a Saudi envelope was the real frosting on the cake."

"I'll go along with that," Goodrich conceded. "The State Department started giving me heat right away about the need to overlook these little lapses by our allies."

Tony could have been correcting a student. "The beauty of it was that it worked both ways," he said with hoarse appreciation. "The Saudis figured they were being landed with the can to cover up an American mess, and they could build up a lot of credit by going along."

Neil Conroy emerged from his review of the past with a burst. "I don't understand you people," he complained. "You assume things about the Saudis, they assume things about you and nobody bothers to find out!"

Ben was thankful Neil had not been present at the airport when he and General Khalid, by their mutual delicacy, had managed to mislead each other so completely. "I admit that you're the only one who thought to ask the Saudis outright," he conceded generously.

Unfortunately, Neil had moved from exasperation to curiosity. "Why no direct questions?" he pressed. "Do you just take it for granted you'll get lies?"

"Tut, tut!" Zinka was being kind but firm with the young. "You do not understand diplomats, Neil. Lying is too direct for them," she said darkly. "With lies there is always the danger that at least one party may know what is going on. By wrapping themselves in a fog, they virtually guarantee that everybody will be confused."

Her husband did not contest her premise. On the contrary, he embraced it. "Sometimes the fog pays off," he announced cheerfully. "And I think I could get to be pretty good at it. You should have heard me with Wellenmeister."

"I wouldn't brag about it," Ben grunted. "You let him get away."

Goodrich shrugged off his failure. "From here on, I stick to dry land."

"Could we get back to the main question?" Peg Conroy pleaded. "You said there couldn't be any continuity at Dorland, Ben. Did you mean because they changed presidents?"

"That was only part of it. The minute Wellenmeister left the company, it was unlikely Dorland would resort to murder because of what he'd done. But after the Paris crash, the probability dropped to zero. They weren't protecting either the plane or Wellenmeister. Mike Atamian's killing was counterproductive from Dorland's point of view. So the only thing to do was assume that the murderer was someone who didn't give a damn about Dorland. He was out to save his own skin."

Tony Martinelli's eyes gleamed with interest. "Which didn't

make a hell of a lot of sense as long as Perini was supposed to be the guy who was bribed. Then Charlie Crowder spoke his piece and whammo!" His lightly balled fingers exploded outward in illustration.

"The murderer had to be General Farrington or Colonel Yates," Ben continued, "but after that it was a toss-up."

"Oh, come on. Don't be so modest," Ursula cajoled him. "The policeman who was with you at the arrest said you were betting it was Larry. How did you know?"

Ben reddened. "I'm not being modest, I'm trying to forget my mistakes. The only reason I was suspicious of Yates was because of you, Ursula. You kept popping up all over the place, with Farrington's aide and out at Perini's house. I decided Yates was nervous enough to keep tabs on the investigation and was using you as his legman. It never occurred to me that you were Neil's inside source."

"That's because my cover was so good," Ursula chuckled. "I hadn't planned to be an undercover agent at the beginning. But when Neil called—and he was stamping mad—to say that they were covering up the VX-92 by blaming his co-pilot, I realized somebody must know what was going on. And as the two most likely men were going to be at the Air Show, I decided to spend my leave there seeing what I could find out."

Nodding intelligently, Ben promptly paraded his ignorance before the whole table. "It was a real piece of luck for you, being picked up by Yates right off the bat."

The intensity of reaction to this simple statement came as a big surprise to him. Ursula was so amazed her jaw dropped. Peg and Zinka stared at him as if he were a mental defective. Even Elsie sniffed and said with majestic reproof, "Really, Ben!"

Half laughing, half indignant, Ursula managed to explain. "That piece of luck cost me a lot of patience. I waited at the swept-wing exhibit for five hours because I knew it was Larry Yates' assignment. And when he did finally show, I picked *him* up."

It was not just the women who were ganging up on Ben. His old friend and supporter Val Oakes also had a word of reproach.

"Things haven't changed that much, Ben. I told you that the real winners like Ursula here are never wandering around alone."

"Thank you for those kind words. As a matter of fact"—Ursula dimpled at Val—"the only hard part was remaining unattached until Larry came."

"I should hope so," Val responded gallantly.

This last exchange clarified a good deal for Ben. He was not denying for a moment that he often required social instruction. But the object of the current exercise was not his education. Val and Elsie had joined the conspiracy to establish Ursula as a pearl of great price. Peg Conroy was being told that her son was a very lucky man.

Deaf to these undertones, Preston Goodrich was anxious to press on. "Fine," he said to Ursula, "so you took Yates in tow. What did it get you?"

"Not much at first. It was when we got back to Washington that things became suspicious. You see, at the beginning Neil just told me that the junior member of his board had committed suicide. Then I picked up the *Post* and learned we were talking about Julian Perini. That didn't make sense at all, because I had known Julian in Germany."

"You knew he had money," Ben guessed.

"And lots of it. So there was no way he would have been interested in that bribe. What's more, Julian had a very quiet, almost apologetic style. I couldn't see anybody thinking he'd swing enough weight to persuade General Farrington and Colonel Yates of anything. On top of all that, Larry let his hair down one evening and told me the air police were asking questions because they weren't satisfied with the suicide. So I dropped in on Julian's sister, and by the time I'd heard her story, I insisted Neil get out there and involve the police."

Ben handsomely admitted that her approach had certainly worked.

"As far as it went," she said. "But you have to remember the headlines I was reading while this was going on. Walter Wellenmeister admitted his part. Then Congressman Atamian was blown up, and all the papers acted as if the scenario was simple. Finally,

Farrington's aide told me that the general had been playing footsie with Dorland, hoping for a cushy spot when he retired from the service. If Julian wasn't the rotten apple, then it looked as if it had to be Farrington."

Tony Martinelli shook his head disapprovingly. "You've got a lot to learn about crooks, Ursula," he rasped.

"What's to learn?' she retorted. "Once a crook, always a crook."

"There are big-time crooks and there are small-time crooks. The trouble with poor Mike Atamian was that he sold out too easy," said Tony, warming to his theme. "And Dorland started treating him like an errand boy. If this general of yours was holding out for a top job, then the last thing he'd do is take twenty-five grand for low-level shenanigans."

Ben was rather pleased to see someone else at the table being instructed in fundamentals, particularly in view of Ursula's blithe self-assurance.

But when she instantly announced she was a numskull not to have thought of that herself, Ben relented enough to say, "Well, you seem to have gotten on the right track in the end."

Ursula wrinkled her nose thoughtfully. "I was paying too much attention to facts. The one thing I overlooked was how well I was getting to know Larry Yates. And it's surprising how damning that turned out to be."

Ben leaned back, prepared to receive the delicate fruits of feminine intuition.

"In the first place, he spent money like water," she announced crisply.

Even Val was stirred to protest. "He was a womanizer, he was trying to impress you."

"Then he should have chosen a girl friend who didn't know to the penny how much a lieutenant colonel makes," she snapped back. "Besides, it wasn't just for women. Larry wanted everything of the best for himself. He intended to stay on in the service, but he didn't want to live on an Air Force salary. Then he was totally self-centered. Lots of divorced men don't care what happens to their ex, but most of them have some qualms about their children. Not Larry. When he decided the domestic scene wasn't for him, he slammed the door on it. The important thing was for him to be free as a bird."

"Now wait a minute," said Ben. "All of this makes him pretty nasty, it doesn't make him a murderer."

"Oh, I agree," Ursula said cheerfully. "It was all just sinking into my unconscious, the way I know that he was planning to use me as long as he needed a shoulder to cry on, and then he was going to ditch me."

Preston Goodrich chose the wrong moment for amateur psychiatry. "Don't you think that may explain your negative reaction to him?" he asked keenly.

Ursula was amused. "When it comes to who was using who, I don't think I've got anything to complain about."

"You can say that again," murmured Tony, who had never been an admirer of the new woman.

High-mindedly, Ursula ignored this contribution. "My real problem was Neil. He was so pleased to have Dorland saddled with the blame for everything he wouldn't listen to my ideas about Julian, and he wasn't even interested when Mr. Crowder's statement leaked. That's when I called you, Ben. If I had to choose between trying to talk sense to Neil or to Mount Rushmore, I'd go with Rushmore any day."

She smiled across the table at her fiancé with great affection.

"I guess I was pretty hard-nosed about it," Neil admitted with no visible sign of regret.

"In fact, I was ready to drop the whole thing," Ursula recalled rather absently as Neil stretched out a hand to enclose hers. "But then I walked into that restaurant, and the whole thing was plain as day. Larry must have left only a minute before I came. The barman told me he'd raced out, and then I looked up and saw the television still on the Wellenmeister story. Just as I stood there, I knew who would kill Julian and plant a bomb on a congressman to protect himself. So I went straight to the air police."

Ben thought they were at the end of her story. "And when they heard you, they called out a helicopter."

"Like hell they did!" Ursula straightened so abruptly the locked hands fell apart. "They thought I was hysterical because I'd been stood up for a luncheon date. It wasn't until General Farrington stormed in that there was any action."

"So that's where he went," Ben cried. "Of course, as soon as he heard the Crowder leak, he was the one person who had no doubt what had happened."

"And what was going to happen. The general demanded that the air police provide Wellenmeister with protection and him with an around-the-clock alibi."

For a moment, they were all silent, contemplating the effect of this double-barreled request from a high-ranking officer. Elsie, whose opinion of the military had been sinking steadily as she sat on the Uniform Weaponry Committee, said grimly, "So much for their cavalier dismissal of your information."

"General Farrington sounded a lot more hysterical than I did," Ursula recalled with satisfaction. "But he did get results. They were so suspicious of him they wouldn't let him anywhere near Wellenmeister. That's why I was bundled into the chopper, because they wanted someone who could identify Larry."

All of Elsie's preconceptions were being confirmed—the air police in the grip of inertia, General Farrington giving way to emotionalism and the solid good sense of a woman saving the day.

"It was certainly fortunate that you got there in time," she said graciously.

Ursula grinned. "Actually, it was kind of exciting. There wasn't much we could do while they were on the expressway. Then, when they turned off and we were looking for a good place to box them in, we'd barely cottoned on to the fact they were being chased by another car when two motorcycles joined in. I was relieved when we were able to stop the whole thing."

Surprisingly the first comment came from Earl Mohr, and it had nothing to do with the larger issues.

"I'll bet it was exciting, swooping down and seeing the whole parade from above. You know," he added wistfully, "I've always wished I could have learned to fly."

Ursula promptly trained the battery of her considerable charm on him. "But, Earl, it's not too late. Neil told me you used to do a lot of high steel work. You're just the kind of man who'd be terrific with small planes."

Earl blinked at this new vision of himself. "You don't think I'm too old?"

"Nonsense!" Ursula's voice dripped honey as she went on. "I've got a wonderful idea. When Neil and I come to Newburg, I'll take you up in a single-engine job and teach you to fly it. I'll bet you take to it like a duck to water."

As Ursula continued to elaborate a plan which involved her spending considerable time with Earl, giving him a great deal of pleasure, and as Neil threw in additional encouragement, Peg Conroy looked at her two menfolk in open dismay.

The spectacle was enough to cause Ben to retreat hastily into a side conversation. "It's just like I thought, Pres," he said, turning to Goodrich. "There was never any need for me to get into that chase. I could have saved myself a lot of trouble."

"What trouble did you have?" Preston Goodrich asked indignantly. "Think about me! For that matter, think about poor Wellenmeister."

"Ha! It'll be a long day before I waste sympathy on him," Ben snorted. "What's happened to Wellenmeister, anyway? There hasn't been a squeak out of him."

Goodrich was still a novice in the machinations of the military-industrial complex. "Would you believe he's back in California trying to persuade George Kidder to put him on the Dorland Board of Directors?"

"Makes sense," Val Oakes grunted with weighty approval. "Wellenmeister and Kidder went to the mat, and Kidder came out top dog. So now Wellenmeister is following some very old, tried and true strategy."

Ostensibly, Val was addressing Ben and Goodrich, but he fixed

217

such a compelling eye on Peg Conroy that, in spite of her other problems, she waited a moment for him to continue, then said nervously, "What's that?"

Val was benevolence itself.

"If you can't lick 'em," he advised her sonorously, "then join 'em!"